For My Mom.
Always loved. Always missed.
You will forever be precious to me.

The sins of the father...are coming back to wreck his world.

Make no mistake, Declan Flynn is not a good man. He's never claimed to be. He's rich, powerful, dangerous...and, apparently, on someone's kill list. When he wakes up one night, tied to a chair in a dank basement, Declan is certainly less than pleased—and in a killing mood of his own. Then she appears. His most unlikely savior.

Marley Jones never expected to be the guardian angel to a man most people consider the devil.

But fate is often funny, and she's in the wrong place at the right time in order to save one very ungrateful and gorgeous billionaire. She's a low-rent PI, he's crime royalty (if you believe the gossip) and she may have just stumbled onto the first big case of her career. Now her job is to protect her new client—and in order to do that, she plans to stick to Declan like glue. He'd better get used to having her around. Intimately close.

First, he could have saved himself. Second, there is no way that Declan ever intends to let Marley go.

Good things—and people—don't come into Declan's life often. And when Marley inserts herself into what will obviously become one very bloody battle, the only thing he can do is protect her...even as Marley mistakenly thinks *she* is protecting him. By saving him, Marley put a target on her delicate back, and he intends to make sure that no one so much as touches a hair on her head. He also intends to claim the brave and fierce woman who calls to a dark and savage hunger that he's buried deep inside.

But an enemy wants vengeance, and he doesn't care about the collateral damage.

Someone wants Declan to suffer. To pay for the crimes his father committed. To unmask the predator who is now hunting both Declan and Marley, they will have to face the hell of Declan's past. Monsters aren't born. They're made. Declan was made into a monster long ago, and this beast will do anything to protect the angel that slipped into his world.

Try to take her from him? He will show you hell on earth.

Author's Note: Some cases are never truly closed, and when it comes to Declan Flynn's past—the nightmare is not even close to over. The Ice Breakers are returning to solve a very cold case, and new Ice Breaker recruit Marley Jones is about to find herself the target of a vicious killer...even as she becomes the obsession of a man who has known very little that is good in his life. A cold case, a hot romance, and a hero who knows all about being *bad* are waiting in CRUEL ICE.

Cruel Ice

Ice Breakers Cold Case Romance
Book 12

Cynthia Eden

HOCUS POCUS
PUBLISHING INC.

This book is a work of fiction. Any similarities to real people, places, or events are not intentional and are purely the result of coincidence. The characters, places, and events in this story are fictional.

Published by Hocus Pocus Publishing, Inc.

Copyright © 2025 by Cindy Roussos

All rights reserved. This publication may not be reproduced, distributed, or transmitted in any form without the express written consent of the author except for the use of small quotes or excerpts used in book reviews. No part of this work may be used in the training of AI models.

If you have any problems, comments, or questions about this publication, please contact info@hocuspocuspublishing.com.

Chapter One

Declan Flynn slowly opened his eyes, and as awareness crept through him, he realized a few very, very important points of information. Important point one...he was not in his hotel suite. Point two...he was not in his plush, king-size bed. Point three...*he was tied to a fucking chair.*

Faint light shone from the far right side of a dank, dark room—a room that he one hundred percent did not recognize. His head turned slowly as he tried to take in the scene around him and figure out just what the hell was happening. Nothing was familiar to him, and the musky scent of the place made his lips twist down in disgust.

His arms were bound behind his back, and he pulled, testing the ropes that held him. *Tight.* The rough hemp bit into his wrists. His legs were tied to the legs of the chair by what felt like the same type of rope. Someone had secured him well, all while Declan had been unconscious.

How the hell did I get here? He pushed against the fog in his mind. He'd had a business meeting. After it had concluded, he'd swung by a club. Then...

Declan could remember heading out of the club's doors. Seeing the long crowd waiting to the side as they vied for their chance to enter Abyss. Eager people who wanted to get in and dance and drink the night away. He'd turned away from them and—

Nothing.

He strained against the ropes. They sawed into his wrists, and Declan was pretty damn sure he felt blood dripping down his fingers. His teeth snapped together. Sure, maybe most people would wake to this nightmare situation and be terrified.

Declan wasn't most people.

He wasn't terrified. He was fucking furious. "What the hell is happening?" Declan bellowed. Someone had to be there, right? Watching? Waiting? The prick who'd kidnapped Declan and hauled him to wherever the hell he was *had* to be close. "When I get out of these ropes, I'm gonna kick your ass!" Had his words just been a little slurred?

Sonofabitch, they had been. He'd been drugged. Yeah, that would explain a few things. Like why the hell he couldn't remember much after walking out of Abyss.

Tensing his body, he began to twist the ropes that circled his wrists. He would get out of this mess, and when he did, he was going to teach his abductor just what a horrible mistake he'd made. *The last mistake of your life, you bastard. No one messes with me. I will have you screaming for mercy.*

More blood dripped down his wrists and to his fingers as he twisted the ropes. Was his knife still in his boot or had the weapon been removed? How long had he been there? Where *was* he? And what fun ways could he torture his abductor? Oh, how he was going to make the fool beg for mercy. Only Declan never showed mercy. Never. Just ask his father.

Oh, wait. You can't ask the dead anything.

Declan kept fighting the ropes. Questions rolled through his mind as Declan—

Soft fingertips fluttered over his shoulder. A husky, feminine voice told him, "I'll get you out."

Declan froze.

Those fingertips swept away but the scent of jasmine—and amber—teased his nose. His head whipped to the right as he tried to get a look at the woman who'd spoken. And who'd just offered to free him.

Is she the one who put me in this damn room? "You're gonna pay," Declan swore in a low rumble. She would have needed help moving him. Maybe she'd had some grunt goons doing the heavy lifting as they hauled his ass into this hell and tied him to the chair. Whoever this lady was, she would soon learn that you did not fuck with him and walk away.

He never forgave, and he never forgot.

"Pay for helping?" A bare whisper. Mostly just a breath that slid to his ear. "Seems odd. Shouldn't you pay *me* for helping?"

Helping? Like he was supposed to buy that? A growl broke from him.

"Be still," she urged him.

He realized he'd jerked his arms.

"I don't want to cut you. I found this knife on the floor, and I'm doing my best to saw through the ropes." Again, all whispered, as if she feared someone else would overhear her words.

His nostrils flared. He pulled in more of that seductive scent. A scent that did not belong in this current hell.

Declan heard the faint sawing of the knife as it bit into the rope. She *was* cutting him free.

Was this part of the game? The torture? Some weird mind fuck? Not like he was going to be foolish enough to trust her. In this world, he trusted no one. A lesson Declan had learned long ago.

"Almost there…" Soft. "You're bleeding, by the way."

Yeah, he was aware of that fact.

"I followed the van that took you. I was behind you the whole time. I called the cops—"

Another growl broke from him. Declan and the cops didn't mix well. Ever.

"But it could be a while before they arrive, and I was afraid you'd be dead before they got here."

Declan had no intention of dying. The pressure of the ropes suddenly eased, and pinpricks of pain shot through his fingertips.

"There." A rush of relief from her.

Declan kept his hands behind his back. He flexed his fingers and made no sound as he let the pain roll through him.

The woman darted in front of him. In the faint light, he could see the glinting blade of the knife that she held in her hands. If she wanted to slice his throat, she should have done that *before* cutting the ropes that bound his hands.

She sent him a quick, nervous smile. Then she dropped to her knees before him. Her hair—a thick, heavy mass that curled slightly—tumbled over her shoulders. It was too dark for him to see the color clearly. Too dark for him to see her clearly.

But she was suddenly right in front of him and reaching out with the knife.

"I'll have your legs free as fast as I can. Watch the door,

will you? If it opens, *tell me*. Don't let some jerk sneak through the door and get the drop on me."

The door behind her.

"I snuck in through the little window behind you. You're lucky I could fit. Otherwise, I don't know how I could have gotten in the basement without your abductors spotting me."

Lucky. A new word to describe him.

Currently, he was still partially tied up in a *basement*. Declan wasn't sure he felt *lucky*.

He heard the faint sawing as she cut the ropes. Then...

A grinding. Growling?

She stopped cutting. Seemed to stop breathing. "Is that someone leaving this place...?" Her head tilted to the side as she appeared to strain toward the sound. "Or arriving? Oh, please, don't let that be someone else arriving—or you and I will both be dead."

Her head turned a bit more as her focus shifted away from him.

"I guess it could be the cops..." She held the knife in her right hand.

He brought his hands forward in a slow, careful movement.

"But wouldn't the cops come in with sirens blaring?" Soft. Uncertain. Her head started to turn back toward him.

Quick as a striking snake, he yanked the knife from her hand. And he put it right at her throat. Her mouth hung open in a round O of shock.

It took a few seconds for her to snap her mouth shut. Then... "What are you doing?" A squeak. "I'm here to help you!"

Did he look like a freaking idiot?

A motor growled. Definitely a motor. But the sound faded as the car left.

Her shoulders slumped. The movement had her pressing too close to the knife. She gasped, and he realized that he might have just nicked her. "Stop moving against the knife." A rasp. A slurred rasp from him.

"Oh, no." Her hands rose and pressed to his chest. As if the woman didn't see the *knife*. "Did they drug you? I thought they might have. You didn't fight much when they put you in the van. Actually, you just kind of slumped."

Anger pulsed in him. "Get the ropes off my legs."

"I was *trying*. Did you miss that part? But then you took the knife." Her hands left his chest. One hand—small, delicate—rose to hover over his as he gripped the knife. "If I'm gonna cut you free, I'll need the knife."

That was precious. She thought he'd just turn over his weapon? "Get the hell back."

Her fingers touched the top of his hand. "If you give me the knife, I'll cut you free."

"Get. The. Hell. Back."

She scrambled back and fell on her ass.

He sawed at the ropes. Might have nicked his legs a few times. Screw it. He barely felt the pain. Barely felt anything but rage. In moments, the ropes dropped from his legs, and he was free.

She rose and stood uncertainly near him. "You're a very ungrateful rescue."

Rescue? What the hell was he? Some kind of abandoned dog? Declan shot to his feet and took a surging step forward.

The world immediately tilted and swirled, and he started to slam straight down toward the floor. But she was there. The woman lunged for him. Her arms wrapped around him, and she braced him against her much smaller body. "Got you," she promised.

Jasmine and amber filled his nose again. The warmth of her body seeped into him. Her hair brushed against the side of his face when he found himself angling even closer to her. And why in the hell was he doing that?

"Did you almost fall because you don't have feeling in your legs due to the ropes or is it because of the drugs?" Her head tilted back as she asked the low question.

When her head tilted back, her mouth moved incredibly close to his. As in, kissably close. He stared at her mouth. Even in the dim lighting, he could see it was a nice mouth. Lush. Sensual. Right there. And...

His lips brushed over hers. A soft, light kiss.

She shivered. "Why did you do that?"

Hell if he knew. Kissing a captor seemed like a piss-poor idea. But he'd just wanted...*her*. Yeah, that was screwed.

What is wrong with me?

"It's the drugs," she said, as if she'd heard his mental question. "They're making you loopy, aren't they? Okay, here's the deal. We *have* to get you out. If that was the sound of their car leaving, then this is our chance. I'll help you walk as much as possible, and, um, do you mind moving the knife away from my throat?"

He blinked. Yep, he'd put the knife at her throat again. Even as he kissed her.

Slowly, he eased the knife away.

Her breath rushed out. "Thank you. Now, any chance you'll give *me* the knife?"

No chance in hell.

She waited, as if hoping he'd just hand over the blade. He did not.

"Okay." She nodded. "You keep it. You were the one

kidnapped, after all. I get where you might have some trust issues, but, see, here's the thing." She angled her body so that she could pull his left arm over her slender shoulders. *Like she's bracing me so I can walk better.* "I'm not the bad guy."

He was. He was the bad guy. Should he tell her that important fact?

"I'm rescuing you. Trying to, anyway. And would it kill the cops to hurry up and arrive?" She tugged him forward. "You aren't fitting through the window I used. We'll have to go up the stairs and hope that we can sneak out without catching the attention of your abductors."

Sneak out? Screw that. He was planning to slice his abductors into little pieces. Thus, the knife. What else did she think he was gonna do with it? Whittle some wood?

And if she's lying to me...if she turns out to be part of this nightmare...

Would he slice her silken skin?

Maybe he already had. That definitely looked like blood dripping down her neck. "Sorry." The word just rumbled from him.

"For what? The kiss? Don't worry. I'm sure it was just the drugs."

No, it had not been. He looked back over his shoulder. Made out a small window. Way too small for his massive form. Partially open. *She'd crawled inside to reach me?*

"I've got an idea," she exclaimed. She kept whispering, and he wondered what she'd sound like when she spoke normally. "You stay here, and I'll slip up the stairs. I'll peek and see how many enemies we're facing."

Enemies?

"And then I'll come back." She began to pull his arm off her shoulders.

"No." He tightened his hold.

Her head turned toward him. More of her scent flooded his nostrils, making his already foggy head feel even foggier. "If you're with them, I'll kill you." A warning she needed to hear. To hear and understand to the depths of her soul.

"Uh, I'm not with them." Rushed and hushed. "No need to kill me. Promise, there is absolutely no need. I'm really, really not with them. I'm Marley Jones. I'm a PI. A new PI, granted, but I'm—"

His hand clamped over her mouth because Declan thought he'd just heard the snarl of an engine. Someone coming back?

Her eyes stared at him. Again, too dark to see clearly, so he didn't know the color. But her eyes were big and deep. *And scared.*

Probably because of the knife he'd just put to her throat yet again. Or the threat to kill her. Or the hand that he had over her mouth so she couldn't scream for help.

She could have screamed plenty before I covered her mouth. And she cut me free. Hell, if she really is playing Good Samaritan, I have to be scaring the shit out of her.

He didn't hear the snarl of an engine again. His fingers slowly lowered.

"I get that this is scary for you," she said softly.

Was she reassuring him? Worrying about *him* being scared when he could feel the fear practically pouring from her body?

"But I'm on your side. I'll help you get out of here. I hid my car close by. If we get to it, we'll be home free."

Why was she bobbing and weaving? Wait. Maybe she wasn't bobbing and weaving. Why was the room spinning?

Oh, dammit. That's me. Dizziness spiraled through him,

and all he wanted to do was shut his eyes and sleep. Declan shook his head, hard.

"We *won't* be home free? You think the bad guys will come after us?"

He didn't think someone had gone to all the trouble of abducting him just so he could walk off into the night. When he wasn't weaving on his feet, Declan would figure out which bastard had done this to him. Then Declan would burn the bastard's world to the ground.

Which enemy did this to me? Because his little PI had been right before. An enemy was definitely at work. Declan had an extremely long list of enemies.

"So, I don't like to tell you your business but...if we're making a run for it, we should do it now. It's really quiet, and I think this is our best shot. Only I'd like to make that run for it without a knife at my throat." A pause. "You can trust me."

He could not trust anyone.

"I'll help you get out of here. I'm not going to leave you."

His chest burned. Probably because of the stupid drugs he'd been given. Not because of what she'd just said. Certainly not because this was the first time in his life that someone had promised not to leave him.

He moved the knife from her throat.

She exhaled. "Thank you. Let's keep it away from my neck, shall we? For good this time. I, um, really don't like knives."

They tended to be his weapon of choice. He always had a knife at the ready. When he wasn't, oh, say, drugged and tied to a chair in a damn basement. Declan kept the knife gripped in his right hand. "I'll go first."

"Um, again, not to tell you your business, but you're

weaving, and I think I'm the one who can maneuver better. Let me go up the stairs first and make sure the coast is clear. I'll be right back." She reached for the doorknob. Twisted it and... "Dammit, it's locked."

He'd expected that to be the case. "Can break it down." His slurring had definitely gotten worse. Those four words emerged as one. *Canbreakitdown.*

"On a normal night, sure, I bet you could. Probably with minimal effort, big guy. However, this isn't normal." She bit her lip as she seemed to consider options. "I'll go through the window. Find a way to sneak inside on the first floor. And come back down here for you."

He shook his head.

"Or I can go back to my car. Get a crowbar and bring it in through the window. We can pry the door open with it. Either way, *I'll be back, I swear.*"

What the fuck?

She squeezed his hand. "Count on me. Trust me."

He trusted no one. But..."Get...away." If she was some innocent...if her story was true... "Get away...from here. Leave me..."

"Screw that. I'm coming back." She spun away and ran for the window. As he watched, she climbed on an old shelf. Shimmied. And slid out of the window.

I have to get out of here, too.

Declan grabbed for the doorknob. He jerked. Twisted. Nothing happened. He lifted up his foot and kicked at the door. Once. Twice. Three times.

He fell on his ass.

Declan hauled himself back up. His breath heaved in and out. *Not a normal night.* Okay, so she'd been right about that part. But maybe there was something he could use in the smelly basement in order to get the hell out of there. He whirled around and almost fell again. Only he managed to keep himself upright at the last second. When his hand hit the wall as he steadied himself, he found a light switch. He flipped the switch, and more illumination flooded the room.

Now I can see what I'm working with. He staggered to the large cabinet on the right.

Maybe the PI should have looked around with him before she went running.

Unless she was lying. Unless this is some weird-ass mind game.

He opened the cabinet and had to do a double take. Because it sure as hell seemed like he was staring at a torturer's wet dream. Blades. Hammers. Saws. Needles. A slew of gleaming, silver instruments that looked as if they'd been stolen from a surgeon's bag of goodies.

Fuck me. Someone has a big night planned.

Too bad that Declan had other plans. He put down the knife and reached for the biggest hammer he saw. Declan curled his fingers around the handle. *This should do the trick.*

The door creaked open behind him. Declan spun and rushed forward with the hammer raised to attack.

"It's me!" His PI—why couldn't he remember her name?—threw up her hands. "Don't hit me!"

His hand—and the hammer—fell back to his side.

"Where did you get that?" She craned around him. Her eyes bulged. Dark, soulful eyes. So deep. Fucking spellbinding.

He blinked. She'd asked a question. Maybe about the hammer? Where it came from? "In the cabinet full of torture gear."

More craning of her head and body. She actually grabbed him so that she could look around him better. "Oh, no." Horrified. "Let's go. *Let's go now.*" She looped his arm around her shoulders and began hauling him toward the now open door and the stairs that waited just beyond that door.

He didn't really need help. He could get out fine on his own.

But she was helping him up the stairs. And soon they were bursting into what looked like an old kitchen. One that hadn't been used in ages judging by the grime and dust and the choking scent of rotten food.

They shuffled toward a closed door.

"I climbed in through the kitchen window," she told him, sounding a little out of breath. Probably because she'd been climbing in so many damn windows or because she'd dragged his wobbly ass upstairs. "Almost missed it. It was partially ajar. People need to shut their windows, am I right?"

No, she was not right. Open windows were leading to his freedom. People needed to leave them open all of the time.

She opened the door and tugged him onto a back porch and into the night. Not a cold night. Too hot, in fact. Maybe that was why the windows had been open. He didn't really care why. He just followed his PI as she staggered toward the trees behind what he now realized was some kind of cabin. He was putting too much of his weight on her, and he should stop.

But he was also having trouble positioning one foot in front of the other so...

"Maybe you should drop the hammer."

He didn't. They needed a weapon. He'd left the knife in the basement. He hadn't meant to do that. He'd planned to bring both weapons.

"What...what do you think they were gonna do with all those scalpels and saws?"

"Cut me into lots of pieces." *Cutmeintolotsofpieces*.

"Oh, God." She seemed to get a renewed burst of energy.

They made it to a VW Beetle. A convertible with the top up. She opened the passenger side and pushed him in before she slammed the door. Then she rushed around the car. Jumped inside and had the motor flaring to life. "Next stop, the police station."

His hand flew out and curled around her wrist even as the car hurtled forward. "No."

"No? Oh, you want to go to a hospital first—"

"Do you know who I am?"

The little car's engine snarled and sputtered because she was really hauling ass. "No," the PI confessed. "I don't. What's your name?"

He squinted at her. "You saved me, and you didn't know me?"

"I saw a guy get shoved into the back of a van. And I just saw *a torture cabinet*. Shouldn't you question me less and thank me more?"

Maybe. "Damn dangerous." A rumble. He was so freaking tired. "Don't ever do that shit again." He stroked along the inside of her wrist. No clue why. He just did it. Then Declan let her go. His eyes closed as he fell back against the passenger seat. "I'm Declan Flynn."

Silence.

The kind of shocked silence that told him the name had just rang a bell for her.

Then, voice squeaking a little, she asked, "*The* Declan Flynn? As in Declan Flynn, the *king of the mob*?"

Hardly. "Don't believe the hype." Even if some of the hype happened to be true. "Cops and I...don't mix."

"But I already called them! You were kidnapped! They're on the way, and we're probably going to run into—"

As if on cue, bright, blue lights filled the road ahead. The scream of sirens pierced the night.

"Them," she finished. "The cavalry is here."

Fabulous. "Whatever you do..." Okay, he wasn't gonna stay conscious much longer. He got that. The darkness pulled at him. "Don't let them throw me in a cell."

"Why on earth would they do that? You're the victim!"

Oh, but his PI was too precious. He just wanted to wrap her up...*and keep her*. He forced his eyes open so that he could see her one more time.

The sirens were louder. The blue lights brighter.

"Thanks for coming back for me," Declan murmured. She'd kept her promise.

"Declan, why would the cops want to put you in a cell? You're a victim!"

She'd just used the V-word twice. But she was wrong. "I'm a killer." Something he would never admit, not under typical circumstances. More like, this was one of the secrets he'd normally take to his grave. But this wasn't a normal time and whatever drugs he'd been given had made his tongue way too loose. "A killer straight to the core. It's in the blood, you know. Always in the blood."

She slammed on the brakes.

He fell into the darkness.

Chapter Two

DECLAN FLYNN SLOWLY OPENED HIS EYES.

Marley Jones perched nervously on the edge of his bed. Biting her lip, she waited for him to take in his surroundings. The bright, white walls. The low hum of voices coming from outside. The antiseptic smell.

His gaze focused on her.

She tried to smile and actually felt like she was mostly successful. Sure, the smile wouldn't reach her eyes. Her stomach was in too many knots for the smile to be real. But she didn't want to panic the man so...

She ramped up her smile a little more. Added a bit more friendly voltage.

His dark brows pulled together as he glowered at her.

"Uh, hi." Marley cleared her throat. "Do you remember me?"

He stared back at her with the most intense, most absolutely *dangerous* eyes that she'd ever seen in her life. It should be impossible for a pair of eyes to be described as dangerous, but his were. A swirling hazel that gazed at her with fierce intent. Not *good* intent. More like...*he's going to pounce on me at any moment.*

Maybe she should move off his hospital bed. Yes, good plan. She hopped up and started to flee toward the relative safety of the nearby chair. Only she never made it to the chair because his hand flew out and clamped around her wrist. Her pulse immediately skyrocketed as the impact of his touch flooded through her system.

Why do I react this way to him? Even last night, in the middle of hell and chaos, her reaction to him had been way, way off the charts. She'd tried to dismiss the reaction as stemming from adrenaline and nerves but...

Nope. I'm still reacting to him the same way.

"I remember you." Gruff. Deep. Rumbling. And no longer slurring. The calluses on the edges of his fingertips raked lightly across her skin.

His words had been running together last night. Probably due to the drugs that he'd been given. The docs at the hospital had watched him like a hawk because Declan had been dead to the world when he came in on the ambulance.

Her breath expelled in a rush of relief because he seemed to be awake and aware and finally back with her.

"You were with me in hell," he added.

Her eyebrows shot up. Okay. So perhaps he wasn't quite so aware.

"The basement," he clarified. "Hell."

Yes, granted, she could see where he'd describe the place that way. It certainly hadn't been heaven for her.

"You came back for me." His thumb brushed along her inner wrist.

His touch makes me feel so strange. Not bad. Not necessarily good, either. Too aware. Too sensitive.

Declan shook his dark head. "You shouldn't have done that. Major mistake on your part." He released her wrist.

But even though he was no longer holding her, she didn't flee to the safety of the chair. Instead, Marley turned back so that she faced him fully. "I shouldn't have come back to save you?" Had the man wanted her to abandon him to whatever twisted fate waited in that horrible basement?

His eyes—that hazel seemed to peer into her very soul. Without blinking, he stared straight at her and nodded.

Her shoulders stiffened. "I wasn't in the mood to leave a man to die." She would never be in that mood. There were enough monsters in the world without her becoming one, too.

"I would have gotten away."

Her jaw dropped. He couldn't be serious. "You couldn't even *walk!*"

"I would have gotten away." Utter certainty.

"I untied you." Maybe he had forgotten some important bits from the previous night. A refresher was clearly needed so he could be appropriately grateful. "You were tied to a chair when I cut you loose. Then I found a way for us to get out of that cabin. I even drove the getaway car." All without a thank you. Someone had clearly never been taught how to express gratitude. Not that she was looking for a shiny medal or anything...

But I did save the man's life. A little gratitude would not be too much to ask.

"You don't know what you've done." He shook his head. "Like I said, major mistake." He sat up in the bed. Winced.

Immediately, her hands flew out and curled around his shoulders. "You should take it easy. I heard one of the doctors say it looked like you had some crazy drug cocktail mix in your blood." Maybe she should call a nurse for him?

His head turned so that he was staring at her hand as it gripped his right shoulder. Slowly, his gaze slid back to her face. "Why are you here?"

Again, no gratitude. "Because you couldn't stay on your own! You were unconscious! Defenseless!" So many reasons. "What if your abductors had come after you again?"

"In a hospital? You thought they'd come at me in a hospital?"

He'd better not be making fun of her. She tightened her grip on what were some very strong shoulders. The thin hospital gown did little to hide the man's power. He probably *should* have looked weak as he sat in the bed. He'd been unconscious for hours.

Only, he didn't look weak. His dark hair was tousled, stubble covered his hard jaw, and his eyes glinted. He appeared...sexy. Strong. Dangerous.

In a hospital bed.

How on earth was he pulling that off? Meanwhile, she probably looked rumpled, wrinkled, disheveled, and generally like something a feral cat had hauled inside.

Declan Flynn was also just staring at her. Right. Because he'd asked a question, and she should respond and not simply gawk at him as she thought about feral cats. "You never know when your enemies might attack. The cops couldn't find anyone at that cabin. I hate to be the one to tell you, but...the people who abducted you got away." No softening that bombshell. It was what it was. "They are still out there somewhere, and they might come after you again." *Let go of his shoulders, woman.* She let go. Cleared her throat. "I didn't want you defenseless while you slept, so I stood guard."

His gaze dipped slowly down her body. Down, then

back up. And his lips twisted into what was almost a half-smile. "What are you?" he asked. "Five-foot-three? Four?"

"Six. I am five-foot-*six*." Important inches in her world. When you were surrounded by towering brothers, every inch counted.

"Uh, huh, and you look like if I breathe too hard, I'll knock you down."

Irritation buzzed through her blood. "I thought that perhaps you were still traumatized from the night before. Or that you were just not a morning person. But I have now reached a new conclusion." Her spine could not get stiffer. "You're an ungrateful ass."

He blinked.

"*My* five-foot-*six* self got you out of that cabin. I got you to my car. I got you to safety. And while I was dragging *your* nearly unconscious self, you didn't knock me down. Not even once." Though it had been a frantic struggle to reach her VW. Not something she'd mention at the moment. No need to give the man more fuel for his fire.

Her words made his smile stretch even more. Why? She hadn't said anything even remotely humorous.

Her gaze lingered on his face. Such a handsome face. Strong. High forehead. Long blade of a nose. Sensual—if just the slightest bit cruel—lips and—

"The scar's a bitch, isn't it?" Flat. Low. His hand lifted and scraped over the right side of his face.

She didn't pretend not to see the scar. It was long, slashing as it cut down his cheek and dipping into the stubble that lined his jaw. Maybe other people pretended they didn't see it. Maybe they politely averted their eyes. She wasn't those people. "It's stupid sexy."

His mouth dropped open.

Whoops. That would be her tendency to be brutally

honest...and say the wrong thing. Marley cleared her throat. "I'm sure it hurt horribly when you received it."

His hand fell away from the scar. "Didn't exactly feel good."

"But it really goes with your whole drop-dead dangerous and lethal air. Most people probably wouldn't be able to pull it off. But you do." Her gaze returned to meet his.

He stared at her with shock clear to see in his eyes.

She shrugged. "I'm very sorry you were hurt so badly that you scarred."

"You *aren't* bothered by the scar, though, are you? Not even a little?"

No. Her tongue slid over her lower lip. "I'm more bothered that you haven't thanked me yet. I expected an uber billionaire to have better manners."

"Who the hell are you?"

Now this was embarrassing. "Ah, see, I worried you might not remember my name. That would be thanks to the drug cocktail in your system." She rocked forward a bit. "I'm—"

"Jasmine and amber." His nostrils flared.

"Uh, no. That sort of sounds like a stripper name. I'm—"

"You *smell* like jasmine and amber."

That made sense. Probably hints of both in her perfume. "I'm Marley Jones, PI." *And this is the important part.* "You clearly need my services, so you should hire me on the spot." *Hire me. Please hire me.* It was hard not to sound as desperate as she felt.

Because she wasn't ready to walk away from Declan Flynn just yet. He needed her.

She was fascinated by him.

"Why would I hire you?" The little line was back between his dark brows.

How many times would the man need to be reminded that she'd saved his life? But she could make her case. Again. "You probably have an army of security personnel."

"Um."

That wasn't a yes or a no. "But I didn't see that army last night. I just saw little old me." Her palms were getting sweaty, so she casually wiped them on the front of her jeans. "I saw the men who took you. I saw their vehicle. And I *will* find them. I will track them down. I will hunt them. I will—"

"*Marley.*"

Her head swung to the right. The hospital door had been slightly ajar—one the nurses had left it open earlier—and now she realized that someone had been eavesdropping on her conversation with Declan. Such an incredibly rude thing to do.

But then, she'd found that Detective Parker Ellis was often rude.

Parker glowered at her from his position in the doorway. He had not exactly been a fan of Marley's since...well, probably since their one disastrous date ages ago.

"The *police* will find the people responsible for abducting Mr. Flynn. That's certainly not the job for some wannabe PI." Parker marched into the room with authority and arrogance oozing from his pores.

That was typically the way he did most things. Once upon a time, Parker had been the quarterback in high school. Then the jock of the moment at the University of Georgia. But an injury had taken him off the field, and these days, he spent his time throwing his weight around at the Augusta, Georgia, police department.

"Wannabe PI," Declan seemed to taste those words.

Her eyes narrowed as her head swung right back to Declan. "There's nothing wannabe about me. I have my license. I'm official. And I have a hundred percent case closure rate." No need to mention that she'd only had three cases so far. Two had been wives who wanted their cheating husbands photographed in the act. The third...that had been a pro-bono case. Caterina Robbins had vanished. Marley had found Caterina in twenty-four hours. So what if Caterina happened to be a Cheshire cat? A successful closed case was a successful closed case.

And I saved Declan Flynn last night. The Declan Flynn. Tech billionaire. Supposed mob royalty. Too gorgeous to be real...Declan Flynn. She'd saved him from getting sliced into lots and lots of little pieces. Oh, but those torture instruments were going to haunt her for days.

"How long have you possessed your license?" Declan asked softly.

"I—"

"Barely a month," Parker informed him with a bit too much satisfaction. "Our Marley tends to pick up and discard jobs pretty quickly. You have quite the resume don't you, Marley? Kids' party entertainer, pastry chef, real estate agent, bartender, and now...PI." Parker shook his head. His dirty blond hair tumbled over his forehead, and his blue eyes gleamed. "And let's not forget Ph.D. candidate. You do like to dabble, don't you?"

"I'm not dabbling." *But you're being a dick.* So she had some failed jobs in her past. Didn't mean that she wasn't going to be a kickass PI. She'd worked her butt off to get her license. She'd trained in self-defense. She'd shadowed other PIs for months. And that Ph.D. candidacy that he just liked to toss out like it was nothing? She'd nearly gotten her Ph.D.

in psychology. She *knew* how criminals worked. She knew all about the devious minds at play in the world.

A faint flicker of fear slithered down her spine as she remembered the incident that had ended her pursuit of her Ph.D. *Don't think about it right now. Focus on the moment. The present. The past can't hurt you.*

"How did I wind up in the hospital?"

Declan's low voice jerked her attention back to him. And when she looked at him, Marley was surprised to find his eyes dead on her. Not on the detective.

"The police met us on the highway." Did he recall that part? The shriek of sirens? The flash of blue lights?

Declan inclined his head.

"You were out cold in the passenger seat of Marley's car." Parker moved to her side. Got *way* too close, frankly. His shoulder brushed against hers.

Declan frowned.

Marley eased away from Parker.

Parker eased closer to her.

Declan's frown grew darker.

"An ambulance was behind the cop cars," Parker told him. His hands moved to his hips. His badge gleamed from a perch on his belt. "The EMTs ordered an immediate transport for you because you were unresponsive. Marley insisted on riding along with you."

Declan was staring straight at her. He kept doing that. And she could have sworn she felt the weight of his gaze like a physical touch. Talk about intensity.

But in response to Parker's words, Marley forced a shrug. She had insisted on being in the ambulance with Declan. "I rode along because I had to keep you safe." Something she had already mentioned to the man a time or two.

Parker laughed. "Uh, yeah. He's safe. You did your due diligence." Then the detective laughed yet again. A deep, booming laugh that some people might like. Marley was not one of those individuals. "It was cute the way you suddenly swore that you were his fiancée and that you had to go with him. Is that how you got the nurses to allow you to keep staying with him overnight? By swearing you were involved with the vic?"

Marley felt the sting of heat in her cheeks. "Desperate times call for desperate measures." There was no way she'd planned to leave Declan alone.

Declan's expression changed. He suddenly looked... *intrigued.*

A shiver slid down her spine. Sort of like when you get a hint that something really, really bad was about to happen to you.

"You told the EMTs that we were engaged?" Declan asked her. No emotion at all filled his deep, dark voice.

Marley bit her lower lip. "I sort of...implied that you would freak out if you woke up without your fiancée at your side." That was not the same as saying she *was* his fiancée.

"Oh, she didn't imply it." Parker motioned toward. "She flat out said those exact words. I was here at the time. '*He will freak out if he wakes up and his fiancée isn't at his side.*'"

"I didn't *say* that I was your fiancée!" Marley hurried to point out that important distinction to Declan. "Just that if you woke up and your fiancée wasn't there—*not that I am your fiancée*—you would freak. Again, I didn't say that I was your fiancée. People just drew that conclusion."

"Because it was the conclusion you wanted them to draw," Declan's rumble cut through her words.

Her breath expelled. "I wanted you safe." If that was a crime, call her guilty.

"And again..." From Parker. "He is safe. Your job is done. So, pretend fiancée, why don't you head on out? I've already interviewed you."

Yes, he had. During the night when Declan had slept.

"And, now," Parker added as his voice flattened, "I need to ask Declan some questions about his— "

"No." Declan's adamant voice came out as a crisp denial.

"No?" Parker's brows rose. His arm brushed Marley's again and—

Declan shoved the hospital covers out of the way. He swung his legs to the side of the bed and surged upward. Marley immediately jumped forward and grabbed him, afraid that he might fall as he'd fallen the previous night when he first got out of the chair in that horrid basement.

But Declan didn't seem to be in any danger of falling. He stood up, strong and powerful, and his head tilted as he stared down at her. His nostrils flared the tiniest bit, as if he were pulling in her scent again.

She realized that she was pressing her hands to his chest. Standing way too close. "I thought you needed me," she whispered as heat stung her cheeks.

His head dipped toward her. "I do," he whispered back.

Surprise rolled through Marley.

Parker reached out his hand and curled it around Marley's shoulder. "You need to—" Parker began.

"*You* need to stop touching her," Declan instructed, and there was a lethal note in his voice. "It's quite irritating. Both to me and my...fiancée."

"That's bullshit," Parker groused even as he dropped his hand. For an instant, he glared at Declan. Anger flashed hard in the detective's eyes before he blinked, and it vanished.

Had she just imagined that emotion? Before she could decide for sure—

"No, it's actually the truth," Declan announced. "Not bullshit. I find myself annoyed every single time you touch her. And Marley doesn't like it, either, or else she wouldn't keep moving away from you."

True story, she didn't like it. She was also still touching Declan, and he might not want her hands on him. She started to move back.

"Touch me anytime," Declan invited her. "I like it when you do."

A lick of heat unfurled within her. *Not the time.* But it was good to know that he felt that awareness—correction, attraction—too. *And what are we going to do about that?*

"I meant," Parker cleared his throat, "her being your fiancée is bullshit. I know the real deal. She's the PI who got lucky and saw your abduction. The two of you don't know each other. You're total strangers."

"I'm the one who got lucky." Declan smiled at her.

Such a killer smile. Her breath left her in a surprised rush. Declan was an attractive man, but when he smiled that particular way...*wow.* She felt that smile in every inch of her body.

"Though, for the record, I truly could have saved myself."

Why was he still spinning that story? "Liar," Marley accused, and for some reason, it almost felt like an endearment when she said the word.

Declan's head moved in the smallest of nods.

I'm still touching him. And I still like it.

Another loud throat clearing came from Parker. "I have

questions," he groused. "I need to know who took you. I need to find the bastards because I don't like people terrorizing others in *my* town."

Marley finally pulled her hands away from Declan.

He turned more toward the cop. "I have no idea who took me. When I think of last night, I remember waking up, tied to a chair." He glanced down at his body, and his face tightened in distaste. "This gown has got to go."

She didn't think he had on anything *beneath* the gown. So if that gown *went* anywhere, she and Parker would be getting quite the show.

"We've got our crime scene team scouring the basement where you were held. We found the discarded ropes. We found the torture instruments." Parker whistled. "Someone was planning for one hell of a party with you."

That wasn't exactly Marley's idea of a party. Her stomach twisted.

The detective pushed, "Who hates you so much that they'd want to do that to you?"

Declan rolled a shoulder.

Marley gaped at him. Was he seriously showing zero concern? When someone had abducted him and clearly planned to spend a large amount of time torturing the man? "You have no idea?"

Before Declan could respond to her, Parker noted, "I'll need a list of your enemies. Both those in the business world and in your personal life."

"That's gonna be one hell of a long list," Declan told him after the faintest of pauses. "I don't play nicely in business...or in my personal life."

Tech billionaire. Declan was supposed to be some sort of mega genius when it came to tech. He had all sorts of secretive contracts with the government, and he'd created software that would allow people to surf on the web and be completely untraceable and he'd—

"Is this abduction related to the mob?" A stark question from Parker. "Because we need to cut through the BS and get to the truth. That setup at the cabin sure as hell looked like something mob organized to me."

The temperature in that small hospital room seemed to drop. Marley shivered because the cold slithered in every direction. No, it seemed to *come* from Declan and slither out to fill up all the other space. His attention was suddenly focused one hundred percent on the detective. "You think I'm some sort of criminal?" Declan questioned in his emotionless voice.

"There have been rumors for—"

"I work with the US government. I have dozens of contracts with them and with foreign entities. My companies provide satellite links, they provide security services, and they provide the needed tech to help keep this world moving." A muscle flexed along his jaw. "You really believe government bureaucrats would approve my contracts if I was some kind of mob thug?"

Not a thug. "Royalty," Marley murmured.

Declan's head swung toward her.

She could have slapped a hand over her mouth. But, come on, why pretend the elephant wasn't in the room? Especially considering what had happened the previous night. Parker wasn't wrong. The abduction did feel like a mob job. A message had clearly been sent. "The gossip says you're mob royalty. That your grandfather and father were involved—that they *created* a syndicate that took power in Chicago and throughout the northeast."

"I am not my father." Cold. No, *chilling*. "Never make that mistake. I'm not my father. Not my grandfather."

She sucked in a breath.

He eased a bit closer toward her. And he'd already been very close. "My fiancée should know better." A low rasp. "If the US government thought I was a criminal, they wouldn't be in so many partnerships with me."

"Not necessarily." Marley just felt compelled to add, "Pretty sure they've been involved with criminals before."

His eyes narrowed. That hazel...back to being *so very dangerous*.

"Not that I'm saying you're a criminal," she hastened to add. *Do not call a potential client a criminal*. That was probably rule one in the PI handbook. If it wasn't, it should be. "I'm just saying...perhaps some of your father's old associates didn't get the memo about you not being involved in what he and your grandfather may have—"

"Neither of them were ever tied to the mob. Those are bullshit stories. Myths to make the family seem more powerful and threatening."

She wasn't looking at a myth. His words sounded like truth, but they sure felt like a lie at the same time.

"You think I'm in the mob?" Declan caught her chin in his hand. "You think I'm some monster, yet you saved my ass anyway?"

There was so much gold in the center of his eyes. Her breath caught, then released in a soft exclamation. "You finally admit I saved your ass?"

"I—"

"*Declan!*" A sharp exclamation that came from the— yep, still open—hospital door.

When Marley glanced that way instinctively, she found a nurse staring back at her. A pretty brunette with wide eyes. But the nurse wasn't alone. A sharply dressed man in a too expensive suit with carefully styled, silver-streaked hair stood with the nurse. His eyes were on Declan. Surprise—and worry—filled his stare. "I saw the story on the news!" A sharp exclamation from the man as he bustled forward. "You're on every channel. You and—" His gaze darted from Declan's hand as it held Marley's chin...to Marley. His suspicious stare locked on her face. "You and her," the stranger finished as his gaze assessed her.

"Why is the patient out of the bed?" the nurse demanded.

"Because the patient fucking felt like getting out," Declan threw back. "James," he said, addressing the man who kept frowning at Marley. "I need clothes. Tell me that you brought my suit because I don't know what the hell they did with my things."

"They were taken into evidence," Parker said. "Your abductors might have left trace materials behind."

Declan was still holding her chin. Marley eased back. She didn't like the way that the James guy was eyeing her.

"I need clothes, and then I need to get the hell out of here." Curt words from Declan.

"The press is outside," James warned him. "The feeding frenzy is in full effect. It's not every day that Declan Flynn is abducted and then saved by—saved by—"

"I'm a private investigator." Marley straightened her shoulders. "I'm the woman who got Declan to safety."

James opened his mouth. But no words came out.

"Oh, she's not just a PI," Declan drawled. "James Henry, meet my fiancée...Marley Jones."

Chapter Three

"I don't understand what's happening here." Marley sat with her delicate shoulders hunched and her hands twisting in her lap as the limo pulled away from the hospital.

"We're getting away from the hospital and going back to my suite at the hotel." Simple enough to understand. Declan ignored the faint headache that drummed behind his left eye. Getting out of that hospital had been a bitch. He'd had to wait hours for the doctor to arrive. There had been more blood work. More tests. And the annoying detective—the one who liked to touch Marley far too much —had lingered the whole time with his too watchful stare as he'd fired off question after question. And during all of those questions, the detective's stare had drifted a bit too often to Marley.

Find your own PI, asshole.

Because as far as Declan was concerned, Marley was his.

"Yes." Marley cleared her throat. "I get that we're in a

vehicle and heading for your hotel. Check. Not having a problem understanding that part."

He would not smile. He shouldn't even want to smile, not after the shit that had gone down the previous night. But there was something about Marley Jones...

She didn't leave me in that basement. She came back for me. Even when he'd told her to get the hell away. She'd come back.

Marley might not get it but...that didn't happen his world. When danger came calling, people tended to flee. No one had tried to protect him before.

Certainly not some gorgeous, sensual, five-foot-*six* angel with curves that begged to be touched, dark hair with streaks of red hidden in its depths, and dark, chocolate eyes that stared straight *through* him. Her skin looked like silk, and all he wanted to do was reach out and touch her. To see if it would be as soft as it appeared.

I touched her in the hospital room. She was so soft. I need to touch her again. Only instead of touching her, his hands fisted.

"What I *don't* understand is why you insisted I come along with you." Her head tilted as she studied him. Locks of her hair slid over her shoulder. "I thought you didn't need me."

Oh, I need you. In ways that he had never expected. "You're the one who keeps saying that you saved me."

"Because I did, in fact, save you."

And now he was going to have to save her. Something she would not understand, not until it was too late. But as James had revealed, the press was, in fact, salivating. *Billionaire kidnapped, held in torture basement.* That headline was too salacious to pass up. Especially because his family had been tabloid fodder for years and years. With good reason. And bad reason.

I am not my father.

At least, he normally wasn't like his bastard of a father. Declan's right fist slowly unfurled. His hand lifted, and his fingers skimmed over the scar that would mark him for the rest of his life.

"I saved you, and now you're carrying me off to your… hotel suite?" She blinked those deep and dark eyes at him. "And you keep telling everyone I'm your fiancée. I get it, I shouldn't have said that bit. My bad."

No, she should not have. A target had been placed on her back the minute that she helped him, and with her claims to the EMTs and the hospital staff that she was personally involved with Declan, that target had only gotten bigger. "You're the one who insisted on staying with me." So this was her fault. She'd also insisted on helping him to escape from hell. "Tell me…" His fingers stroked once more over the scar before his hand dropped. "Do you always risk your life to save people you don't know or am I special?"

Her long lashes flickered. "I feel like you're playing with me." She turned away. Slithered a bit across the leather seat and then her hand was rapping on the window that separated them from the driver. "I'm just going to get out now. I don't enjoy being someone's joke."

Lightning fast, he closed the distance between them and caught her hand mid-rap. "I could never think of you as a joke." No, she was far too important for that.

He heard the faint catch in her breathing.

"You feel the attraction, too," Declan noted. *Good. I sure as hell don't want to be alone in this madness.*

The screen that separated the front of the limo from the back slowly lowered. "You need something, boss?" His driver—and bodyguard—Andy Greer stayed focused on the road ahead of him as he asked the question. Marley had been right when she said that he normally had an army of guards around him. A man in Declan's position required protection.

Except, last night, he'd ditched the protection. *And someone had been watching. Waiting for that mistake.*

But the thing about Declan—he was an extremely fast learner. And he never, ever repeated the same mistake twice.

"Yeah, I need something," he told Andy. "Gonna want you to make a pitstop by Marley's place so that she can pick up her luggage." He couldn't help but glide his fingers along her inner wrist. Her pulse raced beneath his touch.

Was that because she felt the surge of attraction like he did?

Or because she was pissed as hell because he'd basically forced her into the back of the limo with minimal explanation?

"What's the address?" Andy asked.

Declan stared at Marley.

"Why do I need luggage?" she whispered.

Tread carefully. "Because I'm hiring you. Didn't you say I needed protection?"

"Uh, boss…" Andy began. "You've got plenty of—"

"The address, Marley," Declan demanded, cutting through Andy's words because Declan was quite aware that he did, indeed, have plenty of protection. Not like he needed a reminder. "Rattle it off, would you? Then we'll talk more."

Though her delicate jaw hitched up, she rattled off the address.

Declan barely held back his smile. He *did* keep holding

her wrist, but with his free left hand, he hit the button to raise the privacy screen once again.

Her gaze never left his face. Her angry, distrustful, and utterly delightful stare.

"Where have you been all my life?" he wondered.

She blinked. Then frowned. "You're still not yourself, are you?" Marley pulled her hand free of his grip.

Dammit.

But then she reached her hand up—both of her hands, actually—and she cupped his face. "You should have listened to the doctor and stayed put in the hospital. The staff there should have kept observing you, but, oh, no, you had to be the big, demanding, billionaire badass who left right away. *Against the* doctor's orders. Do I have to remind you that you were drugged?"

Yeah, he was quite aware. No reminder necessary. "Someone slipped something in my drink." A mistake— theirs and his. "I saw the bartender prepare the drink myself." Which just meant that the SOB had been damn good at slight-of-hand tricks. A real magician, that asshole.

Her lips parted in surprise. "You didn't mention that to the detective. You told him last night was still *blurry*."

Bits were blurry. True story. "I don't remember how I got to the basement. Who tied me up. That shit is blurry."

"But the bartender isn't. You remember him, don't you?"

He did.

Her gaze never left him. "Parker wanted to know where you'd been before you were abducted. You didn't name any club or bar, but you do remember exactly which places you visited, don't you?"

Declan inclined his head. "Place. Singular. And I

thought I might revisit the location with a certain intrepid PI that I will be hiring."

Her hands slid away from his cheeks. Then *she* inched away from him. Marley returned to her original seat in the limo. "Don't play games with me."

"Why not? Don't you like games?"

A negative shake of her head. "This is life or death. Not Monopoly."

So good of her to point out the difference. He slid his index finger along his lips to hide the quirk of his mouth.

He could practically see the wheels turning in her head before she muttered, "Parker said the cops should be in charge of the investigation."

"Um. I did hear him mention that a time or twenty." He'd also picked up on a few things like... "The detective doesn't like you."

"He doesn't like that I wouldn't sleep with him when we went out."

Every muscle in Declan's body tensed.

"But I don't screw every man who buys me dinner, and, for the record, it was a crappy dinner."

Breathe, Declan. Breathe. A sudden, red haze seemed to have clouded his vision. Hell, maybe it was the drugs he'd been given. Because the heat flooding through his body didn't feel normal. It actually...hell, did it feel like jealousy? Was this what jealousy was?

"He's held a grudge since then. And..." An exhale from Marley. "I am a new PI." A bit of a forlorn confession. "Parker has that part right."

He doubted if Parker had anything right. "Did you know who I was when you gave chase after the van?"

"We've been over this before. No, I didn't." She didn't

even blink. "All I saw was three men. Two were trying to drag your rather large and slightly floppy self into the back of a van. I saw the back of your head. Dark, thick hair. I screamed for them to let you go. They ignored me. They shoved you inside and hauled ass away." A delicate roll of her shoulders. "So I gave chase. I called the cops along the route, but those creeps in the van were moving helluva fast. And going down some seriously snaking roads. I lost the signal on my phone twice. Once I thought I'd lost the van. I had to be careful. I kept my lights off a lot because I didn't want to tip them off that I was trailing. I was afraid that if they realized they were being followed, they might panic and do something foolish."

"More foolish than kidnapping me?" Because that would prove to be a fatal mistake.

"I thought they might panic and kill you. Then they'd just toss your body out of the rear of the van and keep driving."

He grunted. "Lovely visual."

A nod from her. "I snuck into the cabin as quickly as I could."

Yes, she had. "Do you often rush straight into dangerous situations?"

Her gaze cut from him. "Danger can be everywhere. You don't have to rush and find it. Sometimes, it will find you." Her shoulders didn't roll in a shrug again. Instead, they straightened with determination. "You do need me."

Yes, I do. But, darling, you need me even more. Something she did not yet realize. Soon enough, she would.

"I can find these guys, I know it. Tell me the bar you visited—describe the bartender to me. I'll go from there. You can keep your guards in place, and I'll track down the people who took you. Count on me for this job."

"Oh, I am definitely counting on you." He spread his

legs out in front of him. "You're *my* PI." Was there a subtle possessiveness on those words?

She'd stiffened.

Okay, perhaps the possessiveness had been not-so-subtle.

"I'm hiring you," Declan told her. "Full-time. While we are together, I will be the only client you have. So any others will need to get the news that you are off the market."

"Uh, yeah, I'll give them that news." She coughed. "Don't you want to know my rates first?"

"I'll pay you three grand a day. Meals and lodging will be provided."

She coughed again. Or maybe choked. Declan wondered if he should lean forward and pat her on the back. He even lifted his hand to help.

"*Three grand a day?* That's like...twenty-one thousand for seven days."

Yes, it was exactly like that. "Is it not enough?"

Her eyes doubled in size. "Dude, I will do the job for twenty-five bucks an hour, plus expenses. You do not need to overpay me. Keep the cash."

Why? "I have plenty of cash."

Her wide-eyed stare swept the limo. "Clearly. But I am not taking advantage of you."

Is that what she thought was happening? So very wrong. "Three grand a day. You move into my world. You stay close to me. We hunt the kidnappers together." There was no way he was letting Marley out of his sight. Not even if he had to chain her to his side. Which was exactly what he was doing, in his way. "In case you missed it, I have money to burn."

"Yeah, but I'm not a fire, so don't throw money on me." She crossed her arms over her chest. "And you're not going to stay a billionaire if you are so careless with your cash."

She fascinated him. "Are you always this blunt with people?"

"No. Usually I don't call people idiots when they try to hire me. I tell them that they are geniuses." A huff. "Look, I'm taking the job. I *want* the job. Finding these guys and stopping them is my goal." Her lips pulled down. "Honestly, I'd hunt them even if you weren't hiring me."

Yes, he'd rather feared she would. Thus, the job offer. "You'll need to move in with me."

"What?"

"Move in. With me." Was that clear enough? He thought he'd enunciated things very well. "While we are in town, you'll stay in my hotel suite. Don't worry, it has two bedrooms." Unfortunately. "No one-bed situation."

"Uh, good to know."

"And if we travel to Chicago, my estate has ample rooms."

"Ample, right. Check."

"Where I go, you go. And, of course, if any reporters get too curious about what's happening and why you're so close, we'll just provide the handy cover story you already created for us." *Hello, my lovely fiancée.*

Her pink tongue swiped along her lower lip.

And his gaze became absolutely locked on her mouth. *Oh, the places I want that sweet mouth to be.*

"Can't we just admit that fiancée stuff was BS? Tell everyone I'm a PI? I'm sure some enterprising person will pull up my job info, anyway."

He wondered what she would taste like.

"Uh, Declan?"

His gaze slowly rose so that he could get lost in that dark stare of hers again. "You're going to marry me."

Her brows rose.

"That's the cover story we are telling everyone. It will allow you to move in all of my circles. To be with me at every moment. No one will think I'm just moving a junior PI into my life. But they'd buy that I was moving my new obsession in close to me."

Obsession. A slip of the tongue.

She bit her lower lip. Dammit. And his eyes were right back on her mouth. *I want to taste her.*

She freed her lower lip. "So this is to be an...undercover mission?"

If that was what she wanted to call it. "Do you have a boyfriend who will object?" Boyfriend, lover, person who Declan needed to make vanish.

"No, I'm not involved with anyone right now."

"You are." Again, he pinned her with his stare. "You're involved with me. Going forward, this will be our story." He paused for a beat. "We were out together. We became separated. You saw the bozos shoving me in the van. Like any concerned fiancée, you followed me and called for help."

"A concerned PI would do the same. I don't see why we need the cover story."

He needed it because it would be another layer of protection for her. When he publicly claimed her as his... *You do not touch what is mine.* Some messages would need to be deeply, deeply understood.

"Declan?"

His chest tightened. His dick hardened. He liked it when she said his name. Too much. "I want you."

"What?"

The limo slowed to a stop.

Declan made no move to leave the vehicle. "I want you. Figured I should just tell you how I felt. If you aren't interested, you say the word right now. I'll make sure things stay completely professional between us."

"A professional PI relationship?" Her voice had gone a little breathless.

"Um."

Her lashes swept down to conceal her eyes. "And if I say that...if I say that I get an electric rush each time we touch, that my heart rate speeds up and I get these images of us together, doing all kinds of...of things in my head...what would you do?"

No one in his world had been this honest with him. Certainly, no romantic partner.

"Oh, God. That's what the three grand is for, isn't it?" Absolute horror coated her face as her lashes swept up. "You're paying me for sex." Red blasted into her cheeks. "I'm a PI, not a prostitute." She lunged toward him, and her index finger stabbed Declan in the chest. "And you can just—"

He kissed her. He'd kissed her in that hell of a basement, but it had been a fast, fleeting brush of their lips. A taste that had tormented him.

Now, he wanted her mouth more than he wanted anything else, so he took it. Declan expected heat. Sensual energy. Desire.

What he didn't expect was the full-on, lust-filled explosion that happened when their mouths touched.

And she tastes even fucking better than she smells.

Her mouth opened wider beneath his, and he let his control slip away.

Chapter Four

Declan Flynn was kissing her.

She was kissing him.

Her mouth had opened wide beneath his plundering lips, and she was greedily kissing him back with wild abandon. Her hands had moved to grab his shoulders and hold on tightly. A moan built in her throat. Need and hot desire spiraled through her. She had never, ever reacted this way to a simple kiss before. Not gone from anger to—to...

Some seriously intense, raging desire. The kind of desire that made her want to jump on his lap, straddle him, and hold on for what promised to be one incredible ride. Quite possibly, the best ride of her life.

What is wrong with you, woman? Get your senses back! One did not lose all control and propriety just from a kiss. Or at least, one didn't normally.

Yet she was.

Her nails sank into his shoulders. Her tongue licked against his.

He—

Lifted his head. "Thanks for saving my life." Deep. Rumbly. Dead sexy.

She blinked. And her cheeks burned even hotter than they had before. "Did you just give me a *thank you* kiss?" They were practically eye-to-eye.

The skin near his eyes crinkled with his smile. "No, I just gave you an I-want-to-fuck-you kiss. But if you're confused, I can certainly do it again."

Yes, yes, do it again. And again.

But...propriety. He was hiring her. Offering her lots and lots of money for her first big case. A case that could prove to everyone just how serious she was about pursuing a PI career. One did not jump clients.

Even if the client can kiss helluva well.

"You want me. I want you." Again, he spoke in that deep, rumbly voice that seemed to sink right through her. "Good to know we're clear on that point."

Wait. Hold on. Marley scrambled away from him. "Just because I kissed you, it doesn't mean that I intend to—that I plan to—that I want to—"

"Fuck me until we're both too tired to move?"

Marley sucked in a deep breath.

"Just know the offer is on the table." He made a show of adjusting the sleeve of his fancy suit coat. The guy at the hospital—James something—had brought the change of clothing to his boss. Declan had ditched the paper-thin hospital gown for a crisp, white shirt, a gray suit coat, and matching pants. His black shoes had gleamed as they tapped over the tiled floor at the hospital. In record time, he'd transformed and appeared as if he was ready to pose on some business magazine cover.

Meanwhile she looked...

Oh, no. Her eyes widened. Her hands flew up to try and

smooth what had to be some seriously out-of-control hair. She'd splashed water on her face in the hospital. Gotten a toothbrush and toothpaste from a kind nurse but otherwise, she was still in the ever-so-rumpled clothing from last night and probably looking like the final girl from a horror movie.

"Why did your eyes go wide again?" His head cocked. "What's wrong?"

"I look like death, and you just made out with me."

A sudden bark of laughter came from Declan. No, not a bark. A full-on, wild roar of laughter. She frowned at him because his laughter was just rude. He could have at least said she didn't look *that* bad. Instead, he had lost it.

The driver opened the limo's side door. He poked his head in, and his stunned expression locked on Declan. "Boss?"

More laughter, but at least it was starting to sound a bit subdued. "Give us...give us a moment, will you, Andy?"

A quick nod. The door immediately shut.

Marley crossed her arms over her chest. "I am so happy to amuse you."

"Most things don't amuse me. Most things piss me off or bore me." His laughter faded as he studied her. "You're different."

He needs to work hard on the charm. Very, very hard. "Yeah, because I'm not a *thing*. I'm a person." A person with feelings that he'd just hurt.

He studied her. "You understand...you couldn't look like death if you tried?"

He obviously did not know her well. "Is that your way of complimenting me?"

"Do you need compliments?"

"No." She didn't.

"Because if you do, just know that I want you more than

I can ever remember wanting anyone. I want you so much that I'd love to fuck you here and now."

She slanted a glance his way. "That could be due to the drugging. Maybe you're just not yourself at the moment."

"I'm definitely not myself with you." Softer. "And it's not due to the drugs. The drugs have nothing to do with how big my dick is."

"Jeez! Don't say things like that!"

He shrugged. "You kissed me back just as fiercely as I kissed you...and you haven't been drugged. What excuse are you going to use?"

"Excuse?"

"Um. Yes. For the attraction we feel for each other. Off-the-charts, isn't it? Or do you normally respond that way to a first kiss with a man?"

It hadn't been their first kiss. It had been their second. Not that she was counting. "Your driver is waiting outside." She peeked toward the window. They were in front of her small rental house. "We should get moving."

"It's okay. Andy is paid a ridiculous amount of money to wait." His fingers tapped along his thigh. "Answer my question."

"Which one?" A quick reply. "You've asked several."

"Do you normally respond that way when you're kissed?"

Respond that way? Did he mean...did her nipples normally get so tight and sensitive, did her panties get damp, and did she want to crawl all over the man kissing her? "No. I, ah, can't say that my response is typically so strong." Understatement of the century. Marley hoped that she sounded suitably cool and nonchalant.

His eyelids flickered. "Good to know. Because I don't

normally go from zero to *fuck-her-now* quite so quickly, either."

She had to try twice in order to swallow the lump that rose in her throat. "Good, ah, to know."

"The other question you didn't answer...what excuse are you going to use?"

"Adrenaline." It was the first thing that popped into her mind.

His lips began to curl.

Do not dare laugh again, Declan Flynn. "It's been a very stressful night. You slept for hours, but I'm still riding the adrenaline wave." And an exhaustion wave because she'd been afraid to sleep at the hospital. Afraid that if she closed her eyes, something would happen to him.

"You kissed me like your life depended on it...because of adrenaline?"

She'd never been a fan of lies. Her shoulders slumped. "I kissed you that way because...I don't know why. My body responds to you. I want you." There. Stark. Bold. "I am coming off an adrenaline surge, but I also had about twenty minutes of sleep last night. I'm not thinking clearly so my control isn't what it probably should be." *Wait. Does this make it sound like I can't handle the job?* Marley immediately straightened the shoulders she'd slumped. "You can trust me to find the people who took you. I'll sleep and be back to one hundred percent, I promise."

His face had become an unreadable mask. "And what are your promises worth?"

"Everything." A whisper. "Sometimes, all you have is your word. I like to think that when I make a promise to a client, it's as binding as a contract."

A slow nod from Declan. Then he extended his hand toward her. "Then let's shake on that contract."

It's happening. Declan Flynn is hiring me. But she hesitated. "The attraction—it has nothing to do with my work as your PI."

"Sex is separate. If it happens, it's because you can't go another moment without having me inside you." His hand remained extended.

She tried to close her mouth. "You say outrageous things."

"I'm trying to be clear with you." His hand never lowered. "I want you. I want to fuck you. But that is separate from my case. I want you as my PI. I want you staying close to me. At all times."

Her hand lifted, but didn't touch his. Not yet. "I have a few stipulations." Though she needed to hurry with them because she didn't like the idea of poor Andy just standing by the car. "First, we are not telling the world that we're engaged."

"And why not?"

Because her brothers would lose their minds. "We can say that we're involved. But I'm not sporting a ring, so I don't think we need to go with the full-on engagement story. I can just be your current girlfriend. The fling of the moment."

His jaw tensed. "What other stipulations do you have?"

"Honesty." There. Done. "It's very important. You're holding back info from the cops." Something that was very dangerous considering what had happened last night. "Don't hold back from me. Tell me everything."

"Any other stipulations?"

"Not at the moment."

"Um." He wiggled his fingers. Long, strong fingers. "Are you planning to ever shake my hand?"

Her fingers pressed to his. Declan's hand immediately

closed around hers. Warm. Slightly rough with calluses. Utterly dwarfing her own hand.

And she realized that, though they had shaken on the deal, he had not actually *agreed* on her terms. Not with his words. "Uh, Declan—"

He let her go. Turned for the door. "We need to grab a bag for you and then get back to my suite. I sent James to keep an eye on our asshole bartender so that the jerk wouldn't leave town. But you need rest before we interrogate him."

You sent James...and you're telling me this, now? As for interrogations, maybe that should be the business best handled by the cops. "About the interrogation..."

Declan had already climbed from the limo. She scrambled to follow him. When she got out of the limo, Marley couldn't help but wince. The limo was hugely out of place on the quiet street. It *blocked* two driveways. And her neighbors were out and gaping as they unpacked groceries.

Marley sent them a quick wave, and then she grabbed Declan's hand and began towing him toward her slightly sloping front porch. The cold had long since withered her flowers. "Be out as fast as possible, Andy," she promised.

At the door, she paused to free Declan and to fumble with her keys only...

The front door was slightly ajar. Ajar as in—the lock had been smashed. "Oh, no."

"*What?*" From Declan.

But he didn't give her a chance to explain. Instead, his hands closed around her waist. He lifted her up and placed her behind him.

"Fuck," Declan swore as he glared at the lock. Then, "Get back to the limo. Get inside it."

She tapped him on the shoulder. His head jerked back toward her.

"My house," Marley informed him. "And *I'm* the PI. You're the one who should go back to the limo."

His look questioned her sanity.

Why? She was being incredibly sane. "Declan, it's *my* house."

"Some bastard broke inside!"

Yes. "And that bastard could still be inside."

"Get in the limo."

Their business relationship was clearly not off to a good start. *"Get out of the way."*

He didn't. He did push open the front door and head straight inside her home. Like he was some fierce cop and not say, oh, a tech billionaire who had no business storming *any place.* But, storm, he did. She hurried right on his heels. As soon as they were inside...

A shocked gasp tore from her as Marley stared around in horror. This wasn't some robbery—what she'd feared when she saw the broken lock. This was—this was...

Destruction.

Chaos.

Rage.

Her home hadn't just been ransacked. Her home had been utterly destroyed. Picture frames smashed. Her TV obliterated into hundreds of pieces. Her couch cushions slashed to bits of stuffing. The floor was littered with wreckage, and as she stared at the remnants of her life, pain knifed straight into Marley's chest.

This wasn't a break-in.

This was a message. This was hate.

She took a step forward, only to have Declan's arm immediately wrap around her waist. He hauled her back against his body. "You go nowhere without me." A savage growl.

He was really missing the PI part of the equation, but she was too busy burning with rage and a strange grief to discuss the point with him. They needed to search the house to make sure the perpetrator wasn't still inside. Her gut said the jerk was long gone. That he must have come under the cover of darkness to wreak his destruction or else her nosey neighbors would have seen him entering her place and obliterating her lock.

"Tell me that you have a weapon on you," Declan rasped. His breath trickled lightly over her ear.

She shook her head. Weapons weren't allowed in the hospital, and she'd had to stay there all night. There were weapons stashed in her car, but since she'd ridden in the ambulance with him and abandoned her car on the side of the road—well, she wasn't too sure where her ride was. Maybe police impound? She'd have to ask Parker. When she was done with her current emergency.

"Good thing I have one," Declan murmured. And the man pulled out a gun.

"Where did you get that?" And when?

"James brought it to me."

In the hospital? Where guns weren't allowed? "That's against the rules."

He stared at her. Just stared. Then said, "I have the gun. That means I lead the search. You stay behind me."

"You give way too many orders for a client." And... "You could always give me the gun."

He wasn't. He was heading through her house. Since someone had to watch his arrogant back, she took care of his six. With every step, rage blossomed more and more inside of her. They slipped into her kitchen.

Every plate was smashed. Every bowl shattered.

Her hand reached out and curled around a knife that had fallen to the floor. As a rule, she hated knives. They reminded her of a time she'd like to forget, but she needed some sort of weapon. A knife was better than nothing.

Her fingers only trembled a little as she gripped the handle of the knife.

They left the kitchen. Trekked soundlessly down the small hallway. The door to her bedroom was ajar. She braced herself before they entered, so she wasn't overly surprised to find the same chaos waiting in the room that had previously been her safe haven.

Bedding slashed. Mattress stabbed open. Every drawer in my dresser and chest pulled out. The contents littered the floor. Her underwear had been slashed just like the bedding. All her clothes—slashed. "This took a lot of time," she whispered.

"And a lot of rage."

Her pictures were broken, too. When she stepped forward, her foot crunched one of the pieces of glass that had been in a picture frame.

"Fucking bastard." A low snarl from Declan.

Her head whipped to the right.

A photo was on her wall. A photo that had previously been in one of the silver frames that she kept on her nightstand. It was a picture of her standing between her two brothers. They were all smiling. Or at least, they had been smiling. It was impossible to see her expression in the photo now because a knife stabbed into her face. The blade sank into the wall behind the photo, pinning the image in place.

Her body tensed. She knew a message when she saw one. She'd *gotten* the message the instant she stepped into her home and seen the wreckage. Someone was very, very angry with her.

Someone wanted her dead.

Declan reached for the knife that sliced into her photo.

"Don't!"

He looked back at her protest.

"There could be prints on it." The person—or people—who'd left the deadly message were long gone, but perhaps some evidence had been left behind. "And I'm not a one-woman crime-scene unit, so we need to call the cops." Parker had to be informed. No way was this a coincidence. She saved Declan and the same night her home was destroyed? You didn't have to be a genius to connect these dots. "The men who took you know that I got you free. Clearly, they are not happy with the turn of events." *Or with me.* Her gaze darted around her bedroom. Everything was destroyed. "There isn't going to be anything here for me to take."

"I'll buy you anything you need." He'd turned away from the knife. Declan still gripped the gun in his right hand. "And I will make them pay for what they did. I promise you, I will."

That was dangerous talk. "Declan..."

He paused right in front of her. His eyes glittered down at her. "And when I make *you* a promise," Declan continued, voice low, lethal, and terror provoking, "you can believe that it means *everything*. As far as I'm concerned, those SOBs are dead. They just don't know it yet."

Chapter Five

Detective Parker Ellis stood on the threshold of Declan's hotel suite. The detective had been pounding on the door, and Declan had reluctantly answered when the pounding persisted. The last thing he felt like doing was talking to this prick again.

But, there they were. Face to face.

Parker raised one eyebrow. "Wanted to come by and update you on the scene at Marley's place." He craned to look over Declan's shoulder. "Marley *is* here with you, isn't she?"

"She's sleeping." And she needed to remain undisturbed. The woman had been up for well over twenty-four hours. Declan didn't like the shadows that darkened her eyes. He also sure as hell hadn't liked the pain that he'd seen flash in those eyes—and on her beautiful face—when she saw the wreckage at her home.

I knew they'd go after her. The minute Marley had saved him, she'd put a giant target on her back. Now, he had to protect her. At all costs.

He didn't need a PI. Hell, he had a whole security team.

No BS. But he did need Marley close. And if hiring her got him what he wanted…

Hello, my new PI.

"Sleeping, huh?" Parker rocked back on his heels. "And here I thought she'd be out tracking down the guys who took you. Being a one-woman army as she tries to prove that she's a real PI."

The detective was such an annoyance. "She *is* a real PI."

Parker's gaze slid to Declan's face. "I can't help you when you're withholding information from me."

I don't particularly want your help. I will locate the bastards on my own. After all, what was the point of having limitless resources if you didn't use them to hunt your enemies? But he couldn't say that to the detective. "We called you as soon as we realized what had occurred at Marley's place." Because Marley had insisted on informing the detective. "She believed the wreckage at her house was tied to my abduction. If the perps left evidence behind, Marley was under the impression that you and your colleagues could find that material."

"That's what crime scene teams are for."

He was well aware of what crime scene teams were for. "I believe we went over all of this at Marley's place." Time to shut the door in the cop's face. "So unless you've come to give me new information…" Declan began to push that door closed.

Parker's hand flew up and slammed against the wood of the door. "I get that you don't like cops."

Oh, he got that, did he? Declan had been mildly worried that the detective wasn't aware of that important fact.

"I also *get* that you aren't some squeaky-clean

businessman." Parker's nostrils flared. "You think I haven't seen your record?"

"My *sealed* record, you mean?" Because any crimes he'd committed as a minor should have been thoroughly sealed. Plus, of course, there was the fact that certain powerful individuals owed him—so those people had made sure Declan's past was as dead and buried as it could possibly be.

Just as dead and buried as my bastard of a father.

Parker's gaze had drifted to the scar that sliced over Declan's face. "Self-defense," Parker murmured. "At least, that's what people say." A pause. "Are they going to say the same thing when the bodies of your abductors turn up? And isn't that the *real* reason you've got Marley close? You know they're pissed at her for interfering. So pissed that they broke into her place and left that lovely knife shoved through her photo. They're coming after her, so you figure you'll be there when they do show up to punish her. And you'll have your chance for some ice-cold vengeance."

He hadn't heard the creak of the bedroom door opening behind him. The suite was huge. The sprawling area included a dining room, a kitchen, a den, and two bedrooms. Plus, a grand piano and a pool table because, why the hell not? Marley was currently sleeping in the bedroom down the hallway to the right. Or at least, she should have been sleeping.

Unless Parker's incessant pounding on the suite door had woken her.

But I didn't hear the creak of the door to let me know she'd tiptoed out of the bedroom.

As for the charge that Parker was leveling at him... Declan rubbed his chin. "Unless I'm mistaken, I believe that *I* am their target. They kidnapped me once, after all. I don't need to use Marley as some sort of bait." He was doing the exact opposite. Trying to protect something that was precious. "I got away, so it stands to reason another attempt will be made on me. Marley is part of my protection deal." No, she wasn't. "When they come after me, I have to make sure they are stopped." Permanently.

"You're withholding intel," Parker gritted out.

Prove it, cop.

"You want to hunt them on your own. You want to make them pay for what they did."

Declan let his eyes widen. "Well, I can assure you, I am a bit unhappy with being drugged, kidnapped, and nearly tortured to death. Don't know many individuals who would be thrilled with those events."

Parker glared. "The cops can handle this."

The cops had better get out of my way. This shit is personal.

"I know you remember more from last night." Parker was a dog with a favorite bone. "You sent your goon running from the hospital fast enough. Gave him orders, and he took off like a hound on the hunt."

"Tell me you're not referring to James." Declan winced. "He will be horrified to hear that you called him a goon. And then a hound. Offended to his very soul. He will never like you again." Not that James had probably ever liked the cop in the first place.

"You sent him running with instructions, didn't you?" Low. Biting. "You told him what you remembered from the night of your abduction. He probably got a team to round up your suspects for the attack."

The detective was not as clueless as Declan had feared.

"Let the cops handle this," Parker urged him. His hand still pressed to the wood of the door. "We will arrest them. They'll be locked away for what they did."

Will they? "They may have already fled the city. If they are smart, that's exactly what they've done. My guard was lowered when they took me." A foolish mistake because he'd damn well been suffocating and had needed an escape. One night to disappear into a crowd and pretend he was someone else. *But that didn't happen.* "It will not be lowered again." Never again. *Kidnap and nearly murder me once, shame on me. Come after me twice, and I'll put you in a grave.*

"We're searching for that van. Marley got a partial on the plates, and we're going to track it down. We will find them." A grim vow from Parker. "Just don't do anything foolish until we do, got it?"

"I'm not a foolish man. Quite the opposite. But thanks for the insult."

Parker grunted. "You think I don't get that you're holding back? That I don't realize you're going for some vigilante justice BS?"

"And the insults keep coming." Declan's voice was mild. James would say that the more mild his voice became, the more dangerous his mood. "Do you always speak to crime victims this way, or am I special, Detective Ellis?"

"We interviewed the bartender at Abyss."

Declan didn't blink.

"Based on the location of where Marley saw you get thrown in the gray van, I had my team backtrack through the area. Cops went in all the bars and clubs. Found a waitress who remembered you at Abyss. I'm afraid that scar makes you hard to forget."

"You don't say. And here I thought it was completely unnoticeable."

A muscle jerked along Parker's jaw. "We pulled in the bartender who served your drink last night." Parker's stare was far to watchful. "Of course, I know *you* don't remember him, right?"

"Um."

"But we brought him in for interrogation earlier. His name's Keith, and Keith swears he served you a completely normal drink. His boss even turned over surveillance footage so we could watch the encounter ourselves. There is no sign you were drugged at Abyss."

Again, Declan made no movement. Nothing to tip off the detective that he did fully remember the name of the club and the SOB of a bartender who'd given him the drink. The only drink he'd had that night.

"You walked out of the place under your own steam. No stagger. No stumble. And you only took a few sips of your drink. You didn't even talk to anyone except the bartender."

The detective had been far more thorough than Declan expected. Kudos to the man. Slightly problematic, but still, he'd have to remember not to underestimate Parker Ellis again.

"Is any of this ringing a bell for you?" Parker pushed.

"The night is still foggy," Declan said.

"That wasn't a yes or a no."

Right. It hadn't been. "Perhaps I will recall more later."

"Perhaps you will." Parker's nostrils flared "We had to let the bartender go after the interview. Keith has no record, and there is no evidence he did anything to your drink."

I'll find evidence on my own.

"Again, this is *not* a vigilante situation."

"Detective." Declan sighed. "What is it about me that makes you believe I am going out to seek vengeance on my own?"

"Your family. Your past. The fact that you're far, far too calm for a man who was abducted and nearly murdered.

Got to tell you, you're not acting like any victim I've ever seen." Suspicion darkened each word.

"That's because I'm not like any victim you've ever seen before." *And the people who made me a victim? Oh, absolutely, they will pay.* "Thank you for the update on my case." Declan looked pointedly at the hand on the door. "Now, if you'll excuse me, I need to get back to Marley."

The hand on the door fisted. "I thought she was sleeping."

"Yes, but why does she need to sleep alone?"

Parker's teeth snapped together. He took a hard step toward Declan.

Declan didn't back up. He never retreated from anyone. Hadn't, not since he was sixteen years old. The year he'd learned to stand his ground.

And the year he'd learned how to kill.

Ah, was it any wonder the detective thought Declan had dangerous intentions toward both Marley and the people who'd made the mistake of taking him? The man was not wrong.

"Is there a problem, detective?" Declan asked, voice silky.

"You aren't her damn fiancé."

"No. I'm not. But I am her new client." They'd even shaken hands on the deal. Not quite a signed contract situation, but he'd be taking care of that technicality immediately.

"Because you're her client, you think that means you're going to fuck her?"

Oh, there it was. Jealousy. Right out in the open. The detective had a very conflicted relationship with Marley, that was clear to see. "I think what we do together—or how often we fuck," a deliberate provocation, "is none of your concern."

Parker's eyes were chips of fury. "Word of warning about Marley."

As if he needed a warning where she was concerned.

"I've known her for a long time."

"Have you." Not a question. Declan would be investigating the detective—and Marley—and soon he'd know them better than they knew themselves.

"She has this tendency to think that she can fix the world."

That seemed right. He'd already noticed that do-gooder trait in her.

"She's drawn to broken things." Again, Parker's gaze dipped to the scar on Declan's cheek.

Oh, you bastard. You think I'm broken, do you? You have no idea. "Good to know." He smiled. Declan knew the smile would stretch his scar in a most terrifying way.

Parker jerked his stare back to Declan's eyes. "Those broken things she wants to fix so badly? They break *her*."

Tension knifed straight through Declan's gut. "She doesn't seem broken to me."

And he heard the creak of a door opening behind him.

"Appearances can be deceiving. If you don't believe me, ask Marley why she isn't working on that Ph.D. of hers any longer." Parker took a step back, finally. "She shattered inside a while back, and she's still weak now. You can't count on her for this case. I told Marley that she should have just stuck with the pastry chef job. It was safe and easy. She's not made for darkness." His head snaked to the side, and his gaze cut over Declan's shoulder. Declan knew the detective had Marley in his sights. "You're not made for this kind of work, Marley. Didn't you learn your lesson before?"

Declan heard her sharp inhale.

"Leave it to the professionals," Parker advised her. "And both of you—don't withhold evidence from me. Put all the cards on the table. I can't help you if you're not shooting straight with me."

Declan could feel Marley closing in, but she didn't speak. The scent of jasmine and amber teased him.

"You aren't Ophelia," Parker added darkly. "She might enjoy fucking killers, but that doesn't mean you have to do the same."

Well, someone had just crossed the line. With his words, and he'd literally crossed back into the hallway enough so that Declan could now—

Slam the door in the detective's face.

And he did. With a smile still curving his lips, Declan shut the door right on the annoying detective. He flipped the lock, pulled in a breath, and slowly turned toward Marley. "Did you have a nice rest?"

She blinked at him. Then looked at the door. "You slammed the door on a cop."

"He was boring me." And annoying the hell out of him. Declan took a step toward her. There were still shadows under her eyes. She'd clearly needed a longer nap. "He woke you up." *Asshole.*

"I never sleep for long." Marley tucked a lock of hair behind her ear. "Do you have questions for me?"

"Questions?"

"About the stuff Parker just said." She braced her legs and straightened her spine. The pose didn't make her look any bigger. With his six-foot-three frame, he towered over her.

Those broken things she wants to fix so badly? They break her. Parker's words rolled through Declan's head. The cop clearly thought Declan was just another broken thing that wanted to hurt Marley.

He doesn't know me. He doesn't know what I want to do with her.

But Marley was staring at him with those big, deep eyes of hers. And he nodded. "I do have questions."

"Fair enough. You're paying me a lot of money for my services, and I want you to know that you can count on me. I will *not* turn and run when things get dangerous. Parker is wrong about me."

He eliminated the distance between them. Almost helplessly, his hand lifted, and his knuckles skimmed over the silk of her cheek. "I know that already."

"You do?"

"You didn't run at that shitty cabin, did you?" It would have been so easy to leave him. Yet she hadn't.

Her fatal mistake.

"No, I didn't." She wet her lips.

He stopped touching her. But didn't move back. "Have a big question for you."

"I'm *not* broken. Well, maybe bent and banged up in a few places, but who isn't?"

Declan shook his head. "The big question I have is... why in the hell did you ever date that prick?" *And what did you do with him on that date? Because if that jerk put his hands on you—*

"Oh, I-I thought he was safe."

His brow furrowed. "Explain."

"He's a detective. No record. He protects and serves. Does the whole routine of safety. And he *is* a good detective, by the way. Thorough and determined. He puts criminals away. He upholds the law."

Not like he wanted to hear her go on and on praising the douche. "If he's so perfect, then why aren't you two in wedded bliss somewhere?" More rage stirred at just the thought. He tamped it down. His voice was mild. Almost bored.

"He's not perfect. Neither am I." Her hands rubbed along the front of her jean-clad thighs. "And I don't like it when someone tells me I'm *broken* and that I should stick to making pastries and that I should never have put myself into a situation that was dangerous in the first place. I don't like it when someone treats me like I'll shatter at any moment." A shake of her head. "Parker and I have known each other since high school. Like I said, I thought he was safe. But I guess safety wasn't what I wanted."

Declan wanted to touch her again. Instead, he shoved his hands into the pockets of his dress pants. "What do you want?"

"I—" Marley stopped.

Say you want me. Say it. If she did, he'd take her right then and there. Nothing would stop him. Not if she just said those precious words.

"I want to solve your case. I want to prove that I can do this job."

Hardly the passionate declaration that he'd craved. But they'd get to that declaration, sooner or later. He could be patient when he wanted something badly enough.

He wanted her very badly.

Marley swallowed. "I want to show that darkness doesn't scare me."

"Darkness can scare anyone."

Her lashes flickered. "You're not a safe man, are you, Declan?"

"Not even close." He wouldn't pretend on that issue. "If safety is what you crave, you should walk away from me now." Because he would never be safe. When it came to Marley, he would be demanding. Possessive. Possibly obsessed.

He'd never had someone like her in his world before.

"I told you, I *thought* I wanted safety."

"But what you really want is to fuck a killer?" The words just rumbled out. *It's what I am. What I've been since I was sixteen years old, and Parker—damn him—knows that dark truth about me.*

She flinched. "Okay, below the belt. Parker is a straight jerk on that score." Her brows beetled. "First of all, my cousin Ophelia is married to the man she's, uh, involved with. And Lane Lawson was cleared of the charges that originally put him in jail. He was not a serial killer."

Lane Lawson. The name rang some bells. A lot of them. Once upon a time, Lane Lawson had been hunted by the FBI because the Feds believed he'd been a serial killer. He'd been locked away, only to later be released. His sister and the lead FBI agent who'd locked him away had been the ones to free him. Except...*wait, didn't the tricky bastard break out of his cell before he was actually cleared?*

"Parker mentioned Ophelia." The lock of hair had slid forward again. Once more, Marley tucked it behind her ear. "Ophelia is my cousin. Second cousin, actually. She's a great PI. It's because of her that I got interested in the work —and in the Ice Breakers."

Okay, shit. The distant bells weren't just ringing. They were clanging hard in this head. "The Ice Breakers?" Surely not. Surely, she was not involved with—

"They are a group that solves cold cases."

Sonofabitch. How could the world be this small?

"They started online. Everyone came from different backgrounds. A reporter, a bounty hunter, law enforcement —you name it. Different people, but the same goal. Closing cases that have remained opened for years. Helping families solve mysteries that have haunted them." She turned away. Walked toward the floor-to-ceiling windows that looked out over the city. "With my background in psychology, I thought I could help build victim and perpetrator profiles. I started working with them thanks to Ophelia's connections, and then I decided to get my PI license as I became more involved."

He didn't speak. Mostly because he wasn't sure what to say. Should he reveal his own connection to the Ice Breakers? Could he trust her with that intel?

"The Ice Breakers have made the news a great deal. The more cases that they solve, the more attention they attract. Like I said, the group started online, but it's grown by leaps and bounds. Now Archer Radcliffe finances the operation. Families in need don't pay a cent. Archer takes care of everything."

He knew Archer. Billionaire. Secretive SOB. Once suspected of murder himself, only Archer had been cleared of the charges. *Courtesy of the Ice Breakers.*

Declan and Archer occasionally traveled in the same circles. Never friends. Business rivals. Sharks who understood not to swim too close to one another.

Declan's gaze skimmed over Marley as she gazed out at the city. Darkness had fallen. It would soon be time for them to hunt.

You don't have to tell her about your connection to the Ice Breakers. You don't have to tell her anything.

She glanced over her shoulder at him. "We should get started on your case. Let's find the bartender. Talk to any other staff members who were at the club you visited. Then we can scout the area around it. We'll hit up any potential witnesses we find."

"I know about the Ice Breakers." A confession he hadn't intended to make until the words actually slid from his mouth.

A nod from Marley. "Like I said, they make the news a bit so—"

"My brother is friends with a few of them." Again, an admission that he hadn't planned to offer. He didn't talk about his brother with anyone.

She's not just anyone.

Marley whipped around and faced him fully. "Your brother? I didn't know you had a brother. I thought I'd read you were the sole heir to your father's—" Marley broke off, as if uncertain how to end that particular statement.

"Twisted nightmare of a legacy?" he finished for her, trying to be helpful.

"That wasn't what I was going to say."

No, of course not. Because Marley was *nice.* "This is confidential information." Once more, he closed the distance between them. "As in, it doesn't leave this room. Understand?"

Her head tipped back as she stared up at him. "Consider me a vault."

And, oddly, Declan thought he could trust her. *Don't betray me, Marley. You won't like the way I respond to betrayal.* "I didn't know my brother was alive." He'd hoped that the guy was but after so many years of searching, hope had pretty much been a memory. "He disappeared when I was a kid." His brother had been two when he vanished.

"Over the years, I hired dozens of PIs to find him. To turn up something that would lead me to him." But there had been nothing. "James told me I had to move on. That my brother was dead. Just like my mother was. They both supposedly died in a fiery car crash. No bodies were ever recovered because the car went down a ravine and exploded. Empty caskets were put in the ground. Everyone else bought the story of their deaths, but I didn't. I couldn't."

She reached out and curled her fingers around his hand. Marley didn't offer words of sympathy or comfort, but he could see both in her expression. She stared at him as if she wished she could take his pain away.

Uncomfortable, he almost stepped back.

Don't retreat. Not from anyone. Declan cleared his throat. "Then I turned on the news one day, and, lo and behold, I saw him. All grown up, of course, but it was him. Hell, it was like looking into a mirror." His free hand rose and brushed over his scar. "Minus one big difference, of course."

She didn't even look at the scar. "You must have been so happy."

Happy? Yeah, he guessed that was how he felt. Maybe. Hard to say for sure because he hadn't been happy many times in his life. *Not real certain what happiness feels like.* Maybe he'd just been stunned. "He didn't remember me." *And I could never forget him.*

Her hold tightened on him.

"He had a new name. A new life. A new family." His lips twisted. "Even a new brother."

She didn't just hold his hand. She threw her arms around him and held on tightly.

"Marley?" Why was she hugging him?

"You can have more than one brother," she declared as

she held him as if her life depended on it. "And you can love them just the same."

His hands hovered over her back. Was he supposed to embrace her, too? The embrace she was giving him wasn't passionate. Wasn't about sex at all. He didn't normally embrace women if sex wasn't involved. This hug was odd. And it made him feel different. Too uncertain.

"Don't give up on him. Doesn't matter who else is in his life now." She gave him another squeeze, then seemed to realize that he wasn't holding her in return.

She pulled away just as he began to curl his arms around her.

Marley took a quick step back. She almost bumped into the window. "Don't give up," she urged again. "Some people are worth fighting for."

He nodded, slowly. "They absolutely are."

Her smile flashed at him, and Declan stopped breathing. It was a real smile. Big and beautiful. Maybe the most beautiful thing that he'd ever seen in his entire life. It lit her eyes. Made the darkness shine, and he realized that Detective Parker Ellis was dead wrong. There was nothing broken about her.

There was only beauty.

A beauty that he would happily kill to protect.

She is going to be mine.

And Declan never, ever gave up what belonged to him.

"Are you ready to hunt the bad guys?" Marley asked him.

Oh, darling. You're staring straight at the worst guy out there. Maybe she'd figure out that truth at some point. Maybe she wouldn't. After all, he was very good at pretending. So Declan just nodded once more and said, "Absolutely."

I'm not just going to hunt these fools. I am going to destroy them. By the time Declan was done, they'd be begging for mercy. Too bad for them, he had never been the merciful sort.

If his father was still alive, he could have vouched for that truth. Sometimes, Declan's father's cries still played in his head. The way his father had begged at the end…

Don't, please…don't!

But his father had died. And Declan had walked away, covered in his blood and with a scar to remind him that a monster had truly been born that long ago day.

"I heard what Parker said about the bartender." She grimaced. "Don't hate me, but I was eavesdropping."

He wasn't sure he could hate her.

"I'm not sure the guy is going to cooperate with us after being grilled by the PD."

"He'll cooperate." Declan was certain on that point. "He'll have no other option."

"You…just so you know, you kinda sound scary."

He laughed. "Darling, I *am* scary."

Chapter Six

THE BASTARD SHOULD HAVE SUFFERED. HE SHOULD have bled. He should have begged. He should have cried like a fucking baby.

And then died choking on his own blood.

But that hadn't happened. Despite all of the careful planning, Declan Flynn had escaped. And why the hell had he escaped?

Some wannabe PI rescued his ass. She was in the wrong place, and she made the worst decision of her life. A mistake that she would soon come to regret.

As she bled. As she begged. As she cried like a fucking baby.

And then died choking on her own blood. She'd get the ending that had been meant for Declan. When she was dead, he'd dump her body—what was left of it—for Declan to find.

But before the PI could be taken out, there were other loose ends that had to be addressed. Snipped before those ends came back to jeopardize too much. Not like the plan

71

hadn't always been to eliminate the hired help. Not like witnesses should ever be left alive.

The door in front of him opened. Two burly men rushed inside. Too muscled. Too dumb. Too willing to do dirty work without asking questions if the money was right.

"You never said we'd be grabbing Declan Flynn! Not fucking him! Shit, man! Like I told you on the phone, you'd better be paying for us to escape to Mexico or else I'll be telling Declan—"

He fired the weapon in his hand. The bullet went straight through fool number one's forehead. His buddy gaped. A gaping that lasted a bit too long before he swung back for that open door and tried to flee.

So the second bullet that was fired hit him in the back of his head. Went through the back and tore out the front. And the bleeding bastard slammed into the floor about two seconds later.

Two down. One more hired hand to go.

Then I'll be coming after the PI, Declan. The woman who'd stayed beside Declan Flynn all night. The woman who the press claimed was his fiancée. A lie, of course. Declan wouldn't allow anyone to get that close to him. He wouldn't put a ring on anyone's finger.

Declan Flynn couldn't marry. Because he couldn't love. He wasn't capable of it. He was too much like his father.

He can't love. But he can obsess. He can covet.

Just like I do.

He stared at the bodies. Kicked the slightly bigger guy with the hole in his forehead just because it looked like the fellow *might* still be breathing. He couldn't take the chance that Hugo survived. The bouncer knew too much.

The kick to Hugo's gut resulted in a grunt. Definitely still breathing.

This time, when he raised his gun, he aimed straight for the heart. A quick, fast burst came from his silenced weapon as the bullet fired.

Another kick. No more grunting. No more being alive.

Time to find the next person on his kill list. A bartender who couldn't be trusted to keep his fool mouth shut.

Chapter Seven

"WE'RE BEING FOLLOWED." MARLEY PEERED THROUGH the limo's rear window.

"Yes."

She swiveled around to face him. "And you're not worried?"

"Considering they are my men? Nope. Not at all worried."

Marley slid closer to him. Closer in the new clothes that had magically appeared for her in his hotel suite. A black sweater that she was pretty sure had to be made of cashmere, black pants that felt like some kind of soft heaven against her skin, and the most awesome, kick-ass black boots she'd seen in her entire life.

And let's not think about the underwear. Or, rather, the scraps that counted as underwear. Who had picked out those particular items?

She cleared her throat. "You didn't mention that you had men following us."

"I didn't? Oh, well, I have men following us. The last

time I ditched my protection crew, I wound up drugged and tied to a chair in a shitty basement, so I figured I'd let the guys do the job I was paying them for."

"Probably a good idea," she mumbled.

His head inclined toward her. What could have been a glint of amusement came and went in his hazel eyes. "But don't worry, they know how to be unobtrusive. They won't interfere in our investigation. Unless I signal for them to approach."

It was far too late *not to worry*. Worry consumed her. As did memories of all those torture instruments in the basement's cabinet. "Just who is in this crew of yours?"

"The two tailing us are former special ops. One was a SEAL. The other was a Ranger. They know how to blend. They also know how to kick ass."

Her eyes narrowed as suspicion swirled through her. "They aren't like...the muscle, are they?"

"Excuse me?"

"The bartender didn't cooperate with the cops. Are you planning to use your 'protection crew' in order to force information out of the man? Are they the muscle that you're gonna use to get the job done?"

He put a hand over his heart. "I am shocked. You think I would do something like that?"

Her eyes narrowed. "Yes." Definitely.

The limo halted.

"I probably would." An easy agreement as his hand fell. "But we'll try your charm first, shall we? And let's see where that gets us."

Her charm? "I don't have a lot of that." She stretched for the door on the right.

He caught her hand. Surprised her by bringing it to his

lips and pressing a kiss to her knuckles. "I disagree. I'd certainly say that you've charmed me."

Her heart immediately started racing—the same way it had raced when she realized they were being tailed by a dark SUV that kept one car between them and the limo as it relentlessly followed their path.

"When we go in Abyss, you don't leave my side." His voice was calm, mild, but his stare was piercing. "We get the bartender. We question him together." Another kiss on her knuckles.

Wait, had she just felt the brush of his tongue against her?

He let her go. "And don't question my methods. Just go with the flow, would you?" Declan climbed from the limo because Andy had the door open.

She scrambled out after him. Marley grabbed Declan's arm. "I am *not* a go-with-the-flow kind of person. In fact, I've never even met the flow. I go my own way."

A sigh. "So I am learning." He stared down at her. "Can I count on you not to freak out tonight?"

What did that even mean? And it sure sounded offensive. "I didn't freak out last night, did I? Stop questioning my professionalism." She sniffed. "It's downright rude."

His lips hitched up. "Oh, I would never want to be *rude*. My apologies." He moved the hand that she'd had clutching his arm. Moved it but didn't let go. Instead, he curled the fingers of his left hand around hers. "Let's get the party started, shall we?"

Marley threw a glance over her shoulder. She wanted to put eyes on his protection team, but there was no sign of the SUV she'd spotted earlier. "I don't think it's a party. Or at least, if it is, we have two vastly different definitions for that particular word."

"And just how do you like to party?"

Her gaze skittered back to his. "I'm not really big on the party scene." She could hear the pounding music coming from Abyss. A line of people snaked around the block, waiting to get inside. The women wore skin-tight dresses and stilettos. The men wore a variety of clothing options—some high end, some dressed in ragged jeans. All stood with plenty of pretend swagger. "Got enough of that during *my* short stint as a bartender." And she'd had more than enough of seeing drunken brawls and watching messy hook-ups.

"If you're not into the scene, then what were you doing here last night?" he asked silkily.

She swallowed. "Chasing down a cheating husband. I got the info I needed and emailed the pictures to my client." *Case officially closed.* "Then I was leaving when I saw you."

"Were you the bait for the husband?"

The what? And why was he all extra growly? "No, I was the one snapping pics of him and his girlfriend while his pregnant wife was at home." She tapped a foot impatiently. "Are we going in Abyss or do you want to grill *me* more?"

"In."

"Excellent plan."

And...toward the entrance they went. He headed straight for the bouncer. Big, covered in tats, and featuring a hoop in his nose. Declan stopped right in front of the man.

"Line's to the left, buddy," the bouncer snapped.

"You weren't here last night," Declan noted.

"Nah. I wasn't. Not supposed to be here tonight, either. Got called in when the prick who should be on duty didn't show." He pointed to the left. "Now like I said, the line's—"

Declan put some cash in the bouncer's outstretched hand. "I'm going in with my lady."

The man looked at the money. Whistled. "Yes, indeed, you are going in with your lady. Tonight and any night you want, my new best friend."

She strained to see just how much money Declan had handed the man, but the money had been shoved inside the bouncer's pocket in a flash.

Declan lingered with his new best friend. "Tell me where the bouncer is who was on duty last night. Six-foot-two, stocky. Black hair."

The description he gave of the bouncer could have easily been the same description for the guys who'd taken him. As she'd told Parker, the men had both been big. Thick with muscle and fat, and their hair had been dark. Or at least, it had appeared dark from a distance and in the poor lighting from the streetlamp.

"You mean Hugo. Guy didn't show up today. Asshole. I was supposed to be with my girlfriend tonight, but that prick didn't come to work. Now I'm here, and who the hell knows where he is?"

Declan slanted a glance back her way.

Marley nodded. Yeah, Hugo's absence was suspicious as hell. She got it. But she didn't speak those words out loud. Declan led her in the club and the music was even more pounding and ear-shattering inside. The bodies were crammed too tightly. And eyes were suddenly on her. She looked up and found men ogling her. Their gazes drifted over her as if seeing her naked.

Great. Fabulous. And this was why she didn't like to party. "I'm not on the menu," she muttered. Why were they even looking her way? Her clothes were *way tame* compared to the other outfits. Maybe they just stared that way at every woman who entered the place. Jerks.

Declan looked over and frowned at her.

"Why were *you* here?" she suddenly demanded. "This does not feel like your scene."

"And what is my scene?" Vague curiosity.

She didn't know. Because she didn't know him that well. But it was hard to imagine that he'd come to this crowded meat market unless...*Oh, crap. Did he come here to hook up with someone?* And was that jealousy gnawing in her stomach? Sure felt like it. "I don't know." A mumble.

He didn't move. And he seemingly ignored everyone else as he focused on her. "I was here because I was bored. Sometimes, you just want to vanish in a crowd." He turned and made his way through the throng of bodies. People immediately moved the heck out of his way. Then they were at the bar. Declan shouldered up to it and made room for her at his side. Lights shimmered overhead.

"Be right with you," a bartender promised.

Her gaze locked on him. On the back of his head. Blond hair. Slim but athletic build.

He spun around. "All right, what can I get—*you.*" His eyes widened as he got a look at Declan.

"Hello, Keith." Declan's voice easily cut through the noise. "You remember me. What a coincidence. I also remember *you.*"

And maybe Keith hadn't said anything suspicious to the cops. Maybe he'd cooperated completely. But he took one look at Declan's face—and the fierce intent he saw there— and terror filled Keith's eyes. He spun and dashed toward the far end of the bar. And toward the exit.

"Sonofabitch." Declan jumped over the bar and gave chase.

For one moment, Marley admired the jump. He'd cleared that bar in a single lunge. Impressive. But her job wasn't to sit around and be impressed. So she gave chase, too. She didn't jump over the bar. Instead, she twisted and snaked through the crowd and made her way for the door marked STAFF ONLY. The same door that Keith was bounding toward.

He rushed through the door, followed by Declan, and Marley was right on their heels. In her experience, innocent people didn't tend to run this way. And the terror that had been in Keith's eyes? Oh, there had to be a reason for his fear.

Up ahead, Keith shoved open another door. She saw the darkness of the night waiting. Keith had raced into the back alley. If he got away...

Declan rushed out the exterior door, too. She slammed her hand into the wood and followed and—

"*Ah!*" Keith hit the ground.

Not because Declan had tackled the bartender. But because James had tripped the guy as he ran. James stepped from the shadows, straightening his suit coat as he did so. Looking dapper and vaguely annoyed as he stared down at the sprawled form on the litter-covered ground. An old light at the rear of the bar flickered on and off. Revealing, then concealing the scene.

"I believe my employer wanted to have a word with you," James declared. "That's hard to do when you're running away."

Keith tried to *crawl* away.

He didn't get far.

Shadows surged from the surrounding darkness even as Declan grabbed the back of Keith's shirt and hauled him to his feet. When the shadows moved toward Declan, Marley rushed forward to put her body between him and whatever threat this was going to be.

"Stand down, PI." A deep, rumbly voice from the dark. "We're part of his security."

Her eyes narrowed. A big shadow had spoken. She had the feeling that the guy was deliberately keeping himself hidden. Another big shadow waited to the left. The shadow to the left sidled forward—staying out of the flickering light—and shut the bar's back door. The better for them to not be disturbed.

"Oh, God." A whimper from Keith. "You're going to kill me, aren't you?"

Declan shoved the bartender against the side of the building. "That really depends on you, Keith."

Wait, *what?* She cast one more worried glance toward the shadows. Declan didn't seem concerned about them, so she figured one shadow must be the SEAL and the other had to be the Ranger who'd tailed them in the SUV. James just stood there, looking completely out of place. As for Declan...

She crept closer and tapped his shoulder. "We're not here to kill anyone, right?"

Declan grunted.

"His PI is confused," the rumbly voice said. "Maybe she should wait in the limo with James."

"I do hate violence," James declared as he picked a piece of lint or string or something from his suit. "My monitoring job is done. I kept eyes on the bartender—even when he was taken in by the angry detective for questioning. Now, he's all yours."

Marley watched as James turned and headed around the building. He didn't look back.

"Hey, PI," the rumbly shadow said.

"The name is Marley," she snapped back. "And we are *not* here to kill anyone." There. Much better. A declaration, not a question. She ignored the shadows and focused on—

"*Please, lady, help me!*" Keith cried. "I haven't done anything! Oh, God, oh, God! You're going to cut off my fingers or something, aren't you? Going to slice me open? Going to put me in damn cement shoes and sink me in the river?"

"Why would you think all of this?" Marley demanded. Declan had one hand on the bartender's chest. The other was loose at his side.

"Because he's the mob!" A high cry.

"You really shouldn't have fucked with him," a shadow noted. "Bad mistake."

"I didn't!" Keith shook his head. "I didn't do anything, I swear!"

Declan did not free the man. "You put something in my drink."

"No, no! I didn't! I gave you exactly what you wanted. I opened the bottle of scotch. *A brand-new bottle!* And I poured you a glass. You saw me open it. You were right there! Hell, you even insisted on the new bottle. You picked it out."

Marley tensed. Her gaze cut to Declan's profile. The light flickered. On. Off. On. She stood to the side, so she only saw the right side of his face. The side with the scar that slashed across his skin.

The light flashed on. Went off. Darkness. So much darkness. Then...on.

The cut of the scar made Declan look both dangerous and almost...evil.

He's not. He's not evil.

Her hand pressed harder to his shoulder. "Declan, let the man go."

Declan's head swung toward her. He looked at her like she was crazy. She wasn't. She was being the rational one.

"He's surrounded," she told Declan. "Not like he can escape, not with your two security shadows waiting to pounce. And the man is clearly terrified." What had Declan called him? Keith? Yes, Keith. Parker had also said the bartender's name when she'd been eavesdropping back at the hotel suite. *Keith*.

Declan didn't let the bartender go. "He ran. Innocent people don't run."

He had a point, but she stood firm and pointed out, "They do if they are terrified. He thinks you're in the mob and that you're here to slice him into little pieces." Maybe that horrifying fear had made the bartender run.

Another whimper escaped from Keith.

"If he's not so afraid, he'll talk more." She believed this. Or hoped it. Whatever. "I have questions I want to ask him."

Declan stared at her.

"You hired me to find the truth, remember? I'm here to help." And not to just, oh, say, watch a man get beaten up in front of her.

Declan glanced back at his prey. "You run again, and you'll pay."

Keith shuddered.

Declan let him go.

"Thank you, lady," Keith whispered to her. "This is all a big mistake. Just like I told that cop. I didn't put anything in this dude's drink. I swear it. I opened the new bottle—"

"Where did you get the bottle?" Marley interrupted to ask.

"I—" Keith stopped. Frowned. "Hugo stocked the new bottles. He works at Abyss. Bouncer. Handyman. Stocker. Whatever we need. He'd just put the bottles in right before..." A wave of his trembling hand toward Declan. "Before *he* arrived."

Hugo. That would be the bouncer who hadn't shown up for work that night. Her gaze darted to Declan. "The scotch you ordered—do you *always* order that same drink?"

"It's damn expensive," Keith said before Declan could reply. He rattled off the name. One she instantly recognized just because of her bartending days. Those brief days. She'd never been a big drinker herself, and certainly not for booze that cost more than a hundred dollars a shot. "Not many people do order it," Keith continued quickly. "Most go for beers or the women like the pretty, frou-frou drinks—"

"I tend to order the same drink." Declan's voice was flat.

She sucked in a breath. "Someone knew you were going to be at this club. It wasn't random." Declan had been holding back on her. "It wasn't because you were bored. *Why* were you here?"

He stepped away from Keith. "I thought I might buy the place. It was on my list of potential acquisitions. Figured I'd take a look around. And I *was* bored. I didn't lie to you."

What was that note that had entered his voice?

"Was doing two things at once," he rasped. "Looking at the place and getting lost in a crowd."

Okay, fine, sure. Two things at once. What mattered to her was that the visit hadn't been random. *You were thinking about buying the place.* "Who knew that you might buy Abyss? Who in your life knew that you'd swing by this location?"

This was important.

Declan didn't speak.

Keith did. "Can I go? Please?" He pressed harder to the building behind him. "All I did was open the drink. You asked for that bottle. I just opened it. Had no idea what would happen." He licked his lips. "Saw on the news... heard you were taken...then the cops came for me. *I didn't put anything in there, I swear it!*" His voice shook with intensity. "You barely had three sips. How can I be blamed for what happened?"

Marley's shoulders stiffened. She thought of the crush she'd just seen in the bar. The bodies piled so tightly. "You know exactly how many sips Declan took?"

Keith sucked in a breath. "I—it was a guess. I *guess* he had three."

But it hadn't sounded like a guess. It had sounded as if he'd been counting. "Where is the bottle that you opened?" Marley wanted to get her hands on it.

"Gone. Trashed. Just like I told the cop!" The words were rushed, and he blinked rapidly. "Trash pickup came first thing this morning—took out all our busted and empty bottles. The thing is long gone!"

"You trashed it?" Things weren't making sense to Marley. "But you said that particular drink was so expensive that it was barely ever ordered." Her old boss would have fired her instantly if she'd trashed something so valuable after pouring only *one drink* from the bottle. "So why would the whole bottle be trashed—"

Keith cut and ran. He ran straight at her and shoved her with heavy strength, sending Marley tumbling back, then down onto her ass. Gravel from the ground bit into her palms. Her head whipped to the left as Keith hurtled past her.

Only to be stopped by one of the very large shadows.

"Boss wasn't done talking to you," the shadow informed

Keith. "And it's not nice to shove pretty ladies to the ground."

"Damn rude," the other shadow agreed.

Declan grabbed Keith and hauled him back. "*Exceedingly* rude," he corrected in a chilling voice. "The kind of rude that will get you an ass-kicking."

Marley brushed off her palms. Her head tilted back as she looked up.

Something just moved on the roof.

Her gaze sharpened. They were in a narrow alley, caged between the club and an old pool hall. She didn't know why someone would be on top of the pool hall but...

Someone is.

"Need a hand up, PI?" A shadow came closer to her. He extended his hand to her.

She didn't look his way. Her gaze was on the roof. And...

The light in the alley was still flickering. On and off. On and off.

But up on that roof...

A flash of red. A red shine that shouldn't be there and if she followed that quick burst of red as it angled down...

It's pointed at Declan as he pins Keith to the wall.

"No!" Marley screamed as she shoved past the shadow that had offered to help her up. She scrambled forward and her arms wrapped around Declan's legs as she hurtled her whole body at him. Declan grunted as he went down.

There was a whoosh behind her. A crack. Then another. A sharp cry sounded, and Marley glanced back.

The lights flashed off. On.

Keith's mouth hung open. He touched his chest.

The light turned off.

"What the hell, Marley?" Declan barked. He tried to push her aside.

The light came back on. Keith was on the ground. Not moving. And...why did his shirt front look so dark? And his head—*oh, no, his head!*

Marley pressed her lips together.

One of Declan's shadows—guards—thundered, "Shooter!"

"On the roof!" Marley cried. "To the left!" And she shoved down against Declan just as something hot streaked over her right arm. Marley hissed out a breath.

Declan heaved beneath her.

"Dammit, stay *down!*" Marley yelled at him.

Gunfire erupted behind them. As in—the shadows were firing up toward the roof.

And Declan was not staying down. He'd rolled and pinned her beneath him.

"You don't fucking use yourself to protect me," he gritted. "Not ever."

Her breath panted out as she stared up at him. Or tried to.

The light turned on. The guards had moved to stand between them and the threat. Their weapons were pointed at the roof.

Rage twisted Declan's expression.

The light flashed off.

"Haul ass!" An order from one of the guards.

But Declan was already moving. He'd grabbed Marley. He took her right arm and hauled her up and she had to bite back the cry of pain that sprang to her lips. He rushed quickly toward a dumpster, and they took cover behind it.

She heard footsteps thudding and knew that the guards were giving chase after the shooter.

She tried to step forward.

Declan shoved her back. "Fuck, no."

Marley blinked. "I need to check on Keith!"

"Keith just took a shot to the heart and to the head. Checking on him isn't gonna help."

A shudder rolled over her body.

"How'd you know?" Declan demanded. "How the fuck did you know when two guards trained in special ops didn't see the shooter?"

"I saw a light on the roof," she whispered. Her arm throbbed horribly, but this did not seem to be the moment to mention that pain.

"Don't *ever* put yourself on top of me when bullets are flying." Low. Lethal. Chilling as the grave.

She wet her lips. They felt incredibly dry. As did her entire mouth. "You have such a terrible way of saying thank you. You did this before, when I saved you at the cabin. And you're doing it now. A thank you would not kill you—"

He kissed her. His lips crushed to hers in a hard, demanding, consuming kiss that she had not been expecting. He kissed her with rage and desire, and it was the strangest combination of her life, but she could *feel* both in the hard press of his mouth. Like they were battling each other.

His mouth tore from hers.

"That still wasn't a thank you," she whispered. "But I guess it was close."

He kissed her again. Harder. Rougher. Need shuddered through her body and confused the hell out of her. *How can I want him...now?* They were in a dark alley. Hiding behind a dumpster. With...

A dead body? A dead body just a few feet away?

But what if the bartender wasn't dead yet? What if Declan was wrong?

She tore her mouth from his and pushed against Declan. "I *have* to check on Keith!"

"You can't help the dead." Savage. "Don't you dare move until this scene is secure. The last thing that I want happening is for you to get hurt."

Her arm throbbed again. "Um, yeah, about that..." Dizziness swirled through her. Dizziness because of the crazy kiss or because...wait, was her arm soaking wet? Wet from blood?

Declan was going to be difficult about this.

But she didn't want him moving from cover until the area was secure, so mentioning the arm injury didn't seem like a good plan. She'd wait until the guards said it was safe. And maybe it wasn't as bad as she feared. Maybe it wasn't even her blood. *Maybe it's Keith's.* That was a horrifyingly gross thought. Did she want to be covered in someone else's blood? *Better than my own?* "This shooting isn't random," she murmured. Declan had to understand this just as she did. "Someone stopped Keith from talking to you."

"The shooter is tied to the fuckers who took me."

Right. Yes. So he understood. Of course. She blinked quickly and tried to hold her head perfectly still to stop the dizziness that kept rolling through her. "We have to call the cops," Marley said. "Get an ambulance for Keith."

"Again...*dead*, Marley. He was dead on impact. I was looking at him when you tackled my ass. I saw it happen."

But maybe he was wrong. "The cops," she insisted as shivers shook her body.

"Why the hell are you cold?" Declan shouldered out of his suit coat and put it around her body. When he touched her right arm...

Agony.

She almost passed out on him then and there.

Was I shot? Seemed like it. This was her first gunshot wound. She was not handling it well. Or maybe she was. Hard to say. Blessedly, Declan had only put the coat around her shoulders. He hadn't tried to tuck her arms into the sleeves. If he'd tried that, she wasn't sure she could have stopped a scream from breaking free.

"Just try saying 'shooter' next time," he groused. "You don't need to launch yourself into the line of fire."

"The red dot was on your back. I saw it. *You* were in the line of fire." The dizziness was fading. Maybe. "Saying 'shooter' wouldn't have done anything but get you to spin around and look at me. Then he would have shot you in the chest." And Declan could be the dead one on the ground, not Keith.

No way could that happen.

Her left hand fisted Declan's shirt. "I don't want you dead."

"I don't plan on dying, so that's damn good to know."

She realized he had a gun in his right hand. The man did love his weapons. When had he even pulled out the gun? "We can't just stay here all night," she told him.

A shrill ring cut through the night.

His left hand dove into the pocket of his pants. Declan hauled out his phone and put it to his ear. He also turned so that his back was to her. Her hand fell back to her side as he took up a protective position in front of her. He wasn't supposed to do that. "You're the client," she mumbled. "I think you just don't understand our relationship." Marley's words were low.

He shot a glare back her way. Or at least, she was pretty sure it was a glare. Too dark to be certain behind the dumpster. "*You* don't understand," he fired back. Then, into the phone, "Tell me you have the bastard."

She held her breath.

"Dammit!"

At that explosion from Declan, she took that to mean, no, the guards had not found the shooter.

"I'm getting her out of this freaking alley. Have Andy bring the limo around for me. I'll cover her six. Tell James we're coming and—"

"The cops," Marley reminded him. "We can't just leave the scene of a shooting." That wasn't the way things worked.

"Call the cops," Declan bit out. "Because some law-abiding PI is about to lose her mind on this issue."

Calling the cops at a murder scene was a normal thing to do. Why was he acting like she was the weird one? Again, she was the *rational* one. She'd have to discuss this issue with him at a later date.

Then the call was over. He spun and grabbed her arm.

Her left, blessedly. Not the right. And he pulled her close. "We're getting you into the limo. It will be pulling up at the end of this alley in about thirty seconds. It's bulletproof, so I'll get you in and you'll stay there, and we'll get the fucking cops. Happy?"

No, she was not feeling happy. "I think you should be the one to stay there. You're the target, not me."

"Don't be too damn sure about that." His hold tightened on her. "*You could have been shot.*"

Maybe she should mention that she was, um, injured. Seemed like a good enough time. "So, don't freak out on me but—"

A screech of tires cut through her words.

"Andy is fast," Declan noted.

The front of the limo stopped about twenty feet away, near the end of the narrow alley.

"You go first. And do *not* argue with me." Declan's grip tightened on her. "I'll be guarding your back."

The client wasn't supposed to guard the PI's back. Before she could argue—and she *had* been planning to argue—more footsteps rushed into the alley.

"Declan!"

Her eyes narrowed as she fought to see better in the dark.

James barreled toward them. "Are you hit? Tell me you're not hit."

"I'm not hit." He sounded annoyed. Pissed. "I'm getting her to safety, now."

"Her?" James's voice rose. "Forget her. Get in the damn car!"

"Thank you!" Marley declared because there was another reasonable person around. "It's about time that someone—"

"Screw it." Declan scooped her into his arms. "I'll take care of you myself."

And it *hurt*. It hurt so much that she couldn't speak because her right side had just crashed into him. Declan double-timed it to the limo, with James covering his back. Andy had the door open and ready, and Declan practically threw her inside.

She sprawled on the seat and tried to catch her breath as the pain rolled through her.

"Don't even *think* of leaving." Declan slammed the door shut.

He didn't get in the limo with her. The idiot had not gotten into the bulletproof vehicle.

She fumbled and pulled out her phone and...because

she didn't exactly trust his guards to do the right thing and call the cops, Marley dialed nine-one-one.

When the operator came on the line, Marley said, "There's been a shooting." She hurriedly gave the address. "Two victims. One down. Possibly dead." She shrugged off the suit coat and tried to eye her injury. The gorgeous cashmere top was soaked with blood and stuck to her arm. "The other vic is injured. Send the cops and an ambulance, would you? And, uh, hurry." She kept the line open even as she looked down at the seat in the limo.

She was getting blood everywhere. Dammit.

Chapter Eight

"HE WAS LONG GONE BY THE TIME WE GOT TO THE roof," Cade Grimm announced flatly as he rushed back to the alley and stopped near Declan. The former SEAL sounded pissed.

Fair enough, Declan was certainly *pissed*, too.

"McQueen is still double-checking the building, just in case, but the place is hollowed out. Totally empty on our first sweep. The pool hall looks like it's been closed for a long time." Cade motioned toward the dead body. "What the hell are we gonna do with him?"

A siren's wail cut through the night.

"That's what we're going to do," James announced. "We're going to let the police take care of the matter." He'd been staring down at the body for a few, silent moments. As soon as he'd arrived on scene, he'd immediately searched for a pulse on the bartender.

Declan had told him it was useless.

And it had been.

"If your PI hadn't spotted the shooter," Cade's growling

voice continued, "then you could be the one on the ground, Declan."

The stupid light kept flickering on and off.

"Is it safe for Declan to be out in the open?" James wanted to know as worry threaded through his voice. "I tried to force him into the limo with the PI, but he refused."

"The shooter is gone." Declan had suspected that outcome long before Cade made the announcement. "He stopped the bartender from talking. He did his job. Then he cleared out."

"I'm not so sure his job wasn't to kill you." Cade crouched next to the dead man. He whistled when the light flashed on, and he got a good look at Keith's bloody form. "The head and the heart? That's a professional job."

More sirens screamed. They were a lot louder. And closer.

Cade rose. "The bullets didn't hit you, boss?"

"I'm fine." His hands fisted at his sides.

"You don't sound fine."

They were huddled around a dead body. Excuse the fuck out of him for being *not fine*. "He's playing with us."

"Excuse me?" From James. He'd taken a step away from the body.

"He could have killed Keith before I arrived. He did that shit right in front of me. He's trying to send me a message."

"Uh, what message would that be?" James asked as his head cocked. The light kept flashing. On. Off. On.

"He thinks he's in control." Tension snaked through every muscle in Declan's body. "He's trying to show me how much power he has."

"Well, he *did* kidnap you," James pointed out. "And the

shooting...shit, just how close were those bullets to hitting you?"

I felt them brush over me.

But once again, his guardian angel had saved his ass. "I want this sonofabitch," Declan said flatly. "I want him dead in the ground." *I will put him in the ground.*

The sirens were shrieking now. Car doors slammed.

"Uh, boss..." Cade cleared his throat. "Better not say things like that in front of the cops. And maybe this should be the point where we all put our hands up so none of the boys and girls in blue get nervous and start firing at *us*?"

"Excellent idea," James praised. His hands were already up.

Footsteps thundered toward them.

"Police!" A shout. "Hands up!"

"This is what I mean." A murmur from Cade. His hands were up.

Declan stepped away from the body. His hands rose even as the uniforms rushed forward—rushed forward, then staggered to a stop as their flashlights hit the body on the ground.

There were a lot of other shouts then. A whole lot of confusion as the uniforms scrambled and their flashlights bobbed and—

"Declan! Declan Flynn!"

Detective Parker Ellis was suddenly right in front of him. "What in the hell happened here?" Parker barked.

Declan kept his hands up. "I was interviewing your suspect."

Parker's flashlight swept over him. Lingered on Declan's chest.

"Someone didn't appreciate my interview," Declan

added with a roll of his shoulders. "Gunshots were fired from the roof of the pool hall."

Parker's flashlight didn't lower. "Is that his blood?"

What? On the wall? The ground? "Yeah, his blood hit the wall and the ground." And, just so they were clear... "I didn't touch him after the shooting."

"Is that his blood on you?"

Declan glanced down and saw that the flashlight was shining in the middle of his body—and that his white dress shirt was stained red.

"Fuck." From Cade. "I thought you said the bullets didn't hit you, boss."

Declan blinked. "They didn't."

Parker moved closer. "So it's the vic's blood?"

"She tackled me when the shots were fired. I didn't get his blood on me. I—" Declan shook his head. *"It's her blood."* An overwhelming surge of fear and fury filled him. It burned through him. Twisted. Snaked. Exploded. He whirled for the limo.

"Freeze!" One of the cops shouted, "Mister, you need to freeze right now!"

Declan threw a glance back over his shoulder at Parker. "It's *Marley's* blood." It had to be. He'd picked her up. Carried her against him. "She's in the limo. It is bulletproof so I put her in there...I-I didn't know she was hurt!" He had to get to her.

"Where is the damn limo?" Parker snarled. "And, Officer Masters, don't even think of firing that weapon, got it? Stand *down!*"

Then Parker and Declan were racing toward the end of the alley. Racing toward the limo that waited. Declan yanked open the side door. The interior lights shined brightly so he could easily see Marley as she huddled against the leather seat. And as blood utterly soaked her right arm.

"Hi." She grimaced at him. "There's, um...something I need to tell you..."

So much blood. Declan could not move. He could not speak. He could not breathe. *Marley had been shot.*

"EMT!" Parker bellowed. "We need an EMT over here, right now!"

Marley nodded. "That's what I needed to tell you."

* * *

"WHY IN THE hell didn't you tell me that you'd been shot as soon as it freaking happened?" Declan demanded as he sat by the hospital bed.

Her hospital bed. Their positions had been reversed. She'd been the one sitting in the chair and keeping watch over him not too long ago and now...

He glowered at her.

"I don't think I need to stay the night. Serious overkill." She had to wince at her own choice of words. Especially considering the dead body that had been in the alley. *Don't picture him. Stop seeing him in your head.*

Only that was a very difficult task. Each time she closed her eyes, the image replayed. Only sometimes, it wasn't Keith's image. It was Declan's. *What if I hadn't gotten him out of the way in time? What if the bullets had taken out Declan? Right in front of me?*

"Marley." Growled.

She blinked at him. "Yes?"

"Why in the hell didn't you tell me that you'd been shot?"

"Because I was trying to keep you safe! Because it all

happened so fast and...I think it was more of a really bad graze than anything else. Not like the bullet went into me." She held up her arm. An arm that sported twelve stitches and a large, white bandage. "I lost a little blood."

"Your blood was everywhere."

"You heard the doctor. Wounds like this can bleed a lot at first. I'm stitched up. I'm fine." She tried a sunny smile. Her arm was numb, and she'd been poked and prodded for hours. Sunny was the last thing she felt, but Marley could fake it for him. "How about you go get me some clothes so I can ditch this hospital gown, and we get out of here, hmmm?"

He'd hauled the chair right next to the bed. He leaned close, his fingers came out and curled around her chin, and Declan very firmly told her, "No."

She blinked. "I don't have to stay."

"You fucking do. You were shot. You were covered in blood. You were shaking."

He had made a few important points. "So, first, I was in shock. That's why I was shaking." No need to go into all the details about how the blood on her body had reminded her of another time, and it had sent her on a psychological spin that had made her dizzy and terrified and—*stop*. Marley sucked in a breath. "Wounds bleed. That's the normal course of things. I've been stitched up. My vitals are good. Staying here is completely—"

"Necessary," Declan concluded.

Not exactly. "I was going to say unnecessary. You forgot the '*un*' part."

His breath whispered out. His thumb slid over her lower lip.

A shiver skated down her spine. The shiver had nothing to do with the icy temperature in the hospital room and everything to do with the man staring so intently at her. "It was also unnecessary to tell the hospital staff that you were my fiancé." Did her tongue touch his thumb? *Yes.*

The gold in the middle of his hazel eyes heated. "You'd already told the lie here once before." His thumb brushed over her lower lip again. "I just repeated it so that no one would be foolish enough to try and kick me out of your room. I'm staying with you, all night."

"I don't need a billionaire to sit and watch me sleep."

"Too bad. You're getting one." His jaw locked. "And don't you ever, *ever* hurt again and not tell me."

"It was a graze. It was—"

"Marley. You don't *ever* hurt without telling me, understand?" Then his thumb was gone from her mouth. And—and his lips were pressing against her. But this wasn't like the rough and demanding kiss he'd given her in the alley. This was different. Soft. Careful. As if he feared hurting her.

"I'm not glass. I don't shatter," she whispered against his mouth.

"No, you're my guardian angel. You don't shatter. But you sure as hell bleed." He pulled back. "Understand that he's a dead man."

Her brows scrunched as she attempted to follow along after that incredibly tender kiss. "Uh, Keith? Yes, I know he didn't survive but—"

"The man who shot you. He won't go inside a jail cell. He'll pay for hurting you."

Marley could only shake her head. "That's not the way things work."

He sat back in his chair, but his fingers tangled with hers. The fingers of her left hand. "That's the way things work in my world."

His world was a very scary place. She stared into his eyes, searching for some hint of softness. Of—of *something* that would reassure her. But there was just cold, hard intent. A deadly focus.

She was staring at a man who was not afraid to kill.

"Do you see me now?" he asked quietly.

A rap sounded at the door. She jumped, and her head jerked toward the hospital door just as it swung open. Her helpful and bubbly nurse didn't appear. Instead, Parker stood in the doorway. Looking extra grim. He shot a thumb over his shoulder in a quick, rough gesture. "I see you have two guard dogs in place."

"Security," came Declan's easy reply. "For my fiancée. Can't risk her being hurt again."

Parker stepped inside and kicked the door shut. "Still singing that BS line, are you?" A tired shake of his head. His gaze zeroed in on Marley. "Didn't learn your lesson the first time, did you? How many brushes with death will it take for you to realize that there are some people you should never, ever get close to in this world?"

The hospital gown was too big. It started to slide off her right shoulder. She hurriedly pulled it back into place. "I'm doing well, Parker. Thank you so much for your concern. Not in any pain. All stitched up. Ready to go."

"She's not going anywhere tonight." Declan's cold and dark promise.

Parker ambled toward the bed. His gaze swept over Marley's face. Then to the large bandage on her arm. "Now you've got a bullet wound to go with the knife—"

"Did you find out anything about the bouncer?" Marley cut through his words. No sense in him airing all her personal business at the moment. "I assume you *did* follow up on the lead we gave you? Because before I was forced

into that ambulance, I told you that Keith indicated the bouncer who worked last night's shift at Abyss was possibly involved in everything that happened to Declan."

"Yeah. I found him. Hugo Webb was dead along with an ex con buddy of his."

She straightened in the bed. "Dead?" The oversized gown slid down her shoulder once again.

Before she could fix it, Declan was there. He grabbed the material. Started to haul it back up, but...

He stopped.

His fingers brushed across the small scar on her upper right collar bone. A scar that was normally covered, just as the others were. "Marley?"

Her head turned toward him. His eyes were on her scar. And he was pulling at the material of her gown, trying to see more.

"*No.*" She slapped a hand over her chest, holding the thin material in place. "This isn't a peepshow."

His gaze never left the old wound. "That looks like the scar from a knife."

Apparently, the man had an eye for scars.

"*Who put a knife in you?*"

Parker cleared his throat. "So, I just announced that I found not one, not two, but...*three* dead bodies tonight. Perhaps we should focus on that news for the moment?"

Declan's eyes glittered at Marley.

"Dead body number one belonged to Keith Long, bartender extraordinaire at Abyss. Body two was that of Hugo Webb, one of the bouncers at Abyss. Hugo was the bouncer who called in sick tonight and who apparently gave Keith the special drink you ordered last night." Parker was right beside the hospital bed now. "And dead body number three was Hugo's former cell mate, David Berry. Thought you'd be interested to know that Hugo was shot in the forehead and heart. A professional takedown if I ever saw it. His buddy must have tried to flee the scene. David took a bullet to the back of the head. Crime analysis guys said it tore through the back of the skull and then erupted out the front of his head. His blood was splattered everywhere."

"Who put a knife in you?"

Declan clearly had a one-track mind. But shouldn't he be far more focused on the dead bodies than on her old wounds? She was certainly focused on the dead and trying not to be sick as Parker revealed his chilling details. "It wasn't a knife," she whispered. And it hadn't been. Not exactly. But pretty close.

"If it helps you focus," Parker offered, "I'll tell you who left those marks on her. And it's more than just one, by the way. If you knew your *fiancée* better, you'd realize she hides quite a few scars beneath her clothes."

Declan's head whipped toward him. His fingers remained brushing lightly over the scar on her collarbone, as if he could somehow take away the old pain. Silly man. There were some pains that never ended.

"It was a guy by the name of Sebastian Glass. A man convicted of killing three women and suspected of murdering at least four more. Sebastian developed a bit of an obsession with the Ph.D. candidate who was interviewing him...and one day, when the guards weren't paying enough attention, he pulled out a shiv he'd carefully made, and he attacked the woman he wanted."

Declan leapt out of his chair.

"Did that help?" Parker asked politely.

Declan's hands were fisted at his sides.

"Or did it just make you want to kill someone else?" A careful question from the cop. "Got to say, I knew you were holding back on me, Declan. When we were in this very hospital, I could see it in your eyes. You remembered one hell of a lot more about your abduction than you let on, didn't you? And like I said, the murders of Hugo Webb and David Berry looked very, very professional. As in, the kind of professional work that a hitman would do. I have to assume that someone with your...connections...would know exactly how to get a hitman to do your dirty work."

Declan took a step toward the detective.

"And Keith Long? The shot to the head and the heart? Same technique, huh? What did you do...tell your shooter you'd drag the guy outside and have him in position for the attack? Then you could act like you were as stunned as everyone else by the gunshots." His gaze flickered to Marley. "But you didn't count on her getting in the way, did you? You probably thought she'd stay out of the line of fire. That she'd never see the shooter until it was too late. After all, she's just a newbie PI. No real threat to you."

Marley hauled the hospital gown back up on her shoulder. "Declan absolutely did not do that! Not any of it!"

"You see him as a victim." Parker nodded. "Because that's how you met. He was tied up and vulnerable, so you don't get who he really is. But I know the truth." He and Declan were practically toe to toe now. "Why don't you ask him what happened to his dad, Marley? Maybe he'll give you all the gory details, and you'll realize he isn't some lost lamb you need to help. He's another sadistic killer, just like Broken Glass."

Broken Glass. The nickname that the press had given to Sebastian Glass.

"And he'll break you, too, if you aren't careful. Thanks to him, you've already got a new scar to add to your collection."

"*Stop it.*" She jumped from the bed.

Declan immediately whirled toward her. "What are you doing?"

Before she could take a step, he scooped her into his arms, holding her ever-so-carefully, and he put her back in the bed. "Do *not* get up again."

Marley rolled her eyes. "My legs are fine, Declan. I just have stitches in my arm." She glared at Parker. "Stop trying to turn us against each other. It's not happening."

Parker put one hand on his hip. "Because you trust this jerk?"

"Because *Declan* would have gotten shot if I hadn't saved him! He had no clue what was happening. The shooter might have been aiming for Keith, but he didn't care at all if the bullet went through Declan in order to make that kill shot. A paid hitman would have been a bit more careful about *not* eliminating the person who was giving him the cash for the job." Her breath heaved out. "Obviously, someone was taking care of loose ends. The two men—Hugo and David—do you have pictures of them? Do they fit the descriptions of the men who pushed Declan into the van?"

"Big and brutal. Yeah, they fit."

A quick nod from her. "They were the muscle. And Keith got eliminated, too, because he was involved. He admitted to trashing the bottle that he'd opened for Declan. Keith trashed the bottle because he *knew* there was evidence left behind in it that could prove his guilt. All three of those men were involved, and now all three are dead." A shake of her head. "But Declan wasn't behind their deaths. The man who planned Declan's abduction was —and you *know* this. You're just pushing and pushing at him because you think you can make him crack. News flash, it's not going to happen. Declan isn't the kind of man who does that. He doesn't break."

She felt Declan's eyes on her. But he didn't speak.

Marley slanted him a glance. "What? Want to say I'm wrong? Do it. I dare you."

"*You need to get away from him, Marley.*" A fierce command from Parker.

Declan settled back into the chair beside her. His expression was cool, almost bored now, and maybe she would have bought that fake mask, if she hadn't seen the emotion glittering in his eyes. "Marley isn't getting away from me." Declan's cool and controlled voice. "She's my PI. Our case isn't over."

His coolness set off alarm bells in her head. *Declan is near exploding.*

"Does she have to die before the case is over?" Parker asked softly.

Declan blinked. The set of his jaw hardened. "Marley won't die. No one will so much as bruise her skin from here on out." His head turned toward her. "There will be no more jumping between me and bullets for Marley. No more putting herself at any risk. Marley understands our arrangement."

No, Marley did not. But she figured they could have this discussion in private. No need to set off more suspicions from the detective. He was already anti-Declan enough.

"She's to act in an advisory role," Declan continued silkily. "And, of course, as my fiancée, she will be receiving full protection from my security team. From here on out, Marley will be monitored twenty-four, seven."

Um, she didn't like the sound of that. And back to her shooting... "So, by any chance, has my small, really-only-aflesh-wound injury been kept from the media?" *Please. Don't let that bit have been leaked to the press.*

"No, it hasn't been kept from them," Parker immediately informed her. "The press knows about the murders and your connection to them. Any story that involves Declan Flynn is guaranteed to attract attention."

Her shoulders slumped. "That's unfortunate." Her family would be pissed. But they were out of the country, so maybe her brothers wouldn't hear the news. A woman could hope. Dealing with Declan was bad enough. Dealing with the worried twins?

After the incident with Sebastian, I thought they were going to lose their minds. And her brothers didn't know she'd recently hung up her PI shingle. That would be another fun surprise for them.

They thought she was happily making pastries somewhere. Their mistake.

"Any other information you wanted to share, Detective Ellis?" Declan lounged back in the chair. "Or do you just have more accusations to hurl my way?"

Steam practically rolled from Parker. "You're not cooperating with the investigation."

Declan raised his brows. "The police were called to the alley. Not like I tried to *hide* things."

Marley didn't point out that *she'd* called the cops.

"You won't provide me with a list of your enemies," Parker fumed.

"That's because the list would be far too long. And I actually don't know anyone who has the balls to kidnap me and torture me." Declan's voice was still mild. Vaguely musing. "That takes a special kind of sonofabitch, don't you think?"

"Yeah, it does." Parker crossed his arms over his chest.

His head turned toward Marley. "You could have died tonight."

She was aware, yes. "But I didn't."

"The way I see it, you've already lost several of your nine lives. How about you stop tempting fate?"

She could make no promises.

The faint lines near Parker's eyes deepened. "If the mastermind is eliminating loose ends, you get that you could be next, don't you, Marley? Maybe you weren't *accidentally* hit tonight. Maybe the bullet just didn't go in your heart as planned by the shooter because you got lucky."

Marley shook her head. No. The shooter had *not* been aiming for her. Parker was wrong.

He was also, apparently, not done. "Because if I were the perp..." A long exhale from Parker. "And I knew one woman was the reason why I had failed in my plan to kill Declan Flynn, then I'd be damn infuriated with her. The kind of fury that would drive me to kill."

She fiddled with the sheet. "Good thing you're not the perp, huh?"

Parker pointed at Declan. "Protect her. If you do nothing else...*keep her the fuck safe*."

"If you believe nothing else I say, believe this—she will be protected at all costs." Flat. Chilling. A vow. "You have my word."

"The word of a killer. Great. Just what I wanted to feel all warm and reassured on the inside." Parker spun away. Marched for the door and hauled it open. "How about we try to keep the dead bodies to a minimum, huh? Three was a damn big day." He swept out.

Marley's breath expelled in a rush. She hadn't even realized she'd held her breath at the end. She stared at the closed door for a moment. Then her head angled toward Declan.

His eyes were on her. Glittering. Intent. So filled with a deadly determination that she had to swallow twice in order to clear the lump that rose in her throat. And even before he opened his mouth, she knew he was going to say—

"Who the fuck is Sebastian Glass? And do you want me to kill him for you?"

Shock rolled through her. Okay, so she *hadn't* realized he would say that last part.

Do you want me to kill him for you?

Chapter Nine

"I HATE HOSPITALS." MARLEY STARED UP AT THE ceiling as she made this declaration.

"Then why did you stay with me last night?" Declan asked as curiosity stirred within him. When it came to Marley, he was discovering that he was far more curious than he'd ever realized. He had a deep need to learn everything about her. Every single secret she possessed.

How many scars do you have, Marley? And would you like for me to kill the bastard who put them on you? Because he would. He could. Easily.

She didn't look his way. Just kept gazing at the ceiling as if it held all of the secrets in the world. It didn't. It was a shitty ceiling with white and gray speckled panels and two overly bright, round lights that beamed down on her.

After a long moment, she admitted, "I stayed because I was protecting you."

And that's the same reason you got shot tonight. Your need to protect me. I need to break you of this bad habit, Marley. He wasn't worth protecting. "Sebastian Glass," he prompted. He should have gotten the background check on her sooner. There was too much he didn't know about Marley.

James usually worked much faster when it came to gathering intel. But Declan *had* put the man on tailing Keith as priority one. For all the good that surveillance had done.

Declan pulled out his phone. Fired off a text to James. *I want every bit of data you have on Marley. I want it now. Marley...and some piece of shit named Sebastian Glass.*

"I don't need you to kill him. Sebastian Glass is sitting on death row. The state will take care of the job soon enough." A soft sigh. "Are you really going to make me stay here all night?"

"Yes."

"Don't let the nurses come in every three hours." Disgruntled. "You know they do that crap. Checking your blood pressure, temperature—all the things. I don't need it." Adamant. "I just have some stitches. I should be home."

The home that had been trashed? Not likely.

"You needed it," she muttered. "You actually needed to stay overnight for care. You were the one who'd been drugged. I just got zinged by a stray bullet."

Zinged, his ass. "Why didn't you tell me that you'd been shot?"

Her gaze finally pulled from the ceiling. Her head turned his way, and those deep, dark, utterly unforgettable eyes of hers locked on him. "I didn't want to be a bother."

"What?" He almost jumped from the damn chair.

She winced. "That was probably louder than you intended it to be. You're usually creepily quiet."

Usual didn't apply to any of his interactions with her. And she wasn't going to distract him. He knew her words had been a deliberate distraction. "The fuck you didn't want to be a bother."

"Right." A nod. "The fuck I didn't want to be. And, at first, I wasn't even sure I'd been hit by a bullet. A lot was happening in that alley. My priority as your PI was to keep you safe."

Screw that. "You need new priorities."

A faint line appeared between her brows. "Are you firing me?" Real alarm flared in the darkness of her eyes. "Because of this little zing?"

Did she have to keep calling it a zing? When she'd been bleeding all over the place, it had hardly seemed like a freaking *zing*.

"Marley—" Declan began.

"Don't fire me. *I'm* the one who spotted the shooter, remember? I can do this job."

He rubbed his chest. "I know you can." Only there wasn't really a job. "There's something I need to tell you..." How to be delicate? Tactful? He had zero clue. Mostly because he'd never been delicate or tactful a day in his life. *Marley, I was bullshitting when I said I wanted you to help me find the SOB behind my abduction. Really, you're in danger. I want you close so that I can protect you.*

Except he'd done a piss-poor job of protecting her so far. She was in a hospital bed. Looking heartbreakingly fragile. "I want to scoop you up," he confessed, voice rough. "Run the hell out of here with you and get you far away from any threat." He could put her on his private plane within the hour. By dawn, he could have her out of the country. Maybe he could take her to some tropical island where she'd have twenty-four, seven protection and then he'd be able to actually breathe without feeling this tight knot in his aching chest.

But Marley just tilted her head to the side as she studied him. Then she said, "If you understand the killer and his methods for selecting victims, you can protect people."

Declan blinked.

"At least, that was the premise I followed when I was studying for my Ph.D. My thesis was on using victimology to help *prevent* people from being chosen by predators. Because that's what some of the most dangerous killers do... they choose their prey. Specific prey. It's not some random event. Specific people are chosen for specific reasons. Sebastian Glass murdered three women. Three that were confirmed kills. We always suspected there were more, just like Parker said."

Declan found that he could not move. His body seemed to have turned into stone.

"Sebastian sliced the women with his knives over and over." She wet her lips. "Their bodies looked like broken glass. Cracks everywhere. Some deep. Some shallow, like spiderwebs on their skin."

Even breathing felt hard to Declan.

"I was interviewing him. His IQ was off the charts. He's what's called an organized killer. There were never any fits of rage with him. Everything was carefully planned out. Perfectly orchestrated. He was probably a psychopath...no regard for the feelings of others. No understanding of the emotions that others possess. Though I suspect he was very good at mimicry." A soft exhale. "Just because you're a psychopath, it doesn't mean you're a killer. Lots of people with psychopathic tendencies are incredible doctors. Their lack of empathy actually helps them." She blinked. Then frowned at him.

Declan wondered just what his expression looked like to make her study him that way.

"What?" Marley rubbed her lips together. Exhaled. "You think it doesn't help a surgeon to be able to hold back emotions when you are cutting into the chest of a dying man? You have a job to do. Emotions can't impact you. All psychopaths aren't killers. All killers aren't psychopaths. And, in fact—" Marley broke off.

He waited.

Nothing else came. She fiddled with the white covers on the bed.

"Marley?" Declan prompted when the silence stretched.

Looking down at her fingers as they fiddled, she said, "Very successful business professionals can have psychopathic traits. When you have to make decisions about firing or hiring hundreds of employees all at once, a bit of cold-bloodedness aids you."

He leaned toward her. A lock of hair had fallen on her cheek. He reached out and tucked that lock behind her ear. Her head tilted up, and her gaze immediately shot back to catch his. Declan's knuckles lingered against the silk of her skin. "Are you calling me a psychopath, sweetheart?" A tender question.

She didn't blink. "Are you a psychopath?"

Declan considered the matter. "Pretty sure my bastard of a father was. He was as ice cold as they come. Ice cold, but sadistic to his core." Declan shook his head, but didn't stop touching her. He couldn't stop touching her. And why was he telling her about his father? He never told anyone about the bastard. "But even though nothing else—no one else—seemed to matter, he *was* obsessed with my mother. So in love with her that he couldn't see reason. Psychopaths can't love, right? Isn't that one of the rules?" *I didn't think it was real love. I always thought it was evil and controlling and I...I didn't want to be the same way.*

So he'd shut off his emotions. Refused to feel. *Did I turn myself into a psychopath? Am I that far gone?*

Except, he didn't feel far gone. Not when Marley was right beside him. He felt far too much when she was near.

"Some research suggests that psychopaths can form an attachment to one other person." Her soft voice. Not soft so much as...gentle. Caring. Why the hell did she care so much about him?

"I believe it can happen," Marley continued in the tender voice that seemed to wrap around him. Sink into him. "Is it love the way that a so-called normal person experiences it? I don't know. But who is to say that everyone feels love the same way?" Her head turned. Her lips brushed over his knuckles.

Heat spiked through him, chasing out the cold that wanted to consume him. "Marley."

"I'm sorry that your father hurt you."

Be careful. I'm not normal, and I don't care how normal people feel love. I care that I feel alive when you're near me.

"I wanted to make the world a better place. I wanted to understand the monsters in order to save the future victims. Instead, I became a victim." Her lashes fluttered. "I could tell Sebastian was fixating on me. He watched me too carefully. Refused to speak to anyone else on the research team if I wasn't present. And then one day, Sebastian said he'd only talk if I was the one doing the interview with him. I was working under the guidance of my college mentor. Three of us would normally go in each time we interviewed Sebastian. But he wanted to change the rules." Her breath came a little faster. "I knew something was wrong, and I said I didn't want to do the interview."

Then how the fuck had she wound up attacked and sporting scars?

"But Sebastian said there were more victims. If I would talk with him, one-on-one, he would tell me about them. Who they were. Where they were buried. He said he could be cuffed—and the cuffs chained to the floor. A guard could be in the room. No one else. Sebastian, me, and a guard. I had to sit across from him. Another condition. If I did, he promised that he'd give closure to other families who'd lost their daughters."

"He fucking manipulated you." *He's dead. Screw waiting for the needle to jab in his arm. He is dead.*

"The DA asked me to conduct the interview. Promised everything would be safe. That I'd be watched at all times. But it wasn't safe. I..." Her head turned. Her lips skimmed over his knuckles again. "Sorry," she murmured. The faintest hint of red came and went in her cheeks. "For some reason, you make me feel better."

Her words sank into his heart.

Way to seal your fate, Marley.

"Sebastian got out of the cuffs. Like Houdini. Did it in a blink. And then he was on me. Had the shiv to my throat before I could even scream. Sebastian told the guard that if he didn't get out of the room, he'd slice my throat open right then and there. So the guard backed out."

"He should *never* have left." He'd be finding out the name of the guard. Anyone who'd ever hurt her, Declan would find out about them. And they would pay. Simple fact of life. No one in this world could hurt Marley and walk away.

"His breath came so hard. I could hear Sebastian panting behind me because he was so excited. He spun me around and I stared into his eyes, and I'd never seen evil until that moment. I'm talking about *true* evil. It was real. Dark. Consuming. He wanted to hurt me, and he was going to enjoy it. I'd wanted to know how he picked his victims, and in that moment, I did. He picked the ones that called to him. The ones he wanted to break. That's what he told me. He took the ones who seemed strong so he could show them the meaning of weakness."

She pulled back. Her hand went to her collarbone. "This was the first drive of the shiv. Then he went to my right shoulder. My stomach." Her hand dropped protectively to her stomach.

Helpless, he reached out. His fingers covered hers.

She glanced down at their joined hands. "He wanted to make me weak. He thought that the terror would break me. He was wrong. When he pulled back to slice me again, I kicked him in the dick as hard as I could."

"Fuck, yes, you did."

Her head rose. Their eyes met. "He was bringing that shiv down again. My blood was dripping from it. His eyes had been so cold and soulless during the previous interview sessions. But this time...this time, as he got ready to kill me, his eyes were blazing. He looked...happy."

His fingers remained careful as he held hers. "You escaped."

"I fell. Slipped in my blood that had dripped on the floor. When I dropped, a guard tased him. Another fired tear gas. My eyes were burning, and I was bleeding, and Sebastian was just screaming that he wasn't finished with me." A long exhale. "But that was the day I was finished with him. They wheeled me out of that prison on a gurney. Rushed me to an ER. And I never went back. I dropped out of the Ph.D. program. I hid with my brothers for the first three months after the attack. I would jump at every creak or rustle of sound because in my head, I kept hearing Sebastian say he wasn't finished with me. If he wasn't finished, then that meant he'd come after me again."

"No, love, he won't." Absolute certainty. "He will never, ever get close to you again." He'd be buried six feet under the ground. Being dead would make it exceedingly hard for Sebastian Glass to get close to Marley ever again.

"I ran away from the education that had always meant so much to me. I ran from the life I'd had planned. It took me time, but I got focused again. I stopped jumping at shadows." A ghost of a smile teased her lips. "The kids helped me get out in public again. I got this job—don't laugh but—"

"I would never laugh at you." *Never. But kill for you? Sure.* Without hesitation or compunction. But he would never laugh at Marley.

Her smile faded. "I played a princess at a kid's party. The parents hired me for the role. The kids were all so happy. They were laughing and smiling, and I felt safe. So I kept at it for a bit. Kinda like dipping your toe in the water again. And then from the kid's party planning role—because I started party planning—I got involved in pastry making. It soothed me, if that makes sense. Spending time alone in the kitchen." A roll of one shoulder. "Then I did the real estate bit because a friend told me it was the best way to make fast cash, but it's—it's not just about cash, you know? I felt off in the job. Like I was still looking for what was right for me. And then I worked as a bartender, but..." Her words trailed off. "There were a lot of fights. I didn't always feel safe in the bar."

"And you feel *safe* as a PI?" No way. "Hate to remind you, sweetheart, but you were shot tonight. That's pretty much the opposite of safety."

"I want to help people. My cousin Ophelia helps people. She and the Ice Breakers make a difference. That was my dream, a long time ago. In a different life. To make the world better. Safer. I'm trying to get back to that dream. Even if I have to take slow, baby steps in order to do it."

There were dark shadows under her eyes. She needed her sleep. Declan knew he should let her go. "Ease back," he rasped. "You need to get comfortable."

She wrinkled her nose at him. "You're going to make me stay here all night."

Yes. "I'm going to make you stay here all night," he confirmed. But she slid down on the bed. He pulled the covers over her. Tucked them in lightly around her, being very, very careful with her injured arm.

"You're tucking me in," she noted with some definite surprise. "Declan Flynn is actually tucking me into a bed."

"Indeed I am." He tucked a bit more.

She shook her head against the pillow. "I don't get you."

Most people didn't. And normally, that was the way he liked it. But, again, nothing with Marley was normal.

"You're rumored to be some heartless mob boss…" A big yawn had her blinking, then her eyelids sagging a little bit. "But I knew that wasn't true from our first meeting."

He stood over her. Stared down at Marley's closing eyes with complete focus. "Was it because I was tied up and you saw me as a victim?" That had certainly been Parker's take on the situation.

Parker was a pain in his ass.

"No." Her lashes fluttered. "It's because you told me to get away. To leave you. You were…" A sigh. "In desperate straits, but you were trying to protect me. It was right then that I knew what you were."

He reached behind her. His fingers brushed against the

button to turn off the too bright lights. As they plunged into darkness, he asked, "And what am I?"

"You're not a monster. You're a hero." Sleepiness slurred her words.

Declan gazed at her in silence for a while. Then he shook his head. "No, Marley. I am far from that. You see, I'm a killer. As twisted and hollowed on the inside as they come. When I was sixteen years old, I killed my own father. And I didn't care when he begged me for mercy. He should have known I would have none. After all, he turned me into the devil I am today."

No response. But then, he hadn't expected one.

He'd waited to give that big confession until her eyes were fully closed. Sleep had taken her, so she didn't know what he was.

She'd confessed to him, and some part of him had wanted to confess his darkest secret to her. A payback of sorts. Equal footing.

But she didn't know because sleep had taken her. And he almost liked that she thought he was one of the good guys. He'd never been one of those before. Should make for an interesting situation.

After a moment—a long moment, granted—Declan grabbed the chair he'd been using earlier. He hauled it a wee bit closer to the bed. He sat down, spreading his legs out as best he could. His gaze remained on her face.

He pulled out his phone and sent another text to James.

Sebastian Glass is a problem.

Three dots appeared on his screen as James prepared his reply. Then...

What do you want me to do about this problem, sir?

Shouldn't the answer be obvious?

He wanted the problem to fucking disappear.

In the bed, Marley slowly turned on her side, moving away from him. *Not* the side with her injured arm.

His gaze swept to her, then back to the phone. He fired off one more note. *Life is always easier when your problems have been eliminated.*

* * *

WHEN SHE WAS on her side—and making sure that she wasn't jarring her injured arm—Marley slowly opened her eyes.

Declan's confession rang in her ears.

I'm a killer. As twisted and hollowed on the inside as they come. When I was sixteen years old, I killed my own father. And I didn't care when he begged me for mercy. He should have known I would have none. After all, he turned me into the devil I am today.

A tear leaked down her cheek.

Chapter Ten

Seven days later...

"I'm bored out of my ever-loving mind." She slammed the fancy office door shut behind her for dramatic effect. After all, sometimes, dramatics were needed in order to get a point across. This was, indeed, one of those times.

Marley stared across the massive office space and watched as Declan slowly closed the laptop in front of him. The Chicago skyline waited behind him. Of course, Declan's office would be on the top floor of the high-rise building. Not like she had a fear of heights or anything.

Oh, wait. I do.

After her shooting, he'd whisked her out of Georgia. He'd used the pretense of saying that he had to return to Chicago on business and that, as his PI, she had to come with him.

Not like she'd wanted her client to be jetting off without her, so she'd boarded his private plane. She'd thought that he would be giving her a glimpse into his life. Letting her meet his employees. Talking to her about business rivals. Providing her with an all-access pass into his world so that she could snoop her heart out and find the perp who'd abducted him.

Only...nope. None of that had happened. Not one single thing had gone as she'd envisioned. Instead, she'd been put in a swanky room at his freaking mansion, she'd been told to rest...and she'd been pampered and waited on by his staff like she was some kind of long-lost princess.

Sure, normally, that sounded like one fun way to spend a few vacation days. Being waited on? Living the lifestyle of the rich and privileged? Hello, sweet joy.

But this was not a normal situation. It was no dream vacation. She had a job to do. And Declan was stopping her from doing her work.

His fingers steepled beneath his chin as he studied her. "How did the doctor's appointment go?"

And that was another thing. The man was obsessed with her small scratch. Stupid bullet. He'd never let her hear the end of that incident. "The stitches are gone. I'm all good. Better than good." She put her hands on her hips and marched forward. "In fact, I'm in a fighting mood."

His gaze swept over her. "I was getting that impression."

Her hands slammed down on his gleaming, too perfect desk.

His hazel eyes immediately dropped to her hands. One dark brow quirked.

"Declan."

He leaned back in his chair and gazed up at her. "Marley."

"I thought I was your PI."

"You *are* my PI."

"Bullshit." She called it exactly as she saw it. "I'm your pampered princess. You lied to me."

His face tensed.

"You brought me here so that you could sideline me." Her hands lifted, and she paced around the desk. The better to close in on her prey.

He rolled his chair back, the wheels not so much as squeaking. As if they would dare. His gaze had gone hooded as he studied her.

She pointed at him. No, pointing wasn't good enough. Her index finger stabbed him in the chest. "I will *not*," another jab of her index finger, "be sidelined." Fury pumped through her. "I knew telling you about Sebastian Glass was a mistake. Now you think I'm some fragile, wilting flower." Or, even worse...*a victim who needed shielding from the world.*

He cleared his throat. "You were shot."

"A scratch."

"Your blood soaked my limo."

"I was only bleeding because I'd saved your ass!" How could he forget that important point? And how could he do this to her? "You're putting me on the sidelines because you think I'm weak."

A slow shake of his head as he gazed up at her. "I don't think any part of you is weak."

"You think I can't handle danger and I—wait, what did you say?" Her mouth hung open in surprise, so she hurriedly snapped it closed.

"I said..." His hand rose so that his fingers could curl around her wrist as she continued to stab him in the chest with her index finger. "I don't think any part of you is weak. I think you're strong. Determined. Brave. Too brave in fact.

You definitely dip into the *foolishly* brave category far too much."

He'd praised her and insulted her, all within the span of a few seconds. Typical Declan.

"I also think you're gorgeous. Probably the most beautiful woman I've ever met."

She snorted. Crap. Not the sound of a beautiful woman, was it? Oh, well. "You've dated supermodels. I've seen your press stories. Don't try your tired lines with me. I'm not gonna fall for them." Hopefully, she would not. But she had caught herself preening a bit when he said she was strong. And determined.

Nicest compliments ever. Then he had to ruin things by calling me foolishly brave. Like that's a thing.

"Can't help but notice, sweetheart, you call me a liar quite a lot."

She hadn't actually called him a liar. Just super heavily implied it. But...*liar.* She was not in the same category as his supermodel exes.

"You are the most beautiful woman I've ever met." His hand lifted her wrist. His fingers curled along the outside, and his mouth pressed to her inner wrist, right over the racing pulse. "The bravest. The most selfless. And the most stubborn."

Her knees got a wee bit shaky when she felt the lick of his tongue along her wrist.

"I *sidelined* you, as you say, not because I don't think you're capable, but because I wanted you to heal."

"A scratch."

His lashes—stupid long for a man, now that she stared closely at them—flickered. *Okay, fine, they are not stupid at all. They are sexy. I find way too much about this man to be sexy.*

A man who'd confessed to murder when he'd thought she couldn't hear him.

In the week that had passed, he hadn't mentioned the confession again. Neither had she. But she'd certainly been digging. And the man who'd been more than happy to help her dig and send case files that *should* have been closed and confidential? Detective Parker Ellis.

He'd emailed the information to her five minutes after she'd contacted him.

Information that proved Declan had been abused by his father for years. That if he hadn't stopped his father that long ago night, Declan would have been the dead one.

At least, that was what the cops had concluded at the time. No charges had been filed. Declan had been able to walk away while his father had been buried in the ground.

Declan's mouth pressed to her wrist again. When the rough, wet edge of his tongue slid over her, she jolted.

"You're healed," he murmured.

Her breath came way too fast. "My scratch—those stitches—they are the reason you've been avoiding me and locking me away in the haunted castle?" Her nickname for his home. It was big and intimidating and heavily Gothic and she loved it. Not that she'd told Declan that she adored the monstrosity that was his mansion. And, besides, he'd been avoiding her. Basically, saying she needed to sit with her damn feet up while he disappeared for hours at a time. "You left me with Alfred."

His hold tightened on her wrist. "Who the fuck is Alfred?"

"Really?" A long-suffering sigh. One that she hoped hid the fact that her breathing had definitely become more erratic thanks to the wicked licks of his tongue on her skin. And what was up with that sexy licking? He'd been super platonic all week. She'd entertained the fantasy of him slipping into her bed late one night. Of him saying he couldn't make it without her any longer. That he *had* to have her.

Only he'd never said those words.

He'd been the perfect gentleman. Damn him. Well, almost perfect. There was one thing that he'd done—

"Alfred." Gritted out from Declan. "Who is he?"

"Batman? Robin? Ring any bells?" She tugged on her wrist. He did not let go. "Seriously, you have to see the similarities. You basically live in Wayne Manor." *Though I prefer to think of it as your haunted castle.*

"I live in my own damn manor. Not Wayne anything."

"Yeah, fine, you're missing the point." He had to know who Alfred was. "You can't tell me that you weren't superhero obsessed when you were a kid. Every guy I know was obsessed with Batman at one point or another. My brothers wanted to *be* him when they were younger. Come on, you must know—"

"I know who fucking Batman is." A growl.

A very Batman-like growl, but she didn't point out that fact. Instead, she did a very soft, lady-like clearing of her throat. "Anyway...James is your Alfred."

"James isn't my damn butler! He did not secretly train me in martial arts and help me track down the Penguin and the Riddler."

She nodded, pleased. "Ah. So you *do* know Batman."

He let her go. "I used to have comics. When I was eleven, my father took them all and burned them in front of me."

Her mouth dropped open. What a horrible thing to do to a child. "Why would he do that?"

"Because he didn't want me wasting my time with

things that weren't real. He wanted to show me that shit like that didn't matter."

Her heart squeezed in her chest. "And in his mind, what did matter?"

Declan's eyes glittered as he stared up at her. "Money. Power. Breaking his enemies and pretty much leaving as much devastation as possible in his wake."

From what she'd learned of his father, yes, he had seemed to leave a lot of devastation behind. She could almost see some of that devastation in Declan's eyes. Then he blinked, and she could see nothing at all but a cold stare —no, an icy one—peering back at her.

"You shouldn't have burst into my office," Declan told her. All emotion had left his voice.

She rolled her eyes.

He blinked.

"*You* shouldn't be working this late," she tossed out. "It's eight p.m. I'm sure the movers and shakers are all gone home for the night."

"Not those in a different time zone."

Seriously? "You've been avoiding me. I'd decided that I'd had enough. Told Alfred to kiss my ass when he tried to stop me from leaving the haunted castle. And here I am."

His lips thinned.

"You have been avoiding me." Softer.

"I've been trying not to fuck you, sweetheart. There's a difference between avoiding someone and trying not to absolutely devour the person." His hands went to grab the armrests on his chair. "You were injured."

He'd been staying away so he wouldn't fuck her? Well, well, well. Now she was most definitely intrigued.

"With your stitches, it seemed...best to stay away." A little gruff. "And if I sidelined you—"

"If?" Marley interrupted. Oh, there had been no *if*. There had been serious sidelining.

"I only did it because I was trying to keep you safe."

Her eyes narrowed. "That's the whole reason you whisked me to Chicago as soon as I got out of the hospital, isn't it? Because you're trying to protect me. You're trying to protect the PI who is supposed to be solving your case." Like she hadn't figured this out. "The two men who put you in the van are dead. The bartender who helped drug you is dead. Three dead bodies. Add to that pileup the fact that someone trashed my place right after I saved you..." Only one conclusion could be drawn. "You think he's coming after me next."

Declan didn't blink.

"You think the man behind all of this is going to target me. Maybe he thinks I saw something that can lead the authorities—or you—to him. Or maybe he's just pissed as all hell that I interfered in whatever sick game he was playing with you." She forced a shrug. "Either way, you've decided I'm next on his hit list. You installed me at Wayne Manor—"

"Marley..."

"Fine! You installed me at the haunted castle."

His brows beetled.

"You put me behind the best security that money can buy. You think I'll stay hidden while you hire someone else to hunt him." She leaned forward. Her hands curled around his shoulders. "Think again."

His head tipped back even more as he stared up at her.

His legs were spread. She was standing between them and...Marley lifted her left leg. She put her knee down on his chair. Right between his spread thighs. Very, very close to his dick. A dick that she'd taken a quick peek at and realized...

Declan wants me. Right here. Right now. The hard, heavy length of his cock shoved up against the front of his very expensive trousers.

"You were trying not to fuck me." Her voice had gone all husky.

His hands clamped around her waist. Did he mean to push her away? Or maybe wildly, eagerly pull her closer?

Um, he did neither. Just held her tightly. Was he still trying to hold back? If so, he needed to stop that nonsense. Stat.

"How do you even know that I want to fuck you?' she breathed. "What if I'm not interested?" She was interested, of course. Very, very interested.

"Marley..." A dark rumble.

Her head bent. Her lips brushed over his. An open-mouthed, not nearly enough kiss. Then against his lips, she whispered, "You snuck into my room every single night." Into the room, but not her bed. *I wanted you in my bed.*

"I was making sure you were okay. And how the fuck do you know that I was there?"

"Because I could feel you." Another soft kiss. "I wanted you to do more than sneak inside the room and stand near the doorway."

Now...he pushed her away. Such the wrong response. "You don't want me." Adamant. "Marley, I am *not* the man you want to fuck with."

"Actually, you are." A firm nod. "You are exactly the man I want to fuck. No one else will do for me. And I don't have stitches any longer, so what excuse are you gonna use now to deny us both what we want?"

"I can't..." A muscle jerked along his jaw. "I can't take you once, then watch you turn away."

But he was the one turning away. Literally turning his face away from her and staring toward the city lights.

Since he'd turned his head, she just let her lips feather over the scar that marked him.

Instantly, his whole body tensed. "Marley, no."

"Declan, *yes*."

His hands flexed against her. "I'm trying to do the right thing here." Grated. A little desperate.

She'd like him a lot more desperate. She'd get him that way, too. "Just what is it that you think is 'right' to do? To deny us what we both want? How can that possibly be right?"

He sucked in a sharp breath.

"Because I want you, Declan Flynn. I'm not the type to sleep with just any guy, FYI. I have a particular set of standards." Another gentle kiss to his scar before she eased back a bit. "I tend to like really dominating bastards who are megalomaniacs and enjoy ordering other people around."

"*What?*" His head swung toward her. His eyes blazed.

Laughter spilled from her. "Couldn't help myself." He was so tense. Almost...afraid. Of her? Of them being together? Why? "What do you think will happen to me, if I'm with you?"

He swallowed. "I don't want to hurt you."

"I don't believe that you could." Yet even as she said the words, Marley feared they were a lie. *He's not looking for happily ever after and forever. If you're not careful, he will break your heart as no one else ever has before.* "Physically, I know you'd never hurt me."

"There are other kinds of pain."

She knew he was speaking from experience. "Your father was a real bastard. He made your life hell."

His fingers tightened on her just the littlest bit. "I don't talk about him. Not with anyone."

Such a liar. He'd talked with her, when Declan thought she couldn't hear him. A confession in the darkness was still a confession. "He hurt you." She wasn't going to back away on this. "He made you think you weren't good enough, didn't he?"

"Good didn't enter the equation. He made sure I could never be good. And someone like me shouldn't be with you." He rose and lifted her at the same time. When he put her down, he stepped back. His hands fisted at his sides. "I'm controlling myself."

She frowned. Did it look like she wanted control?

He stood there, all tense and towering, all sexy and dark and brooding, and rasped, "But it's the hardest thing I've done in my life. I want to strip you. I want to lift you onto the desk. And I want to fuck you here and now. So turn around, walk out of this office, and go back to damn Wayne Manor or the haunted castle or whatever the hell you want to call my home."

She wore a long, black dress. Flat ballerina shoes.

He wore his expensive, I-cost-more-than-a-month's-rent pants and a tailored, white shirt. The first few buttons of the shirt had been undone. A light coating of stubble covered his jaw. The glower remained on his face. But his eyes? Feverish intensity had slipped back into them. Lust. Hunger. So much need. For her.

Marley took a breath and a chance. "I stormed over here to tell you that I will *not* be sidelined. The cops in Augusta have made zero progress on your case. As far as they know, the mastermind of your abduction—and the person who likely committed those three murders—the perp is in the wind. He could be anywhere." A fun conversation with Parker had brought forth this unfortunate news. The cops had jack and shit to go on in their investigation. Seven days and already, the case seemed cold. Zero leads. Zero suspects.

I need the Ice Breakers on this.

Her shoulders straightened. Technically, they'd already been straight. They straightened more. "I'm not going to play pampered princess while he hunts you again. He went to all that trouble to target you. He won't give up. He *will* come again."

And Declan? He just shrugged. As if having a killer stalk him was a normal occurrence.

Suspicion had her gaze narrowing. "Is that another reason why you came back to Chicago? Because you knew he was hunting you?"

His eyes gleamed at her. Then he slowly smiled. The smile was the cold grin a shark offered his prey right before his mouth opened and he took a big, lethal bite.

"This is my turf," he said. "My guards are everywhere. My security—everywhere. I have contacts that stretch all over this city. Good, bad, and everything in between. If he's coming after me, this isn't territory that he can control. This is where I will absolutely annihilate him."

Her heart thudded hard in her chest. "Planning to, uh, catch him and turn him over to the proper authorities?"

That smile of his was chilling. "If it helps you to think that, sure. Let's say that's what I'm planning to do."

"Declan!" She grabbed his arms. His hands were still fisted. His body rock hard. "You are *not* taking matters into your own hands. You can't hunt this guy down and get vigilante justice." Seriously, could he be more Bruce Wayne? *Stop it, Declan. Stop.*

"If he's coming at me, if he's coming after you...then I will do whatever it takes to stop him." A tense pause. "Touching me right now is probably not the best idea you've ever had. Might want to let go. Back away. Head out of my office."

Oh, was that what she should do? She gave him her own smile. Not a shark about to attack. Something sweet. Sweet enough to kill. *Kill him with kindness.* She gave him that smile, then she let him go. Stepped back. She made her way around his desk. Her dress swirled around her ankles. Her steps were slow and certain as she headed for the door. She pulled it open. Popped her head outside. "Pierre?" Marley called to the assistant she'd met earlier. The man she'd had to fight to get past.

His head whipped up. He clutched a phone to his ear. Glared.

Oh, had she interrupted his phone call? No wonder he looked extra pissed. "Declan is done for the day. He apologizes for keeping you so late. He hopes you have a wonderful night."

Pierre jumped to his feet. He also hung up the phone and shoved it into his pocket. "Declan never apologizes."

"We'll be working on that flaw." She waved. "Good night. Great meeting you." Especially when he'd tried to physically stop her from getting to her goal. So much fun. Not. The man had truly tried using his five-foot-two-inch, super slender self to block her path. As if he could have stopped her.

While Pierre continued to gape, she very firmly shut the door. Then she locked it. "I listened to your idea," she announced without glancing back at Declan. "But I have a way better one." She spun to face him, and, as she did, Marley caught the naked longing on his face. Her breath shuddered out because no one had ever looked at her that way. Like he needed her more than anything. Like he had to have her. Like—

And it was gone. The longing vanished. His face became hard and unreadable.

Declan certainly excelled at hiding behind a mask.

But he'd slipped up.

She sent him her sweet smile again. All innocence. He still stood behind his desk, with the chair rolled back near him. She headed toward him. Her steps were slow and certain. Just as they'd been when she strolled *for* the door. Deliberate. Pausing beside him, she trailed her fingers down his chest.

"Don't play with me, Marley."

"Who's playing?" She shoved his laptop aside and hopped onto the desk. That big, shiny, intimidating desk. Marley raised her dress's skirt to her thighs. "I'm telling you *my* idea. My genius idea. I'm sure you heard that I told your assistant to go home. I also locked the door. It's freaking Fort Knox impossible to get up to this level of your building, so I think we're safe. No one is going to disturb us." She wet her lips. "My idea..." Her heart drummed madly. Her stomach twisted. Nerves made her voice breathless as she explained, "My idea is that I don't walk away. My idea is that I stay here with you. And you make love to me. Right here. Right now. On this desk. The desk where you work so very hard all the time." She needed him to do something. To make a move. *Don't reject me. Don't.* "Because I came here to do two things. One, to tell you that I will not be sidelined..."

He surged toward her. Stepped between her spread legs. His hands flattened on either side of her body.

"And two..." She pulled in a deep breath. Far too late to turn back now. "I came here to tell you that I want you. I want to be with you. I want you to—"

His mouth crashed onto hers.

* * *

THE VIPER HAD RETURNED to his den.

He hadn't been surprised when Declan Flynn had gone running back to Chicago. Back to his protection and perceived power. Back to the cronies that jumped to do his bidding and the fools who shuddered with fear when his name was whispered in the dark.

Too many people were afraid of Declan Flynn. That was one of the reasons he'd needed to strike while Declan was in unfamiliar territory. The dumb muscle he'd hired to help him in Augusta hadn't even realized who their target was.

And when they did discover his identity...

They were fucking terrified. Calling me and telling me they'd beg Declan for forgiveness. That they'd offer me up as the sacrificial lamb if I didn't give them enough money to flee to Mexico.

He hadn't given them anything but a bullet to the brain. Exactly what they deserved for their epic screwup. They should never have been tailed to that cabin. Certainly not by some amateur PI.

A PI that Declan had taken back home with him after a bullet had sliced over her arm.

Oh, yes, he now knew plenty about Marley Jones.

What an interesting past you have, Ms. Jones. One soaked in blood and fear. She should hate monsters just as much as he did. And yet...

Yet she'd saved Declan Flynn. Not just once. Twice.

At first, he'd just thought to eliminate her quickly. During her big rescue mission of Declan at the cabin, he couldn't be sure she hadn't overheard the two morons talking about things they shouldn't. *Things like me.* Or that she hadn't seen something that would lead her to him.

So, yes, a swift death had seemed fitting.

He'd sent the morons after her. She hadn't been home. What had they done? Trashed her place. Reached an even higher level of stupidity. Because with the trashed house, Marley had known that she was now being hunted, too.

Then she'd done the unexpected. In the alley, she'd spotted him. A surprising feat for a junior PI. The guards with their fancy training hadn't done jackshit to save their boss.

Instead, a delicate female had hurtled her body at him. She'd knocked Declan out of the line of fire. She'd taken a hit.

She'd allowed Declan to cheat death twice.

Do you think you've found yourself a good luck charm, Declan Flynn?

He'd decided to learn all he could about Declan's new charm. And the deeper he'd dived into her life, the more intrigued he'd become by Marley Jones.

A woman who had long been fascinated by monsters. So fascinated that she'd spent years studying the behavior of psychopaths and sociopaths and deviant behavior. Until she'd become prey even as she'd been surrounded by guards and prison personnel.

She'd hidden after that. Retreated. He wondered what the attack had done to her...mentally. She'd stopped trying to understand the monsters. Ended her studies.

You can't understand them. The only thing you can do is kill them. That makes the world a better place.

Some people belonged in the ground. It was a lesson he'd learned long ago. It was a lesson he would be teaching Declan Flynn.

But as he stared up at the Chicago skyline—and at one high-rise in particular—he wasn't as focused on Declan Flynn as he had been in the past. Declan had been his mission for quite some time, but Marley...

What did the attack by Sebastian Glass do to you? Did you realize they can never be changed? That they are wild beasts who just live for blood?

But...something that nagged at him even more... *Knowing how evil they are, why did you save Declan?* He got the first save. Sure. Maybe she hadn't realized who Declan was. It had been dark. She probably had only seen Declan from the back as he was forced into the van.

By all accounts, Marley was a good Samaritan type. Loved kids. Dogs. Volunteered. Helped those in need. Did the whole bit that he found utterly exhausting.

So maybe the first rescue had just been *her*. Her trying to help someone because she knew what it was like to be a victim. But the second rescue?

Why the fuck had she done that?

Didn't she understand what Declan was?

Didn't she see the monster that lived and breathed beneath his skin?

His hands drove into the pockets of his black peacoat. Marley was in the high-rise with the monster right then and there.

What were they doing?

And...

How can I show you what he really is?

Chapter Eleven

WHAT IN THE HELL WAS HE DOING?

Declan's lips pressed hard to Marley's. A hot, open-mouthed kiss. His tongue thrust into her mouth, and the little moan that rose in her throat had to be the sexiest sound that he'd ever heard. His hands shoved down harder against the surface of the desk as he leaned into her. She tasted decadent and sweet at the same time. A heady taste that drove him ever closer to the edge of his control.

For the last week, he'd tortured himself with dreams and fantasies of Marley. She'd been in his home. In the bedroom right next to his. He'd slipped into her room to check on her, yes, but...

Each night, I wanted to touch her. I wanted to kiss her.

Hell, it wasn't about some sweet and tender romance.

I want to devour her. To possess her completely. To own her. To take some of the goodness that was pure Marley and keep it, forever.

To keep her.

But he'd tried to do the right thing, dammit. Tried to tell her to walk away. He'd planned to keep his hands off her.

He could avoid wrecking something—someone—in his life, just this once. And then...

I want you.

Marley's words rang in his head. His right hand lifted. Moved to her thigh. Bunched up the soft fabric of her dress. Touched her skin that was even softer. Silk. His mouth tore from hers, and he kissed a path down her throat. Her hands were curled around his upper arms. Her legs had widened so that he could ease closer.

It would be so easy to shove the skirt of her dress up higher. To yank away her panties and thrust deep into her. *To take my fantasy.*

And with every second that passed, his control shredded a bit more. He skated closer and closer to the edge. *Stop me, Marley. Stop. Me.*

"Why would I want to do that?"

He jerked back from her, stunned that he'd actually voiced the words that had been rolling through his head. The voice of a conscience that should have been long dead. Only that conscience had seemed to creep to life once again when Marley entered his world.

"I didn't do the whole routine of shredding my pride and confessing my desire so that I could stop you." A shake of her head. "You think I do this all the time? Hop on the desks of men and try to seduce them?"

"You'd better fucking not." A savage growl. The scent of jasmine and amber was making him lose his mind.

"I don't. Haven't actually been with anyone in two years now, if you want the truth." Her lips were red. Swollen from his mouth. He got distracted by her delectable mouth, so it took a bit too long for her words to register and actually process in his lust-soaked brain.

Did she say two years?

"After the attack by Glass, I pulled away from everyone in my life. My boyfriend at the time—Zane Patrick—he kept telling me that I should never have been in the prison. And the way he looked at me sometimes...I knew that he didn't like the scars. Zane said they'd always be ugly reminders of my mistake."

Her mistake? The sonofabitch. "You're fucking perfect." *Zane Patrick.* Another name to add to his list. People didn't just get to wrong Marley and walk away scot-free, not on his watch. They didn't—

"He wasn't right for me. I knew it even before he showed me what an asshole he was." Her fingers slid down Declan's right arm. "But, if you don't mind, I'd rather not talk about him. Especially when I am trying so hard to seduce you."

He'd love to never talk about any man who'd touched her before him. *No one else will. You're going to be mine from here on out, Marley.* A bad guy could only try to do good for so long. He'd exhausted his goodness.

Time to take some of hers.

You want to seduce me, love? You want me? Then I am yours. Declan's hands deliberately fisted in the softness of her dress's skirt. He lifted it up higher, inch by slow inch. His gaze dropped to her thighs. Gorgeous. Sexy. Another inch. Another. Until he could see the black silk panties she wore.

"They match the dress," she said, voice breathless and husky and utterly tempting. "So does my bra."

"I'll be seeing that matching bra soon enough." He'd been seeing every single inch of her soon enough. But first...

His fingers moved between her legs. He stroked her through the silk of the panties, rubbing right over her core.

She jerked, as if he'd startled her, but a quick rush of air escaped her lips. "That feels nice."

Nice? Fucking nice? Oh, things were about to feel a whole lot better than *nice*. Maybe that was what it had been like with that prick of an ex she had, but not with Declan. "I don't do nice."

Her long lashes fluttered.

"Remember that," he told her, and his fingers curled around the panties right before he yanked the underwear down her legs.

Her shoes hit the floor. Two soft clatters. He'd stepped back just enough so that he could rip the panties away completely. He tossed them down near her shoes. Then he put his hands on the inside of her thighs. Slowly tracked upward until he reached the spot he craved. This time when he touched her, there was nothing between them. Nothing but her hot, tight sex waiting for him.

One finger dipped inside. She gripped him greedily, and a husky moan slid from her.

His thumb rubbed over her clit. Stroking softly and then...

I'm not the soft type. He'd told her he wasn't *nice*.

He shoved her back, spread her out right on top of his desk, and he bent to replace his hand with his mouth.

"Declan!"

She was crying out his name, but not in pleasure. More like shock. They'd get to the pleasure part soon enough. His tongue stroked her. Slid against her clit over and over and over even as he worked two fingers into the tightest, hottest heaven he'd ever experienced. Her hips heaved up against him. Her hands grabbed for his shoulders. Missed. Her fingers stroked through his hair.

Was she trying to pull him closer? Or stop him?

He feasted more, insane for her taste. Sweet and decadent, that was his Marley. A taste that addicted him. He could not get enough of her. Her breathy moans filled his ears. His tongue replaced his fingers and thrust *into* her.

Her hips heaved.

He lapped her up. Went back to her clit. Worked her relentlessly because he was not stopping until he could taste her pleasure on his tongue.

"Declan?" Surprise. Then, *"Declan!"*

Her body jolted. She cried out as her orgasm lashed through her, and he greedily drank up her release. He didn't stop licking. Stroking. Kissing. He kept up the frantic pace as her orgasm trembled and rocked through her whole body. She went bow tense, then seemed to collapse against the surface of the desk.

Licking his lips, he slowly rose to tower over her. Her dress was bunched at her waist, leaving the lower portion of her body naked. Her lashes lifted, and her breath heaved out as she said, "That...that was..."

"A taste." His taste. Of her. He'd be getting lots more tastes. Because he'd just found his favorite treat in the whole world. Marley. But for now...

I want to fuck her more than I want to breathe.

She was sitting up. He grabbed the dress. Yanked it over her head and tossed it to join the shoes. And, sure enough, she was wearing the promised matching black bra. A bra that cupped her breasts and offered them to him like a freaking gift.

His fingers skimmed over the lush mounds. He unhooked the bra. Ditched it. And then she reached for him—

"No." He pushed her back down onto the desk. "Not done with my turn yet." She was spread out on the desk.

The sexiest vision in the world. How the fuck was he ever supposed to work at this desk and not remember her? Remember this moment?

Her tight nipples tempted him, and he had to put his mouth on them. Had to suck and lick and her hands grabbed for his shoulders again. He felt the bite of her nails, and, in return, his teeth grazed her.

She shuddered beneath him.

His hands slid back down between her legs even as he began to lick and suck and kiss her other breast. Her body quivered and jerked, and his dick was so damn hard that he thought he might explode at any minute.

In her. Get in her.

But he'd wanted to make sure she was ready. There could be no regrets. Marley wasn't getting a *nice* bout of sex from him. He intended to give her the fucking of her life.

She was wet and sensitive from her orgasm. So hot. And tight. She was going to feel incredible around his dick.

And she was going to be his.

"Declan! I want you *in* me!"

Like there was any other place he wanted to be.

But first...

His lips skimmed over her scars. Brief kisses. *I will make him pay. No one marks you and walks away.*

She stiffened when he kissed her scars. Then her hands flew down. She caught his face. Pulled him up to her. Marley kissed him with a wild abandon as their lips met in a frantic collision. He hauled her to the edge of the desk. She arched against him and rode his dick through his pants.

Not good enough.

He pulled away.

"Declan!"

He unbuttoned and unzipped his pants. Hauled out the

dick that ached for her. He had a condom on seconds later and the head of his dick pressed into her.

Her hands fell to grasp his upper arms. "You're...uh, bigger than I'm used to..."

Compliments, compliments. "I'm gonna fuck you harder than what you're used to, as well." A savage promise.

She'd been staring down at their bodies. Watching as his dick pushed slightly inside her. But her head lifted at his rough words. A faint smile teased her lips. "I'd like that."

He was a goner. His control shredded in the face of her soft smile and those three words. He grabbed her hips, hauled her against him, and sank balls deep into her. In that instant, when she surrounded him with her tight, hot, insane core, reality fell away. Nothing mattered but her.

Nothing.

He had her on the edge of the desk. In and out, he thrust. Fast pistons of his hips against her. One hand slid between them to mercilessly stroke her clit as he plunged into her. Again and again and again.

A quick scream erupted from her. One that she instantly tried to muffle with her hand. Why muffle it? He liked it when she screamed for him. Liked it even more when he felt the ripples of her release squeezing his cock.

He pounded into her. Couldn't get inside her far enough. Wanted more. Wanted everything. He scooped her into his arms. Took a few steps with her as he remained buried deep in her heat. Her legs wrapped around him. Her arms. He pressed her against the wall. Lifted her up. Drove into her. Took. Claimed.

Fucked her against the wall and had her crying out in pleasure for him yet again even as his own orgasm barreled through him. It hit in a blinding blast, and pleasure erupted in every cell of his body. He sank into her, kept thrusting, kept fucking her...

When the fury ended, when the release still hummed through his body, and he could actually see past the driving, consuming need, he stared down at her.

She gave him that smile again. Her sweet, innocent smile. Then she said, "You did fuck me harder."

Yes, he had...shit, had it been too hard? Had he hurt her? Had he—

"And I liked it." Her arms were around his neck. "Can't wait for you to do it again."

Chapter Twelve

Where are my panties?

Marley straightened her dress for what had to be the tenth time as she stood—okay, *hid*—in the lush, private bathroom attached to Declan's office. She'd rushed in there after what had truly been a phenomenal fucking.

I think I came three times. An absolute record for her. Usually, she was lucky if she managed to come once. So much for nice sex. She was done with that, thanks very much. She much preferred Declan's style.

She preferred Declan.

A rap sounded at the door, making her jump. Marley whirled around and flipped the lock before she opened the door. Declan was waiting for her. Fully dressed because—right, he'd never taken off his clothes as he made love to her on the desk.

An eyebrow quirked as he lifted a bit of black silk and let it dangle from one finger. "Missing this?"

She snatched her panties and fisted them.

A rumble of laughter broke from him. "Hate to break it

to you, love, but those are unwearable. Some bastard ripped them in his haste to get them off you."

She stared, with her mouth open.

"I'll buy you more," he promised, voice going gruff. "I'll buy you any damn thing you want."

Marley shook her head. "Your laugh."

A line appeared between his eyebrows.

"You have a really nice laugh, Declan." Heat stained her cheeks when he stared at her as if she'd just grown a second head. She hadn't. "You should laugh more." She peered down at her hand. Unfisted her fingers. Yep. Ripped. Sighing, she tossed the panties into the trash. "Is this routine?" Marley had to ask. Really had to say the words. The gnawing in the pit of her gut made her do it. The absolute fear that while the whole universe might have just realigned for her, the encounter had just been a typical night for him. "Do you normally have sex with women in your office and have them toss their panties in your trash when it's over?"

His hand curled under her chin. He lifted her head and turned it at the same time, so that she was staring straight at him. "There has been nothing routine about you from the moment we met."

The gnawing tried to change into a glow. But... "You had condoms in your desk." That meant he'd had sex with other women in the same office. Her shoulders straightened. "Your life. Your business. I don't know why I'm getting all jealous and weird and—" She stopped. Mostly because he'd been shaking his head.

No.

"Didn't have them in my desk, sweetheart. I pulled the condom from my wallet. It's the only one I had in there."

His thumb brushed along her lower lip. "If I had more, I'd be in you right now."

Oh. *Oh.*

Another slow, sensual brush over her lip with his thumb.

Her lips parted. Her tongue just decided—totally on its own, without her permission—to lick at his thumb.

His eyes heated with intent. "I haven't fucked anyone else in this office. I don't normally bring any...acquaintances here."

Her breath whispered over his thumb. "You didn't bring me here. I invited myself."

"You mean you barged that sexy ass in, plowing right past my assistant?"

Yes, that was what she'd meant.

His hand fell away from her. "Let me just be very clear."

That would be wonderful. The clearer, the better.

"Wherever I am, you are welcome to be. Consider that an open invitation. You aren't an acquaintance. You aren't a quick fuck."

"What am I?" Oh, no. Why had she even asked the question? Marley shook her head and brushed by him. With every step, she was acutely conscious of the fact that she wore no underwear. A little quiver shot through her.

His steps followed behind her. "You're my—"

"PI?" she asked as she turned back toward him.

"My Marley."

His voice had gone extra deep and rumbly. And it poured over her in all the wrong and right ways.

"And, for the record, I don't typically laugh much." His hand sawed over his face. His fingers brushed against his scar. Lingered for just a moment. "Hasn't been a whole lot in my life to laugh about."

No, she didn't imagine there had been. "Maybe we can change that."

He advanced toward her. His slow, stalking steps eliminated the distance she'd created. "Marley." He spoke her name like a caress. "I will never be the guy who is the life of the party. I won't be telling jokes. I won't be laughing and fitting in with all the BS that is tossed around in life. I *don't* fit in. I'm not like everyone else. I don't feel like everyone else." His lips curled down. "You—above all others—know that monsters can pretend to blend in. I don't give a fuck about blending. I am what I am."

"I like what you are."

A muscle flexed along his jaw. "You can't."

This time, she was the one to touch him. Her hand rose. Pressed to his cheek. "I do."

She didn't know how to describe the expression in his eyes. His gaze glittered. Lit with so much unnamed emotion that the gold in his hazel eyes blazed at her. "I like you," she said softly.

"Fuck."

Her lips curled. "Does that mean you like me, too?"

His hand took hers. His fingers threaded with hers. "*Like* doesn't enter the equation."

Oh. Her smile faded.

He hauled her out of his office. Turned off the lights. Locked it. Paused a moment to tap something into his phone and then used the secure elevator entrance—the one that needed a special code to get up to his level. She'd gotten that code after badgering James forever.

The elevator doors closed, sealing them inside as the elevator began its descent.

Declan pushed her against the elevator wall. He caged her there with his body. "*Like* is far too tame a word. I want to own you. Possess you completely." His mouth took hers. His tongue swept inside. Tasted and teased and consumed. "*And fucking keep you.*"

He'd let go of her hand when he caged her against the wall. So her happy hands curled around his neck. One even moved to sink into the softness of his hair. When his mouth took hers again, she was so ready. He kissed her with a consuming focus that swept away everything else. As if she was truly the only thing that mattered in his world.

Her heart drummed. Her body tightened. And her sex got way eager and wet for him again. *Not wearing panties. He could lift me up against this wall. Shove the dress out of the way. Take me right here the way he took me in his—*

Ding.

His head lifted.

It took a slow moment for that *ding* to register. And then the elevator doors were sliding open. She couldn't see them, but she could hear the faint rumble as they parted.

"Ahem." A throat cleared.

Declan let her go. Turned toward the now open elevator doors.

She saw the deadly duo waiting for her. Cade Grimm and Hunter McQueen stood a few feet from the elevator. *Hunter—such a fitting name.* She'd gotten to know the two former special ops men pretty well over the last few days. Apparently, getting that wee graze from the bullet had made them respect her. Whatever. Now they were being all nice and concerned—almost suffocating, in fact.

They'd been tailing her when she made her way to the high-rise. A total waste of their time because they should have been with Declan. She'd told them that fact. On multiple occasions. They needed to stop tailing her and go protect Declan. But Cade had been adamant—they'd been given orders. They would follow them. And their number one order was to make sure she stayed safe.

When she'd demanded to know who was keeping Declan safe, he'd assured her that Declan had plenty of protection when he was at his office. After she'd gotten a look at the security staff there, she'd agreed.

"Guess we're calling it a night, huh?" Cade asked, a faint smile tilting at the corners of his mouth.

Declan took her hand again. "You could've given me a warning that she was coming."

Hunter grimaced. "I told him to."

Cade rocked back on the heels of his feet. "Thought you might appreciate the surprise."

Declan grunted. He tugged her out of the elevator.

Can they tell we had sex? Jeez. They can. She caught the knowing glint in Cade's eyes. If he said anything...

"Don't," Declan snapped.

Cade nodded. "Not even thinking it." He turned to the right. "This way, sir. The limo is waiting."

"Smartass, you know you aren't supposed to do that bullshit and call me 'sir.'"

Cade just laughed. He took up a position leading them out, and Hunter fell in at the rear of their little group. They swept past the security guards at the front desk, and then Cade opened the glass doors that would take them out into the night.

Car horns blared and voices drifted in the air. Laughter. Distant music. People rushed by on the sidewalks, most not so much as giving them a double-glance. But there were two men in black suits who waited near the limo. More security, she was sure. They made certain to clear a path for Declan and her. But Declan ducked back, indicating she should go in the open door of the limo first. She bent to enter—

"Declan!" An angry shout.

She whirled around.

A tall man in a battered, leather coat rushed toward the limo.

Cade sprang forward. "Buddy, you need to back up, now!" His hand went to his own coat. No, to his waist. Was he reaching for a weapon? He had to be.

"Get in the car!" Declan barked at her. "Now!"

She grabbed his shirt, ready to pull him in with her even as Hunter closed in on the shouting man and—

"I'm his fucking brother!" A bellow from the stranger as he stepped under a streetlight. The light hit his face, and Marley sucked in a sharp breath at the stunning resemblance. If Declan hadn't currently been attempting to shove her into the limo...

I would have thought this guy was Declan. They could be twins. Except for one very important difference.

No scar snaked down the stranger's cheek.

"Bullshit," Cade said, but he sounded uncertain. Probably because of the freaking near perfect resemblance. "My boss doesn't have a brother!"

"Uh, yes," from Marley because Declan had gone statue still and wasn't talking at all. "He does. Declan told me about him."

Cade sent her a questioning frown.

She was half-in, half-out of the limo, and they were attracting too much attention. "Let's go for a ride, shall we?" She pointed at Declan's brother. "Hop in." But she bit her lower lip as her gaze flickered to Declan. "Unless there's a problem I need to know about with him?" Because if this man was a problem for Declan, she'd let

Hunter and Cade go right back to their tough guy routine with him.

But I heard the longing in Declan's voice when he talked about his brother. I know how much he missed him. Now the long-lost brother was showing up, practically on Declan's doorstep. His *business* doorstep, anyway.

Can we trust him? She trusted her brothers, one hundred percent. But what did she know about Declan's brother?

"No problem." Declan's flat voice. "Get in the car, Royal."

The man he'd just identified as Royal bobbed his head in a nod but shot an angry glance toward Cade. "Want to get the hell out of my way or should I move you myself?"

"I'd like to see you try." A low taunt from Cade. But he backed away. Well, backed away just so he could sidle close to Declan and demand, "Boss, are you sure it's safe to be in the limo with him? You'll have Marley in there, and I know she's priority one."

Her brows shot up. She was priority one? "Uh, no. Declan being safe is priority one." They should all make a note of that important fact.

"I can ride along," Cade assured him.

But Declan shook his head. "Royal is no threat to me." He seemed certain of that.

"I wouldn't count on it," Cade muttered. Clearly, Cade was not as certain of that fact. And Hunter just silently watched. He did that a lot, took in things. Watched. Weighed. There was always so much seeming to go on behind the intense darkness of his eyes.

Physically, Cade and Hunter were opposites. Both men were tall and strong. Muscled. But Cade had a beach boy, perfect looks thing going on. Wide smile. Commercial model material. Looked friendly as heck, but Marley knew that friendly demeanor was mostly BS. The man was icy on the inside.

As for Hunter...while Cade might be the chattier of the duo, Hunter tended to exude an aura of menace. Golden, tawny skin, dark eyes and hair, and features that never seemed to soften, the Ranger didn't ever smile. And sometimes, she thought he might just look haunted. *That man has painful secrets.*

But both Cade and Hunter were very serious about their jobs. And, at the moment, they were staring with serious suspicion at the man who wore Declan's face. *Brothers.*

"Cade and Hunter, follow us to the house." Declan's hands pushed gently on Marley. He was still trying to get her in the limo.

Fine, if getting her in also got him inside...

Marley ducked into the limo.

Declan immediately joined her. He sat down right beside her, his leg and hip against her. The heat of his body reached out to wrap around her. "You okay?" she whispered.

He didn't get a chance to answer. Royal climbed into the limo. The door slammed shut behind him. Royal took up a seat opposite Declan. Faint light shone near the floor of the limo and around the well-stocked bar in the back. The light let her see Royal's tense expression as he studied Declan.

Immediately, she stiffened. *He looks pissed. No wonder Cade didn't want him getting in the car.* "You'd better not even think of hurting him," she snapped.

Declan put his hand on her thigh.

Royal's eyes widened and those wide eyes turned to

fully assess her. Then he nodded. "Right. The PI. The one who saved him from the torture dungeon." Then his stare dipped to her thigh. Or, rather, to Declan's hand as it touched her thigh. "And I think I get why you're still around my brother." He cleared his throat. "So...someone want to tell me what the fuck is happening?" His jaw—so very like Declan's—hardened. "And just who the hell is it that is trying to kill you?"

"I—" Marley began, her voice strained because she did not like the man's tone with Declan. Not one bit.

Declan squeezed her thigh. "This doesn't concern you, Royal. You need to go back to Savannah and your family."

Uh, oh, there had been just the faintest hit of emphasis on *your family*. As if...as if...*as if they weren't real family, even though this guy is Declan's brother*.

The limo pulled away from the curb.

Royal crossed his arms over his chest. "I saw your story on the news. Big, bad Declan Flynn. Imagine my surprise when I learned that my long-lost brother had nearly been killed not once, but twice...and no one bothered to inform me of the incidents."

Declan shrugged. "They're being handled. The perpetrator will be found."

"Three people are dead."

Declan shrugged. Again. "Two of those men helped abduct me. As for the third? He most likely helped drug me. They were loose ends that I believe someone was eliminating."

No change of expression from Royal. "Were you the one cutting those loose ends?"

Her mouth dropped open. Had he seriously just accused Declan of murder? "How dare you!" A fiery eruption. "You don't climb into *his* car and start accusing him of killing people!"

Declan's head turned toward her.

"I don't?" Royal asked. "Even when I think he might be guilty as sin?"

Guilty as sin.

"He's innocent," she snapped back. "Declan did not kill those three men. I know—I've been with him the whole time. He's the victim."

Soft laughter from Royal. "Victim, huh? That's a fun word."

"No, it is not particularly fun." She didn't know that she liked this long-lost brother. Not at all. The heat of Declan's touch warmed her thigh. "Where's your concern? Where is your 'I'm-so-glad-my-brother-is-alive' relief?"

Royal considered her. "She's interesting."

Her eyes immediately narrowed. *Interesting* sounded like an insult to her.

"For the record, I am glad you're alive, Declan," Royal said.

She grunted. About time he said those words. Had it killed him to say them? No.

"I'm also pretty damn happy to be alive myself," Royal continued. "Considering that someone tried to run me down just last week. Seems that you and I have both attracted a sudden enemy."

She felt the utter stillness of Declan's body. Stillness and rage. The rage practically vibrated in the air around her.

"What. The. Fuck?" Low. No emotion at all. But Declan's voice still sent a shiver cascading over her. She'd come to realize that when his voice went low, he was in an extra lethal mood. Not a good sign.

Royal settled back against the lush seat in the limo. "Didn't quite catch what I said? Then let me repeat... someone tried to run me down last week. The asshole came plowing right for me. I made it out of the way with scratches and bruises that piss me the hell off as I kissed the sidewalk. Figured it was some drunk dick at the time. Then I learned that two attacks have been made on my brother's life. Got me to being all kinds of suspicious." He quirked a brow. "So, let's circle back to the fact that we both may have attracted the same enemy." He paused. And suddenly, his face looked...darker. Harder. *Evil*. "Just who the hell is it that wants to kill us both?"

Chapter Thirteen

Royal let out a long, low whistle. "So, yeah, I knew you were rich." He did a slow spin in the middle of the cavernous foyer. His feet tapped over the gleaming, white marble floor. His head tipped back as he gazed up at the antique chandelier that hung a good twenty feet above his head. "But then there's rich and there's...whatever the hell this is."

Declan slanted him a glance as he kept a hand on the base of Marley's spine and led her into the den. He didn't want to stop touching her. Almost felt like she was the one link that allowed him to hold onto his sanity and keep the rage and enveloping darkness away.

She offered me her body, and I swear, I think I touched a bit of her soul. Marley was good. Bright. She saw the best in people. An admirable, noble trait. But she was delusional when it came to him. The woman had called him a hero.

Hero, my ass. He was a monster. No doubt about it. But sometimes, the monster got to keep the fair maiden. Hadn't that shit happened in *Beauty and the Beast?* Once upon a time—a lifetime ago to be precise—his mom had read him fairytales before bedtime. *Beauty and the Beast* had been a particular favorite of hers.

He'd always roared and pretended to be the beast. While his brother...hell, his two-year-old brother had bounced and clapped and loved every minute of the tale.

Now his brother was all grown. No longer was he called Garrison Flynn. Instead, he was Royal Boudreaux. A new name. A new life. A new family.

And a new pain in the ass.

Because *Royal* was whistling and acting like he'd stumbled into some alternate universe because the damn house was big. Declan led Marley to the couch. Waited until she was curled up on the cushions, then he turned back to his brother. "Don't be a dick."

Garrison—*dammit, Royal*—had followed them into the den.

At Declan's growled words, Royal quirked a brow. "Some things are just a natural talent I possess. I don't have to try. I just am."

He just was a dick. Uh, huh. "You're rich as sin in your own right. You own at least half a dozen clubs. You have piles of cash stashed in plenty of offshore accounts. You don't need to pretend with me. The house doesn't impress you. I doubt that anything does."

"You'd be surprised." Royal shoved his hands into the front pockets of his jeans. His gaze darted around. Skimmed right over the thick, dark curtains that covered the doors leading to the attached terrace. "But like I said, there's wealthy, then there is whatever the fuck this is."

Still being a dick. Maybe it was a family trait. Declan knew he could be a dick without trying, too. "You know half the estate is yours."

"I know that our father barely had anything by the time

he was shoved into the ground. *You* rebuilt from the ashes he left behind. You created your own empire with those scary tech skills of yours." Royal's eyes—a shade so similar to Declan's—had returned to lock on Declan. Their father had possessed those same eyes. "The way I see it," Royal added, his tone flat, "the money is all yours."

Half of the money was going to his brother, whether he wanted it or not. "My lawyers are working on reallocating things. You're getting half. You do whatever the fuck you want with the money. Give it to charity. Spend it on a stripper—"

"My Violet would be very pissed if I did that. She's the jealous type. Ferociously so. Just wants to keep me all to herself." A shrug from Royal. "But I understand. After all, I only have eyes for her. Don't really care about seeing anyone else dance around a pole. But if Violet feels like doing it for me..." A lazy roll of one shoulder. "I'm all in. She is truly an incredible dancer, FYI."

"Excuse me." Marley rose from the couch. Dammit, hadn't he just put her down there? When he reached for her again, Marley glowered. "Do not make me remind you that I don't break."

But she could bruise. She could also bleed. And she'd bled a freaking lot in his limo after she'd been *shot.*

Royal coughed. "Hate to say it, but you literally *did* just remind him."

Marley swung toward him. "You."

"Me...what?"

"*You.* You stop talking about strippers and poles and focus on the fact that someone is after you and Declan! Someone wants you dead! This is not a joking matter." Her hands rose angrily into the air before falling back to her sides. And fisting.

Royal's gaze slowly left her and returned to Declan. "He's the one who brought up strippers."

How had such a sweet two-year-old turned into such a pain in the ass? "Burn the money if you want. I don't care," Declan retorted. "But you're getting it. Deal with the fact." *Stop being a shit about it.*

"You want me to have it because it's blood money?" Ever so emotionless. Royal began to poke around the den as he strolled around the room. He paused to peek out the curtains and peer at the terrace. "I did some more digging on the family tree. Turns out we're fucking diabolical. Twisted as hell. And with more than a slight murderous streak." He let the curtains fall back into place. Royal turned toward Declan. Took a step forward.

Declan didn't speak.

Marley did. "Declan *isn't* diabolical." She moved in front of him, putting herself between him and Royal.

Oh, sweetheart, I am definitely diabolical.

"He's not twisted!" she denied. "Why would you say something like that?"

If she only knew the things he wanted to do with her. Absolutely twisted. Having her in his office? Fucking her on the desk *and* against the wall? That had just been a prologue. He had so much more in store for her. If he had his way, he'd fuck her for hours. Days. Until neither of them could move.

He wanted to be so imprinted on her that she could never, ever be free of him again.

He wanted her to beg. To moan. To scream. To never be satisfied again unless he was the one driving between her legs.

Really, was that too much to ask? Declan thought not.

But...

"And he does *not* have a murderous streak!" Marley slammed her fisted hands on her hips as she faced off with Royal. "Who the hell goes around saying things like that? What is wrong with you?"

Royal looked at her. He cocked one eyebrow. "Ah, Declan. I see that you went out and found yourself someone just as protective as my Violet. The protective streak is awfully hot in a woman, isn't it?"

"Who is Violet?' she demanded. Then caught herself. Her shoulders stiffened. "Wait a minute. Hold up. Are you talking about Violet Murphy, the ballet dancer who was abducted in Savannah a while back?" She glanced over her shoulder at Declan, and he could see the confusion in her eyes. He could also see what appeared to be a few dots connecting in her mind. "I followed the story. The Ice Breakers were involved. I remember—dammit, of course, *Royal.* You were involved. You—" She swung her attention back to Royal.

"I was the man who originally pulled her out of the trunk of the car before the sadistic freak who'd taken her had the chance to hurt my Violet." There was nothing flat or unemotional about his voice now. Rage underscored each word. "I'm not really one for heroics, so consider it a very unusual deed for me. But Violet was special. She will always be special."

"You work with the Ice Breakers, don't you?" Marley asked.

"I do now," Royal conceded. "They think I bring a rather...unique...skill set to the crew. I can't say that they are wrong."

I should have told her about my link to the Ice Breakers before. I didn't. What the hell is she thinking now?

"What skill set would that be?" Marley asked in an ever-so-careful voice.

Royal laughed. "Don't think you want to know." A careful clearing of his throat. "Don't think I trust you enough for you to know." A clarification. "Though a bit of digging has told me that you're a new Ice Breaker recruit, too. How funny is that? Isn't life a bitch?"

She drew in a shuddering breath.

"The Ice Breakers are growing by leaps and bounds," Royal continued. "And we're all working on different cases. Cases that others in our bloodthirsty group know nothing about."

Another shuddering breath.

That one eyebrow quirked again. "If you don't mind, I'd like to speak privately with my brother. Not that I trust *him*, either. But I'd really like to get back to the little matter of someone trying to kill us both. And, fuck me, is that a Van Gogh?" His eyes had locked on the wall to the right. A framed painting waited, with a little light underneath it to show the art off to the best degree.

While Royal investigated—and got side-tracked by the painting—Marley spun to confront Declan. "You know the Ice Breakers."

Guilty as charged. "It's a small world."

"No, it's not. It's a giant world with well over eight billion people in it." A long breath. "Is your connection to the Ice Breakers just through your brother? Do you know about them only because of Royal?"

Declan's lips pressed together.

"No." Royal's lazy reply. "I'm helping him with a case."

Her eyes widened. Her wide eyes did not leave Declan. "You didn't think that was important to mention? The fact that you're working with the Ice Breakers on a case? *While* someone is attempting to kill you?"

He didn't speak.

"The Ice Breakers are working over thirty cases right now," Royal announced. "You can't know every case other operatives are investigating—and is it okay if I call you Marley? That's a rather interesting name by the way."

"My parents loved *A Christmas Carol*." She spoke that part as if distracted. "Named me after Jacob Marley. My brothers are Ebenezer—Eb—and Jacob—Jake. Jake was named after Jacob Marley, too. Jacob Marley was always my mom's favorite character." Marley fired a suspicious glance Royal's way. "Why do I get the feeling you already know all that about me? You been digging into my life, Royal?"

I've been digging into your life. Declan didn't speak that truth.

Royal sent her an innocent smile. "Like I was saying, you can't know every case that the Ice Breakers are working. And this one? It has a particular classified designation. In other words, Declan didn't want anyone but the select few working it to know the truth."

Declan saw her delicate jaw harden as her swirling gaze returned to him and seemed to darken even more. "Declan." His name came out as a sigh. An angry one. "You're being hunted by someone, and you've got the Ice Breakers stirring up a cold case. They're looking into—what? A disappearance? *Murder?*"

"Both," came the response from Royal. He practically had his nose to the painting now. "I don't buy that you'd have a fake *anything* on display in this creepy house of yours—"

"Haunted castle or Wayne Manor," Marley said with a fast wave of her hand. "But it is not creepy."

Soft laughter rumbled from Royal. How could the guy laugh so easily? Declan knew just how bleak and dark Royal's past was. The man should be just as twisted as he was. And yet...

And yet Royal fell in love with Violet. He has a whole other life down in Savannah. A different brother. A cop friend who'd take a bullet for him. Royal has played in the darkness more times than anyone else I know, yet he still laughs and smiles and loves and...

I'm so fucking jealous of him.

"Hey." Marley reached out and curled her hands around his arms. Declan hadn't even realized she'd closed the small distance between them. "I don't know where you just went, but I don't like the sadness I saw on your face. You stay here with me, got it? Even if I'm pissed at you, you stay here with me."

He blinked. No, no, there could not have been sadness on his face. He wasn't sad. That was ridiculous. He was—

"He's sad because the Ice Breakers are looking into our mother's disappearance-slash-murder."

Damn but Royal had a big mouth on him. Big and loud and his tendency to overshare was going to get him in serious trouble.

"Our mother is his tie to the Ice Breakers. When I was two years old..." Royal had finally turned away from the painting. "I vanished. Courtesy, we believe, of our dear, dead mom."

Her lips parted. She didn't let Declan go. If anything, her hold tightened on him.

"Not sure how much he's told you about me," Royal continued.

"Not enough," she responded. Still, she did not let Declan go.

He realized his jaw had locked. He should explain. But he didn't typically explain. Didn't talk about his past with anyone.

She's not anyone. And she was staring at him with a gaze gone soft with compassion and worry. She didn't need to feel compassion for him. Not worry, either. He wasn't worth it. "My mother was afraid. She ran away. Took Garrison—uh, Royal—with her. I believe she was going to come back for me, but she didn't have the chance." Did he believe that? Really? Or did he just say that shit when in all honesty...

Maybe she left me behind because she feared I was already too much like our father.

He swallowed.

"Why was she afraid?" Marley asked.

Easy. "Because our father was a sadistic and controlling sonofabitch. I told you before that he was obsessed with her. His version of love. But if she did anything he didn't like, if she violated any of his strict rules, he'd punish her. He punished us all." *Until I was the one to finally punish him.*

"Declan." A sigh. Then she wasn't just gripping his arms. She was hugging him. So hard and tight. As if she wouldn't ever let go.

A lie, of course. Everyone eventually let go.

"Ahem." From Royal. He'd sauntered closer. "I am certainly no expert on these matters, but I think you're supposed to raise your arms and hug her back. Sure, hugs probably aren't exactly typical in a client-PI relationship, but I'm getting that things aren't typical with you two."

His hands began to lift. Not that Declan had needed the guy to tell him to hug Marley. He knew how to hug someone, dammit.

Carefully, his arms curled around her. Circled her. He

pulled her even closer, though she'd already been close before. Her body crushed against his. Warm and soft, and jasmine and amber filled his nose.

He pulled in a deep breath. Let it out.

"I'm so sorry about your mom." Her soft words. "And, of course, Declan, *of course,* she was coming back for you. Never, ever think anything different."

His chest ached. His head bent, and he brushed his face against the softness of her hair.

"If you two need like...a minute, I can go explore the house. See what other pieces of priceless art you just have hanging around like they're family photos. Which, by the way, I notice there are none of."

He'd destroyed all the photos of his father long ago. As for his mother's photos? His father had ripped them all down and burned them right after Declan's mother had vanished.

Declan slowly forced his hands and arms to release Marley. He straightened his spine. "Take any art you want. Already told you, half the fortune is yours."

"Yeah, I don't want it. I prefer to make my own way in the world. Like I already told *you,* I also know our father didn't leave much behind. All of this..." A wave of his hands to indicate the house. "It's because of you. Otherwise, the creditors would have taken it all when you put our father in the ground."

"How is Royal alive?" Marley questioned haltingly. "But your mom isn't? What happened?"

"Thought they were both dead." Had he told her that part before? Everything seemed to blur, and his chest wouldn't stop aching. The past wasn't supposed to hurt, but his felt as if it had just stabbed him in the heart all over again. "I was told they'd died in a fiery car crash. Their vehicle fell into a ravine. Exploded. The bodies—there wasn't really much left. That's the story I was given so long ago. We buried two caskets that always remained closed."

Her breath shuddered out.

"I didn't give up." He wanted to hug her again. Instead, Declan clenched his hands into fists. "Hired plenty of PIs over the years." He'd told her that truth before.

"You mean I'm just the latest in a long line of PIs for you?" A faint, wan smile tilted the corners of her mouth.

Her question gave him pause. "You are nothing like the others."

A wince as her smile faded in an instant. "I worried you'd say that. It's because I'm so new to the gig, isn't it?" She turned away. "Okay, Royal, how did you—"

Declan's hand flew out and caught her wrist. He spun her back toward him, and, in the next instant his hand rose and curled under her chin. Gently, he lifted her head toward him. "The others can't come close to you. You are special, Marley Jones."

A little smile tilted the corners of her lips. "I think you're pretty special too, Declan Flynn."

She did?

"Okay." A long and loud exhale from Royal. "Before I get nauseous or before you two start ripping off each other's clothes, let's get back to business, shall we? Someone is trying to kill Declan. And me. That attempted murder bit pisses me off. When I get pissed off, bad things happen. It's just the way of my world."

It was the way of Declan's world, too.

"To help get back to our focus, how about I sum some things up? That good for everyone in the room?"

Marley moved to Declan's side. They both watched Royal.

"As a kid—hell, I was barely walking around at two, just a damn toddler—I wound up in New Orleans. On Royal Street." A mocking smile came and went on his lips. "Thus, the name."

Marley's hand reached out. Her fingers pressed against Declan's fist. Surprised, his hand opened. Then immediately, his fingers locked with hers.

"I thought I'd been abandoned. That no one wanted me. I grew up on the streets of New Orleans. Made my own family with a very protective and annoying brother, Beau LeBlanc. Lived a life that wasn't typical. Did shit that would give you nightmares. Raised lots of hell. The usual."

Hardly. Declan knew that Royal's particular talent—the unique skill set that had landed him a job with the Ice Breakers? It centered around the fact that Royal hunted killers. Hunted them and stopped them, by any means necessary. A very unusual and dangerous side gig. But then again, Declan had discovered that his brother was unusual and dangerous. *Far too similar to me.*

Royal cleared his throat. "Here I am, living my unconventional life, and then, one day, this billionaire with my face appears in Savannah. Pretty much right in the midst of carnage because some deadly shit is happening. He sees me standing over a dead man, and you know what he says?"

Marley shook her head.

Royal's gaze was on Declan. "He asks if I need help burying the body."

Declan waited for Marley to snatch her hand from his. She had to be horrified by his brother's revelations. After all, Royal wasn't bullshitting. He was telling the cold, hard truth. *I did offer to help him bury the body. And I would have done it in an instant.*

Not like it would be the first time that Declan made a body vanish. Not the first, and certainly not the last.

"The dead man was a killer," Marley said. "I told you, I am familiar with this story. Just didn't connect the Ice Breakers—and you—to Declan. I should have."

"I didn't know the dead man was a killer at the time." Why had he just pointed out that fact? Declan didn't know.

"You were being a good brother," she assured him.

Uh, no. He didn't think aiding and abetting counted as a brotherly duty. "I don't think *good* entered the equation," he returned.

"I appreciated the offer," came Royal's wry voice. "And in return, I wanted to help out the man wearing my face. So when I learned he was looking into our mother's murder—well, I said I'd be happy to assist. That I could connect some friends to probe into the events of that long ago time. After all, I want the truth, too. I want to know how I got ripped from my brother's life and how my mom wound up in the ground when, apparently, all she wanted was to protect her sons." Grief and pain flashed in his eyes only to be quickly masked.

"The Ice Breakers." Marley nodded. "They are the friends. You've been using Ice Breaker resources to help."

"Yes." Royal crossed his arms over his chest. "But like I said, this is a very classified case. But the small team I've assembled has been digging. Stirring up the past. Trying to figure out just what happened—or rather, who the hell forced our mother's car off the road and sent her to a fiery death. Declan thinks it was our sadistic freak of a dad. That the man couldn't handle the fact that his wife was leaving him. And so far, all signs do point to that version of events."

"So whatever the Ice Breakers are doing," Declan had to point out, "it's not related to my abduction. Because my mother's killer seems to be dead." *I killed him.* "And the dead can't reach out from the grave and kill again."

"They'd better not," she muttered. Her shoulders squared. "Okay. Fine. We'll let that investigation remain separate, for now. But, Royal, I want to know everything about the recent attack on you. Every detail you can remember. Maybe you and Declan just have a family trait of pissing off dangerous people and having them go ballistic. Could be two separate enemies gunning for you."

"I do have plenty of people who hate me," Royal confessed, seemingly modest. "But this particular attack...so close in time to what is happening with Declan...hell, I can't help but be suspicious."

Declan was plenty suspicious himself.

"Me, too," Marley revealed. "I'm highly suspicious. And in order to get to the truth, you two..." Her gaze swung between them. "Need to both be completely honest with me. No secrets. No lies." Her shoulders rolled back. Squared. "Who out there hates you so much that torture and death is the path of vengeance that he's taking?"

* * *

SOMETIMES, you could kill two birds with one stone. Wasn't that the old saying? As he waited in the darkness and peered at the distant lights of the mansion that belonged to Declan Flynn, rage twisted and seethed inside of him.

Garrison Flynn had come home. Not that the man called himself Garrison these days. *Royal Boudreaux.* That was his new name. But names didn't matter. It was the bodies—the souls that mattered. And Royal would have a soul as twisted and dark as Declan's.

Just like their father's soul.

He'd seen Royal outside of Declan's high-rise. Watched the man slip into Declan's limo. Watched him be welcomed into that limo when he did not belong in Declan's world.

He hadn't followed them right away. What would be the point? He'd known exactly where they were heading. And there had been other business to attend to. Another loose end to cut. With Declan gone from the high-rise, with security lowered for the night, it had been so easy to get inside and leave a few surprises behind.

He did enjoy surprises. Would Declan enjoy the surprises as much? Probably not. But wasn't that the point?

There are lots of forms of torture in this world. Some were the physical tortures. The ones he'd planned for Declan in that basement. Breaking bones. Ripping skin. Pain that would make you shriek.

But other forms of torture were emotional. Psychological. *That's when you are playing with your prey.* Sometimes, those methods of torture were the worst.

So he'd played a bit. He wanted Declan to know there was no one in his life that truly gave allegiance to him. *You are surrounded by enemies, Declan.* And even the pretty Marley Jones wasn't safe.

She intrigued him. Fascinated him. But...disappointed him. Because she was supposed to see evil, yet she ran to Declan at her first chance. She should have left. Turned from the monster. Instead, she seemed drawn to the darkness. *Such a mistake.*

He had planned to be fairly merciful with Royal Boudreaux. A quick end because the man was just in his way. *You should have died when you were a child. Then I wouldn't have to hunt you now.* But Royal had seen the SUV coming as it barreled toward him on the Savannah street. He'd escaped the attack so quickly. Only been left a bit bloody and with bruises. The driver he'd hired for the attack had been apologetic. He'd sworn that he wouldn't fail a second time.

I don't give second chances. He had given the man two bullets. One to the chest. One to the head.

Royal had left Savannah. Probably hadn't even learned that a dead man had been found inside an abandoned SUV. And now Royal was here. In a place he should not be. The man should have realized that it wasn't safe to come home, not ever again.

Maybe I'll kill two birds with one stone.

Or maybe, maybe if he played things just right, the world would think the two birds had killed each other.

Sometimes, blood was just bad. Evil. Tainted. And the only way to destroy that evil? Kill the whole fucking family line.

Chapter Fourteen

"Did you really offer to help him bury a body?"

Royal was gone. The door had just shut behind him as he exited, and Marley hadn't been able to hold back the question another moment. She needed the truth, and it was long past time Declan spilled all of his secrets to her.

Declan's hand pressed to the wood of the giant door. Two heavy, wooden doors made up the entrance way. Both had elaborate carvings on them. Roaring lions.

Declan had offered to let Royal stay the night. Royal had refused. He'd made a quick phone call and had a mystery friend waiting to pick him up. Royal had stayed only long enough to ask some questions about Declan's abduction. Like Marley, Royal had wanted to know one main thing...

Who hates you so much that they abduct you and want to torture you in a dirty, dank basement? Because when it came to hate, that was on a whole other level of twisted. A level that terrified Marley.

But Declan had given no answers. Other than...*I have a lot of enemies.*

"I offered to bury the body. Seemed like a helpful thing to do." His broad back was to her. "You should go up to your room."

Or she *should* stay exactly where she was. Marley chose to stay. "The house seems extra quiet tonight. No staff are here, are they?" They were alone, she knew it.

"The minute Royal got in the limo, I sent a text ordering everyone else to leave."

"Including James?"

"Everyone. No one can know my brother's secrets."

She rocked forward onto the balls of her feet. "I was here while you grilled him. And while he grilled you. I know the secrets that both of you possess." Though she felt as if she'd only skimmed the surface with the two men. *I want more.*

"You're my fiancée. Sooner or later, you'll know everything about me." He shoved away from the door. Turned toward her. "Every single dark part. You'll wish you didn't know, but it will be too late by then." A reckless smile curved his lips as he began to close in on her. "Maybe it's already too late."

Her breath came out in a fast rush. "I'm not your fiancée. I'm your PI." An important distinction.

His smile dimmed. "I fucked you three hours ago."

One hand fanned her face because she suddenly felt hot. "Has it been three hours? Already?" And he'd been keeping track?

He stopped right in front of her. "You're not wearing panties."

Her thighs tightened. Her sex clenched. "Good of you to remember that important piece of information." It had been way awkward talking to the men minus underwear.

But if she'd left the room to correct that situation, she might have missed vital intel.

The wall was right behind her. He put his hands on the wall, on either side of her body, caging her as he leaned in close. "How many times do I have to tell you? *Good* has nothing to do with me."

Her hands rose to press lightly to his cheeks. "And how many times do I have to tell you...*you don't have to lie to me?*"

He blinked.

"You are not your father. I get that he was screwed up." Oh, boy did she get it. Talk about a deranged mind bent on causing pain and wreaking havoc. "I get that he hurt you. I get that he—"

"He probably fucking murdered my mother. You get that, too, don't you? She left him. Got sick of being the wife of a killer and a monster and a freak who only knew obsession, not love. She ran away, and he couldn't let her go. He could never let go of the things that belonged to him. So he chased her down—or he had his men do it—and they ran her off the road. Her car exploded. She died in a fiery blaze, and I was left without my mother. Without my brother. I was left to be raised by him." His expression seemed cut from stone. "What do you think that did to me? What do you think he made me become?"

"Declan..." Her hands remained on him. And, helpless because his pain hurt her more than she would have believed possible, Marley did the only thing that she could think of to stop the sorrow and rage that poured from him. She rose onto her toes. She pulled his head toward her. Her mouth pressed to his. Tenderly, softly. *Lovingly.* Did he get that? Did he get that she didn't see him as some terrible evil? Because he wasn't. The more she was with him, the more she saw him as...

Her Declan.

"You don't want to do this," he growled against her mouth.

"Do what?" Marley breathed right back. "Kiss you?" *Love you?* A bit too late for that part because Marley feared she was falling fast. Being pulled deeper and deeper into Declan's web with every moment that passed and every painful secret that was revealed.

Declan thought he was evil. He was so wrong. She'd stared evil dead in the eyes. She knew exactly what it looked like. She knew how evil's touch felt. She knew the pain evil could bring.

Declan didn't bring pain. He brought pleasure.

"I want to fuck you right now." A savage rumble from him.

Did it look as if she was going to say no? "Um, I'm kissing you." Another tender kiss. "Please take the kisses as a clear yes for what happens next."

But his head lifted. His gaze—oh, that hazel burned. The gold was the strongest color blazing at her. "You kiss me softly, and I just want to fuck you hard."

Marley swallowed.

"Right the hell here. I want to lift you up against the wall and fuck you *here.*"

Emotions swirled around them. Dark needs. Desires. Tension. "What's stopping you? As you already noted, I'm not wearing any pant—"

He lifted her up. Pushed her until her shoulders hit the wall. His tongue thrust into her mouth. No tender kiss. No softness or comfort. Just hard, driving lust. A desire that was unchecked. A need that would consume her.

He pinned her to the wall even as he yanked up her dress. Shoved it toward her stomach. She heard the hiss of a zipper and knew he was going to do it. Fuck her right there. No preliminaries. No foreplay. Just fucking. Maybe it was what they both needed. Oblivion and then—

"No!" Declan's head whipped back.

What? He didn't want to have sex with her? Pain iced her heart. Why did—

"Pleasure first for you, always." Then he was lowering her back down. No, wait, he was dropping to his knees before her. He parted her thighs. Lifted her up, angled her, and he—

His tongue slid over her clit.

"*Declan!*" A choked scream.

He held her easily, with a strength that was both ferocious and chained and sexy all at the same time. Her shoulders hit the wall again. Her head tipped back as she gasped and moaned because his tongue was utterly relentless on her. Again and again, he licked at her clit. Wild strokes of his tongue as if he could not get enough of her. And then his tongue swirled and dipped into her.

Her heart thundered. Her eyes squeezed tightly shut as her whole body tightened in preparation for the orgasm that barreled toward her. He was working her clit again. Strumming her with his tongue. Sucking and kissing with his lips and she was—coming. Coming against his mouth on an explosion of pleasure that detonated through her body.

She could barely pull in a breath. The pleasure hit her in waves that churned and crested. Over and over. An orgasm that just didn't seem to stop.

And he—he was rising. Lifting her even higher. Her eyes opened. Her legs wrapped around his hips. Her dress was hiked up at her stomach, and he was pushing the head of his cock into the slick, eager entrance of her body.

His face had locked into a tight mask of primitive need. A lust that couldn't be controlled. Just the broad head of his cock had dipped into her, and it wasn't enough. Not nearly enough.

"Marley..." Guttural.

She loved it when he said her name that way.

Her hips slammed against him, and she took every inch of him inside. A flash of discomfort filled her—because there was a whole lot of Declan—but oh, that discomfort vanished in an instant and then there was only pleasure. So much consuming pleasure as she rode him. As his hands bit into her waist and he lifted her up and down, up and down. Faster. Harder. His hips pistoned against her, and her hands clamped around his upper arms as she held on for the wildest ride of her life.

Another climax hit her. Blasted without any buildup or notice, and she could only cry out as the pleasure pulsed through her.

"Feel you...squeezing me." Each word was thick with lust. "So fucking good...every inch of you...perfect. *Mine.*"

She could feel him. All of him. Driving into her ruthlessly. Over and over. And—

"Tight. Hot. *You're all around me, sweetheart. That tight pussy is—fuck!*" Declan stiffened.

Her eyes had closed once more. She opened them. His stare had turned even more ferocious.

"There's nothing between us." His jaw clenched. The words were bitten off. "Nothing. I have to—"

He started to pull back.

She squeezed him even harder.

"*Marley...*" Declan withdrew.

"Come in me. I want you, *in me*."

He slammed deep again. Savagery covered his face. He withdrew. Drove into her. Withdrew, drove and—

He pulled out of her.

"No!" Marley cried. She'd wanted to feel him inside her when he came.

And...

He shuddered against her. Snarled her name. She felt something wet on her inner thigh.

"Fucking coming on you," he rasped. "Wanted to be *in* you. Fuck, yes, but I didn't have a rubber. Might have already been too late. Sonofabitch, what am I going to do with you?"

What an odd question. "Keep me, of course." She wrapped her arms around his neck as a languid tiredness crept through her body. "What else would you do?"

He blinked. Stared at her as if he'd just—

"Yes." Soft. "What else would I do?" Declan straightened his clothes. Pulled down her dress.

She frowned at the stickiness on her skin. But then he was sweeping her into his arms and carrying her up the stairs. And she just settled against him. "I've never wanted anyone the way I want you." Her soft confession. He wasn't the only one who would give up secrets. She'd share hers with him, too.

He hesitated. "Marley." Deep. Dark. Rumbly. "I'm carrying you up the stairs right now. How about you don't say things that might cause me to stumble and drop you?"

"You wouldn't drop me." Her eyes closed. "I trust you."

Silence. But he was moving again. Going up the stairs. Holding her tightly, but tenderly. "Yes, I can see that."

He strode forward. They must have reached the landing and were headed to the bedroom. She forced her eyes to open even when she really just wanted to sleep. Apparently, a whole lot of good orgasms in one night could wreck a woman. Who knew?

Me. I know now.

But this was important. She needed to ask him a big question. "I trust you," she said again. "Do you trust me?"

He entered the bedroom. Not the room she'd been using. A bigger, darker room. Heavy furniture. Lots of books on overflowing shelves. A laptop on a desk to the side. His room.

He put her in the bed. Stripped her. Stripped himself. Got a soft, wet cloth and carefully wiped her body. Then crawled in bed beside her. He pulled her against him, and it felt right to be there in his arms. Warm and safe.

And it was only as she drifted to sleep that Marley realized Declan hadn't answered her question. But maybe his silence was the answer.

He didn't trust her.

Was there anyone in the world that he *did* trust?

Chapter Fifteen

"You're making a mistake."

It was after two a.m. Declan had never been one to sleep easily. Marley was in his bed. Curled up. The dream he hadn't even realized that he wanted. And he should be with her. But her words had haunted him.

Do you trust me?

He hadn't told her everything about himself. But he wanted to.

James paced in front of the fireplace in Declan's study. James had texted him about thirty minutes ago, telling him that he had news for Declan.

That they had to meet.

"You're letting her get too close, but the woman is more dangerous than you realize."

A glass of whiskey sat in front of Declan. He hadn't touched the drink. James had come in and poured them both glasses. It was James's favorite bottle. Aged twenty years. It would be a waste not to touch something so valuable.

Yet Declan didn't touch it. Maybe because the last time

he'd had a drink, he'd woken up tied to a chair in a damn basement. Experiences like that one tended to sour a man on alcohol.

"Declan."

Declan looked away from the amber liquid.

"She's wicked smart. IQ off the charts. Don't let the fact that she's bounced around doing bullshit stuff like dressing as a party princess or making fluffy pastries fool you."

Anger swirled in his gut. "It's not bullshit." New rule in his world—no one would ever say a fucking negative word about Marley. "Working at the kids' parties brought her comfort. The pastry making gave her peace and helped her to move forward. She needed that work."

James blinked. "Sonofabitch, no, please tell me this isn't happening." He slammed down his drink. Drops of the liquid scattered across the desktop. "It can't be happening. Not to you. I didn't think you'd find someone who made you act—" But he broke off. Clamped his lips together.

"What?" *Don't leave me hanging, James. Say what you think.*

The silence lasted a little too long, and then, in a rush, as if he had to get the words out quickly, James said, "You're just like your father."

Declan stiffened. "No."

But James nodded. "I could see it in the hospital, that first night. The way you looked at her. The way you refused to leave her behind. Something about Marley Jones clicked for you, didn't it?"

Clicked?

"That's what your father said about your mom. That he saw her, and he knew she was supposed to be his. And when he saw something he wanted, nothing stopped Conor Flynn. Nothing and no one could ever stand in his way."

James swallowed. His Adam's apple bobbed. "Until you did. Until you, son." James lowered into the chair across from Declan. He suddenly looked very, very weary. The lines on his face etched deep grooves into his skin. "I certainly wasn't ever strong enough to stop him."

Declan's shoulders stiffened.

"I ran." Shame darkened James's words. "I knew what he was, and I ran, and I left you with him, and no matter what I do, I can't shake the guilt. It drags behind me like chains scraping against a grave."

"You had no responsibility to me," Declan said. No emotion entered his voice. When had he stopped letting the emotion slip out? Because he felt emotions. Anger. No, rage. Grief. And maybe even—*no*. He shut down the thought as fast as it whispered through his mind.

"I did. I owed you, Declan, and we both know it. I was the closest thing to an uncle that you had, and I ran. I suspected he'd done something to your mother, and I couldn't stay. Dammit, I—" A ragged exhale. "I ran," he said again, miserable as his shoulders slumped. "I ran like the coward I am." He stared at the glass before him. At the spilled whiskey that dotted the desktop. "I was always afraid of him. From the moment he came into the house. My mom was telling me I should be excited, that I was getting a new brother."

"Stepbrother," Declan corrected. An important clarification. There was no blood link between James and Conor Flynn. James was nothing like Conor. "That was the third marriage for Conor's father." And it hadn't lasted long. Liam Flynn, Declan's grandfather, had burned through wives. Five total.

"Conor scared the shit out of me. I woke up on the second night he was in the house." James's cheeks hollowed as he sucked in, then blew out a hard breath. "He had a knife to my throat. Told me that I was going to do what he said. I'd jump when he wanted me to bounce. That he controlled me, and I'd never be free." He licked his lips. "Even after our parents divorced, I was still scared of him. Still doing what he said. I took the job he offered me after college because I was too fucking afraid not to do it—and because the money was good." His eyes squeezed shut. "There was so much money back then. Money makes you overlook a lot of things. You can close your eyes..." His eyes opened. "And pretend you don't see so much. That you don't see the pain and the evil that is right there in front of you."

Declan still didn't touch his drink. "You always thought he killed my mother."

James nodded. "Yes."

"And you ran because you thought he'd kill you next."

"I gave her five grand." A hoarse whisper. "I helped her to leave. I figured I would be next on his attack list, so I vanished. I hid. I stayed hidden and then...then Conor was gone. Dead. By your hand. You were sixteen. All the money was gone. The big monster from my past was gone. And you needed a guardian."

"You were the closest thing to family I had." There had been no one else.

"I either stepped forward, or you went into foster care." James grabbed his drink. Drained it in a gulp. "I'd run before. I wasn't going to run again."

"You stayed by my side. All these years."

He saluted with the empty glass. "Well, eventually, the money became good again." He lowered the glass. It clinked on the table.

"You didn't stay for the money." Was that really the story James wanted him to believe?

"Well, it certainly wasn't for the company." James made a show of straightening his tie. "You're generally pissy and disagreeable."

Declan grunted. He was both of those things on a very general basis.

"And you seriously needed help with fashion. I shudder when I remember the ragged jeans you used to wear every single day." James sniffed. "Someone had to keep you in style. Someone had to *give you* a sense of style."

Declan glanced away from him. He stared into the fire that danced and swayed in the fireplace to the right. He wasn't particularly stylish at that moment and didn't give a flying fuck about that fact. He'd hauled on a pair of black jogging pants for this meeting. A black t-shirt.

"Someone has to stick close to you and be brave enough to tell you when you're making a mistake." Careful words from James. "All the other employees are too afraid. They know you'll kick their asses to the curb if they dare to speak up."

"And I won't kick you to the curb?" Vaguely curious.

"No." Certain. "You won't. You haven't."

He kept watching the fire. "Tell me, do I scare you the way my father did?"

Silence. The silence that lasted a bit too long before... "Sometimes. When I think your focus is too dark. When I know that you're slipping between the line that separates right from wrong."

"It's a thin line."

"Is it?" A pause. "It's not so thin for most people."

But he wasn't most people, and they both knew that.

"I think," James continued carefully, thoughtfully, "that

the line between right and wrong might be particularly thin for you."

Declan's focus remained on the flames. He liked the way the fire moved. Swayed. Teased. "Marley Jones is no threat to me."

"Isn't she?"

"She saved my life. Twice." That didn't make her a threat. As far as he was concerned, it made her his freaking guardian angel. Who would have thought that he'd ever have one? And, unfortunately, her saving him had also put Marley in the crosshairs of a killer. "She has a target on her back. The bastard who took me is eliminating loose ends. He'll come for her."

"And is that the reason you brought her with you to Chicago? Because he's coming for her?"

Slowly, Declan turned his head until he had James in his sights. Step-uncle. One-time guardian. Employee. Annoying conscience. Some days. "What are you suggesting? That I brought her along as some kind of bait?"

James stared back at him. "Did you?"

"The freak kidnapped *me*. I'm the one he had tied up in his torture basement. He might be pissed at Marley for interfering, but I'm the end goal for him. He'll come for me. And I'll take the bastard out."

James rose. "You mean, of course, that you'll let the cops take him out. They'll arrest him. They'll put him in a jail cell. Justice will be served."

No. "I meant exactly what I said. If you have a problem with the bloody aspects of my life, you shouldn't have hung around so long." He reached for the glass. Swirled the liquid with a roll of his wrist. "You didn't want me to turn out like him, and yet, here you are, saying I'm doing the same shit he did."

"Becoming obsessed with one woman? Moving heaven and hell to possess her? Yes, that is the same."

"Hardly heaven and hell. I simply hired her to be my PI." Declan considered the matter. "And then I made her my fiancée."

James shook his head. "Not that lie again."

"I can assure you, it's not lie." *Or at least, it wouldn't be for long.* Declan fully intended to marry her. *How can I possibly let her go?*

"That—that was some bullshit story she gave to ride along in the ambulance and stay in the hospital with you. She's not—she isn't—"

"As of now, Marley Jones is officially my fiancée. Feel free to spread the word to the proper PR places, would you? You've always been good about knowing who to contact in order to get the best press coverage. When it comes to charm, you are top notch, even when you're working with the reporters who hate me."

James didn't move. "I repeat my earlier warning. This is a mistake."

"It doesn't feel like one." It felt like the best move of his life. Unfortunately, Marley hadn't actually agreed to be his fiancée. Something he would have to correct at the earliest opportunity. She could act like it was just a ruse, if she wanted. He'd go along with that story. For now. Soon enough, though, the fiancée bit would be real.

He would need to acquire one big-ass diamond for her.

No. Not a diamond. Marley isn't ice. She was more like fire in his arms. Maybe a ruby? But how would she feel about a ruby engagement ring?

"I told you before, she's dangerous to you." James seemed even more worried. Typical.

"Right." He put down the drink. Steepled his fingers

beneath his chin. He could feel the rasp of his stubble. Declan made a mental note to shave. He didn't want to hurt Marley's skin.

Especially not when he had her legs spread, and his mouth was devouring her.

I pulled out at the last minute. Could have been too late already. Marley...what will I do if Marley becomes pregnant with my child?

And wasn't he the selfish bastard because he'd known the risk was there? He'd been in her bare, and it had been the hottest sex of his life.

No one felt like his Marley.

"She can see evil, Declan." James had his hands fisted at his sides as he delivered his grim and dark words. "Evil was her specialty. She practically has a Ph.D. in it."

"I think her Ph.D. was almost in psychology but having a Ph.D. in evil does seem more fun."

James just looked even grimmer. "The woman studied killers. Got up close and personal with them until one almost took her life. You think she won't be able to see what you are? You can only hide from someone like her for so long. She *will* see the real you. It's just a matter of time."

"The real me? The monster that lurks just beneath the skin?" It was Declan's turn to rise. And when he did, James automatically backed up a step.

He's always feared me a little bit.

Because Declan was his father's son.

"She'll turn you in to the cops. You give her any reason...if she sees too much...a woman like her will run straight to the cops. Hell, she's already been talking to that detective ex of hers for days."

Anger hummed in Declan's blood. "What?"

"Parker Ellis? She's been calling him. Texting him. And

he's been calling her, too. Just so you know..." Another step back, as if James feared revealing this news. "She got him to access your father's case. She already knows what you did to him. Hell, she could just be biding her time with you right now as she works with Parker. They could be trying to bring you down. Cops have been aiming to bring you down forever. And Parker? He has a special reason to want you to burn."

"How do you know that?"

"Because I dug into his past like you asked! And you're not gonna like it, but that collateral damage your dad was so good about leaving in his wake? He did it to Parker Ellis, of all people. Now isn't that one hell of a coincidence?"

It was.

"His father was a Fed. He was working undercover to bring down one Conor Flynn. Only the man was murdered. Did you hear what I said? *Parker's dad was found murdered.* A bullet to the heart and to the head. Sound familiar?"

Yes, it did.

"Parker and his mom moved down to Georgia after his dad's death, but I guarantee you, that cop *hates* you. And now he's the one working your investigation. The one cozying up to your *fiancée*. This scene has trouble and betrayal written in big, bold, glowing letters."

"Marley won't betray me."

"She may have *already* betrayed you! That cop wants you locked away."

"No current charges are pending against me. I'm an upstanding member of the community."

James snorted. "Bull. Everyone knows that the cops think you are—"

"I fucking work with the US government on more contracts than I can count. I have more connections than you can dream of. Some local cop doesn't worry me." Not the total truth. The more he learned about Parker Ellis, the more Declan realized the man was going to be a problem for him. "How do you know she's been in contact with Parker?"

"Because you wanted me to dig on her, too. I dug. I may have also...monitored her conversations a bit. Sue me."

Declan strode from behind the desk.

"You wanted me to pull up everything I could on her. I did. I have. She and the detective have a history. A long one. They went to high school together. Dated briefly after her attack by Glass. The cop is actually the only guy she's dated since the Glass attack. The woman went into hiding after that creep sliced her. A hiding that came courtesy of her brothers. And speaking of them?" A soundless whistle. "They are a whole other mess of trouble we don't need. Pretty sure one of them might be CIA. The other is some adrenaline junkie who specializes in hostage rescue. True blue assholes who will not understand your way of life."

"What about Glass?" Declan wasn't concerned about the brothers. They would not be getting in his way. "Anything else I need to know about him?"

"He's in Georgia, locked away in a maximum-security prison. Mostly kept in solitary confinement. The man is not some easy target."

Declan inclined his head. He'd already known all of that information, but he still said, "Thanks for the intel."

"I—what?" His brows beetled. "That's it?"

"Glass isn't a concern any longer. Mark him off your list."

"Shit." James raked a hand over his face. "What have you done?"

He needed to see Marley. "Why accuse me? Here I am, being an upstanding citizen—as I keep having to remind you I actually am. I'm in Chicago. You just told me Glass was in a maximum-security prison down in Georgia. I can't possibly get access to him." A roll of one shoulder. "But, sadly, prison riots happen all the time. And sometimes, even people who are supposed to be in solitary get pulled into the fray."

"Shit," James said again. Then… "Shit."

"Is there anything else? Because I thought this doom-and-gloom meeting would yield more drama." *And more information that I did not already know. You're slipping, James.* The Glass intel had been disappointing, and Declan had actually already been aware of Detective Parker Ellis's link to the Flynn family.

I am well aware of my father's crimes. And sometimes, the ghosts of the past can come at you when you least expect them. Parker had stared at him with a bit too much hate that first night in the hospital. The glance had set off alarm bells for Declan. He hadn't just left the digging to James.

Sometimes, I prefer to do my own dirty work.

James shook his head. "You're going to crash and burn with Marley Jones."

Now he smiled. "But won't the fire be fabulous?"

* * *

THE BEDROOM DOOR OPENED. The faint sound had her eyes opening. Marley stared into the darkness.

The door clicked closed.

Footsteps padded silently toward the bed. Her back had been to the door. She'd awakened a short while ago. Gotten out of the bed to dress. Rummaged in Declan's closet until she'd found something that worked and returned to bed.

Then she'd rolled onto her side. Snuggled up against the pillow. And started to drift off again.

Declan hadn't been in bed with her. But she knew that he was now walking toward her. In moments, the bed dipped a bit. Had he taken off some clothing? She'd heard a few rustles. Marley thought that perhaps he had. He slid into the bed. She could feel his warmth, but he didn't touch her.

She wanted him to touch her.

"Do you see evil?" he rasped. Such low words. "I know you saw it with that bastard Glass. Will you see it with me?"

She held her breath. Was he about to make another big confession? Because if so...

She rolled toward him. Put a hand on his heart. No shirt. Bare skin. "I won't pretend to be asleep this time."

His hand covered hers. "Marley? What are you talking about?"

"I don't see evil when I look into your eyes. I see you, Declan. You." Enough of this. Touching him wasn't enough. She threw off the sheet, and she climbed on top of him. Marley straddled him. She was wearing one of his over-sized shirts. He seemed to be wearing a pair of jogging pants. The soft material brushed against the sensitive skin of her thighs. No shirt for Declan.

And his dick bobbed eagerly toward her, shoving against the front of his jogging pants.

Tempting her to take him, to go wild with him but... not yet.

"I heard you when you said you killed your father," Marley confessed. Time to just get that out in the open. If she didn't want Declan to keep secrets from her, then she could not keep secrets from him.

His hands flew up and locked around her waist. "What?"

"I wasn't sleeping. I heard you. And I'm still here. I didn't go running. *I am still here.*" Her hands pressed to his chest. Such a warm, powerful chest. "I don't think you're some big, bad monster, Declan Flynn. I don't care what the world says. I know you. The real you."

He shook his head. Darkness covered the bedroom. Shadows. But her eyes had adjusted to the dark, and she could see him just fine. *I'm not afraid of the dark any longer.*

"You didn't kill your father in cold blood." She knew this truth with utter certainty. "I read the reports."

"Courtesy of your *friendly* detective."

Oh, was that a bite of jealousy? It just might have been. "Yep, courtesy of him. When your father died, he'd been attacking you. You had four broken ribs. You had bruises all over your chest. You had two broken fingers, plus a fractured wrist. And your father had taken his knife and sliced your face." Her head tipped forward, and her hair slid over her shoulders. "I saw the pictures. I saw what he'd done to you."

"Fucking Detective Ellis."

"Your father was beating you, Declan. If you hadn't stopped him, he would have killed you!"

He shot up. Rolled them. Had her beneath him on the bed. He braced his body on his arms as he loomed over her. His legs were between her spread thighs. His strong form dominating hers. "I wasn't going to let him kill me." Cold. Calm.

But he didn't feel cold. The heat from his body practically singed her.

"I took the hits from him. I fucking took them like I'd always taken them. He liked giving pain. I'd done something that pissed him off. Gotten a ninety-five on a test when I should have gotten a hundred."

Her lips parted.

"I had to be perfect. Nothing less was acceptable. Not for Conor Flynn's son."

Tears stung her eyes.

"So he hit me. And I took it and then...then I didn't." Flat. Still so cold. "I realized I wasn't ever going to just *take it* from him again."

There is nothing cold about Declan. I know it. The coldness in his voice is a lie. The colder he is, the hotter my Declan burns.

"He used his boot to break my ribs. He was getting ready to kick me again when I rolled. I caught his foot. I jerked the bastard to the floor." A heave of Declan's breath. "He fell. The knife slid from his fingers, and I grabbed it. In the next instant, I had that knife at his throat. His eyes went so wide. I swear, I think the bastard looked *proud* for a moment."

She wanted to throw her arms around him and hug him but...

His hands had moved. They'd curled around her wrists. He pinned her hands to the bed. Almost as if he was afraid she would touch him.

"Then he started to bleed. Don't know if anyone had ever made Conor Flynn bleed before that night. He didn't like it. He told me to stop. Tried to shove me away. Only I was done being shoved by him."

His words still held no emotion.

But I can feel his rage and his pain and I wish I could take it all away.

"He twisted and punched. I fought back. I used his knife, and I drove it into his stomach. Then drove it in his shoulder. He screamed for me to stop. He *begged* for me to let him go."

Her body had gone taut.

"I didn't. I didn't let go. He tried to headbutt me. We shoved and punched and the next thing I knew...the knife was in his heart."

"Declan."

He brought his face close to hers. "I drove a knife into my father's heart."

"He was *hurting* you. You were sixteen! You had to protect yourself."

"He begged me to let him go. Even as he begged, I knew I was killing him. I wasn't ever going to let him hurt me again. Not me. Not anyone else. And you want to know the last fucking thing he said?"

What she wanted was to wrap her arms around him and never, ever let go.

"My mother's name. And he *smiled*. He shouldn't have smiled when he died. He should have been terrified. Hell was waiting, and he *smiled*."

Her wrists twisted in his hold. "Let me go."

He jerked. "Marley, I—" Declan let her go. He backed up. Went to his knees on the bed. "I tried to warn you that I—"

She shot upright. Her arms flew around him. Her body collided with his as she held him as tightly as she could. "I'm sorry." She pressed a kiss to his cheek. To the scar that marked him. "I'm so sorry you were trapped alone with him for so long. I'm so sorry he hurt you." Another kiss. "I'm sorry I didn't know you back then because I would have helped you."

His hands brushed her shoulders. "Marley?"

Another kiss on his cheek. Then her hands rose to press

on either side of his face. "Declan Flynn, you saved yourself. You protected yourself. Do not feel guilty for what you did. Do not try and pretend you're some big evil killer. You are not. I won't believe it. Not you." This time, she kissed him on the lips. Soft and sweet. There had not been enough softness in his life. She was certain of this. "I would have helped you," she said again.

I would have driven the knife into him myself. And she never, ever would have believed that thought would race through her head. But the idea of someone hurting Declan...

When I saw the pictures of sixteen-year-old Declan, I wanted to kill his father.

Declan shook his head. "Marley..." The faint click of his swallow. "You don't know the things I've done since then."

"I don't see a monster when I look at you, Declan. I don't."

"What do you see?"

"The man I want."

This time, his mouth took hers.

Chapter Sixteen

She shouldn't want him.

She shouldn't hold him. Comfort him. Touch him. Shouldn't offer him the sweetest hope that he'd ever had in his entire life. Because when she did those things, she just sealed her fate all the more.

Oh, who the fuck was he kidding? Her fate had been sealed for some time. Ever since she came back for him in that basement. Or maybe when he'd opened his eyes in that hospital room, and Marley had still been there, holding his hand.

"You're marrying me," he said against her mouth. That delectable mouth. The mouth that kissed his scars and told him that she would have helped him destroy his father.

No one else had ever tried to stop Conor Flynn. But Declan actually believed that a teenage Marley would have.

Though his father probably would have just hurt her.

A growl built in his throat.

And I would have just killed him quicker. No one will ever hurt my Marley again in this world.

"Is this the cover story again?" Marley's breathless voice

asked as she pulled back. "You really want to talk about the cover...now? Because Declan, I want to take your pain away."

His own breath froze in his chest.

"I want to give you pleasure and no more pain. I want us both to have pleasure. Make love to me, Declan. Right now."

Like he had to be told twice to do it. His tongue slid past her lips. Tasted the sweetness that he craved. She'd risen in the bed to hold him. But now she shifted positions as they kissed. Her legs wrapped around him. Her hands tightened behind his head.

His eager dick shoved toward her. He'd stripped off his t-shirt but kept on the jogging pants when he climbed into the bed with her. The worn material did little to disguise his need for her. Still, the pants were definitely in the way. They needed to go. She was rocking her hips and riding against him. When he'd been gone from the room, she'd changed at some point. Put on one of his shirts. He could feel the softness against him even though the darkness in the bedroom made it impossible for him to actually *see* which shirt she'd picked.

The material was oversized on her. It carried the faintest hint of his cologne.

I want Marley carrying my scent. He wanted to mark her. To put a ring on her finger. To bind her to him so that the entire world would know—

What? That one person out of eight billion doesn't think you're the devil incarnate?

He tumbled her back on the bed. Kept kissing her.

No, I want the world to know that this angel wants me. Loves me.

But...she didn't love him. She wanted him. He could

make her go wild with passion. Already, his fingers were sliding between her legs. She wore the t-shirt, but no underwear, and he strummed her clit the way he knew would make her crazy. Strumming wouldn't be enough. Not for him. He needed his mouth on her. Needed to taste her pleasure before he drove inside of her.

She doesn't love me, and I don't know that I can ever love anyone. I'm too much my father's son. Too much—

Her fingers fluttered over his back. Then darted between their bodies. She stroked him softly through the jogging pants. Her mouth broke from his. "I think you'd better grab some protection this time."

In the darkness, he stared down at her. "What if I don't?"

No, fuck, he shouldn't have said—

"Then I might get pregnant, Declan, and you'd have to marry me for real. No charming pretense." She didn't sound worried. In fact, he couldn't tell how she did sound. Odd, when Marley had always been so easy for him to read in the past.

Wasn't that something he enjoyed about her? No pretense. What he saw was what he got. Marley told him how she felt while he...

While I trick. I lie. I hold everything back from everyone in this world because I can't trust anyone.

His body had frozen.

"Grab a condom, Declan." Soft. Her fingers still stroked the dick that ached for her. A dick that was far, far from soft. His body had locked, but his dick was still big and damn near bursting for her. "I want you *in* me."

"I'm going to marry you." A flat promise. "It was never pretend."

"What?"

He pulled back. Kicked the covers out of his way that wanted to tangle him up, and then he was pushing her legs apart. The powerful pounding of his heartbeat seemed to echo in his ears. The blood poured through his veins like lava. Everything felt heightened. Too intense.

His fingers were shaking as he pushed her thighs wider apart. When he put his mouth on her, a tremble skated over her body. He'd been careful until that instant. Using a soft touch. Because this was Marley. But, when his mouth pressed to her, when her taste hit his tongue and she began to moan his name, something seemed to tear loose inside of him. No, not tearing. Like a wall, breaking. Crumbling. Smashing into a million pieces so that it could never, ever be rebuilt.

His mouth turned feverish on her. Licking. Kissing. Taking. Harder and more frantic. She twisted beneath him, and his hands just caught her hips to hold her down. He took and he took and she came against his mouth. Once.

Not enough.

He lapped her up, too greedy and desperate to take every single bit of her.

She came a second time. "Declan!" Sharp. Gasped.

Another lick. He could taste her pleasure. Nothing else in this world would ever be as good.

But he was nearly exploding. He ditched the jogging pants. Rolled from the bed to grab a condom from the nightstand.

Don't want it. Want to be bare in her. Want to make her pregnant. Want her tied to me forever. Only…

What if the child turned out like me?

Fear slid through him when there should only be pleasure in this moment. His hand curled around the handle of the drawer, and he yanked it open. He grabbed for the box of condoms and pulled out one packet. He turned back for the bed.

Marley slipped from the bed. Her knees hit the carpet, and her fingers curled around his dick.

"Marley—"

"Not fair that I have two...and you have zero so far." She pumped him. Base to head. Once. Twice. And then... "Let's fix that problem."

She took him into her mouth.

His hand flew out. Hit the lamp. Turned on the light because he had to see this. Marley, taking his dick into her mouth. Those lush lips parting for him. Pulling him in. And the way her tongue felt...the wet heat of her mouth...the way she gave that little moan as if she loved having his dick and—

He curled his hands under her arms. Lifted her onto the bed. Tossed her down. She laughed when she bounced. Marley's laughter—it was as beautiful as she was.

And some bastard shot her. Her blood was fucking all over the limo, and I thought my world was ending. Who would have thought that just one person could end the entire world?

He tore open the condom. She helped him roll it into place. Mostly just so she could stroke him and tease him and torment him more. But the time for torment was over. He pushed her onto the mattress. Captured her hands and caged them the way he'd done earlier. But this time was different.

Her hips arched toward him, and his dick knew the way home. He plunged all the way in one powerful stroke, and she lifted from the bed with a gasp of his name. Declan leaned forward. Licked her tight nipples through the t-shirt.

Licked and bit even as he thrust. Over and over. Deep and hard. Relentless.

She was so wet and eager. Still so sensitive from his mouth, and when she started to come again—*third time is the charm, sweetheart*—he stopped holding back. His drives were deep and plunging. Claiming and consuming. His hands touched her everywhere. His mouth locked to her throat, and he sucked the skin. He would leave a mark.

Marley. *Mine.*

He came inside her.

* * *

DECLAN'S ARM was curled around her. Her ass was snuggled back against him. His chest was to her spine. Who would have thought this could be the most comfortable position in the world?

Sleep pulled at her. But she needed to say a few things. Important things. Things like...*Hi, Declan. So...I'm worried I might be falling in love with you.*

And it wasn't just about confusing great sex with love. Not that she'd had a whole lot of great sex until Declan. But a woman could tell the difference between pleasure—even really amazing, heaven-touching pleasure—and love.

Love was scary and consuming and deep, and it made you do all sorts of reckless, wild things...

Like seduce a billionaire megalomaniac in his office when you have zero seduction experience. But, even before that...when she'd been in that alley and realized Declan might get shot, the fear that she'd felt had floored her. It hadn't just been about protecting her client. Ha. Not even close. Her lunge to cover him had been instinctive because...

No one can hurt Declan. Not her Declan.

She swallowed. He'd turned off the lamp again. *After* he'd brought a soft, warm cloth and gently cleaned her. A faint smile had curved his lips when he got a look at the t-shirt she wore. An old college shirt. Faded and worn. She'd found it in the back of his closet. She'd raked past all the too expensive items and picked this one.

No real reason why. But...

It made her feel warm. She could swear she smelled his scent on it.

You need to say something. You can't just hide in his arms forever and pretend danger isn't coming. "Probably won't always be like this." The husky words came from her, and really, they had not been what she meant to say. "I'm sure we won't always make love this many times a night." *Make love.* That was how she thought of it. He probably didn't. That was okay. She knew exactly what she was doing.

I'm falling in love with Declan Flynn.

"You're right." An easy agreement. She felt him brush a kiss against the back of her head. "It will probably be more."

Her eyes widened, then she laughed because he was joking, wasn't he?

"I love the sound of your laugh. It's like a little light." Gruff. "When so much is dark."

Holy crap, that was poetic. Poetic from Declan? The man had layers. She rolled into his arms. His features were so shadowed and dark. "Are you always so, um, quick to rise? Because I didn't think most men—"

"There is no always. This is how I am with you. The way I am with you is different than the way I am with everyone else in this world."

She suddenly realized he was not just talking about sex. This felt deeper. "Declan?"

"You're going to marry me."

Back to that, were they? "Declan..."

"James is already sharing the news with certain media sources. By morning, the world will think that Declan Flynn fell madly in love with the woman who pulled him from hell. He proposed, she accepted, and they are going to spend the rest of their lives in married bliss."

"He's *already* sharing the news?"

"I was talking to him downstairs before I returned to you."

So that was where he'd vanished to—a meeting with James.

"You and I talked about the cover before. Your original idea, remember, love?"

Love. A pang shot through her. One she pushed aside, for the moment, so she could focus on the engagement and cover story. The fact that she'd told a few EMTs they were engaged was going to haunt her forever. "We don't need a pretend story. Unless..." Her fingers skated over his chest. Paused over his heart. Such a powerful chest. Such a strong, driving heartbeat. Wait, was his heartbeat a little fast? "Declan? Are you spreading the story to draw out the person who took you? Is he already here in Chicago? Do you know something I don't?" Her hand pressed a bit harder against him. "Don't hold back on me. Remember the whole talk about not sidelining your PI?" Did she need to go over things again?

"I lied to you."

Her eyes narrowed in the dark. "Not cool, Declan. Not cool."

"I never needed a PI."

Oh, wait, was that statement supposed to be a stunner? "I've seen your security team. Kind of figured that part out on my own." But she'd wanted the gig desperately and not just because he would have been her first major client. Though, sure, that had been nice. *The* Declan Flynn and all that. Only...*I wanted to make sure he was safe.* Just like in the hospital, when she hadn't been able to leave him because she'd been so worried about an enemy sneaking in and hurting him.

No one can hurt Declan.

"I can protect myself, Marley."

"Well, you *did* wind up drugged in a basement."

He curled his fingers around her wrist. "You have a giant target on your back."

She actually didn't have anything on her back but his shirt.

"You saved me, Marley. He's going to try and kill you."

"You think I didn't figure that out when my place got trashed? It was certainly easy enough to connect the dots." And as for the dots... "You whisked me away to Chicago because you were trying to protect me. Being your PI isn't about me helping you to solve the case." Damn him. "It's about you protecting me."

Silence. Then, "You're sure I'm not using you as bait to draw him in? He's eliminated three people already. You got in his way—twice—so he'll be determined to eliminate you, too. Maybe I have you close because I want him to come for you...all the better so that I can trap him."

She snorted. In the dark. Pressed to him. "Don't be ridiculous."

"Didn't realize I was." So mild.

"You would never use me as bait. You're hardly the type of man who would do that."

"Marley, Marley, Marley...you're back to saying you think I'm good."

Actually, she hadn't said that. She'd just said he would not use her as bait. "You're the main target. Doesn't make sense that you'd need to dangle me like a worm on a hook. You hired me because you were trying to protect *me*. You brought me with you to Chicago for the same reason. Now you're getting James to tell the world that I'm your fiancée because that's like a neon sign way of saying...*don't dare touch what belongs to me*."

"You do belong to me."

"Because I'm your PI." *I want to be so much more to you.*

"The engagement doesn't have to be fake."

Now she was the one stunned into silence.

"I can give you anything in this world that you want. More money than you will ever spend. The biggest houses. The fastest cars."

"I tend to bargain hunt," she whispered. "Can't stand to buy something if it's not on sale. And big houses just require a lot of cleaning. I also don't drive fast. Speeding is against the law."

"Right. You always follow the law."

"And you...don't?"

"I have broken more laws than I can count. To keep you with me, I'd break *any* rule. I intend to possess you completely, Marley."

Possess. Possessing something or someone wasn't the same thing as love. And he'd warned her before that he didn't think he could love the way others loved. *But who is to say that the way Declan loves is wrong?*

"Marley?"

She'd been silent too long. "I didn't hear a marriage

proposal." She turned away from Declan, but caught his arm and pulled it around her as she snuggled back against him. "You should work on that. Do better next time, and maybe you'll get a different response from me."

A jolt went through him. Shock? Maybe. She was pretty shocked herself. For now, though, time for bed. She wasn't sure she was up to sharing more of her soul with him at the moment. "It's late. We've got a killer to hunt tomorrow. No more sidelining. Your brother is a target, too. From here on out, we go on the offensive. We don't wait on this creep any longer. He's not slipping away."

"I...wanted you to be clear from the doc."

Was he talking about those stitches again? Like a few stitches—or a dozen—would slow her down for long. "I can hunt with you just fine. Time for you to cough up your list of suspects. I want to know your enemies, Declan. I want to know every secret that you possess. Share everything with me. That's the only way for us to get to the truth. I need to know it all. Good. Bad. All the sins that you want hidden, you have to share them with me."

His hold tightened on her.

He didn't speak. Just held her. The minutes drifted past. Slumber pulled at her. Her eyelids sagged closed. Declan kept holding her close.

And, just as she began to drift off, she heard... "Be careful what you wish for, sweetheart. Very, very careful."

Chapter Seventeen

Marley paused beside the empty desk just outside of Declan's office. She'd expected to see Pierre sitting there with his back perfectly straight. With his eyes glinting at her from behind the frames of his glasses. A slightly angry glint. Maybe a judgy one.

She'd prepared for battle.

Only...

Pierre wasn't there.

Declan strode past the empty desk and toward his office.

"Probably giving someone hell someplace." He unlocked his door. "Pierre is good at that sort of thing. Come on inside."

But Pierre's computer was turned off. And the desk chair was in the exact position it had been in the previous night. She remembered because she'd glanced over to make sure Pierre was long gone when she and Declan had left. "I don't think he's been here yet today."

Declan waved her inside. "Why are you obsessed with Pierre?"

She did not go inside his office. "Because your assistant strikes me as the type who is never late. I mean, the man was still here with you at 8 p.m. last night. Everything about Pierre screamed devoted-to-the-job." And something just nagged at her. "Has he ever been late?" Because it was nearing ten a.m. Declan had just wanted to swing by the office to collect files to use in their investigation. Or at least, that had been his story.

They'd been trailed by Cade and Hunter all the way to the elevator on the lobby floor. The men had just stayed below because they'd been certain the building was secure.

But the nagging continued as she eyed the desk.

"Pierre is always on time." Declan ambled away from his now open office. Frowned. "Maybe he's sick?"

Maybe. And maybe... "He really did not like me yesterday."

"Pierre doesn't like many people. That's why he's good at his job. He's great at telling people to fuck off when I'm not interested in talking with them."

Yes, she could see where Pierre would excel in that department. But she could also see... "He's your personal assistant."

"Uh, yeah. The term he prefers is executive assistant."

"He knows everything about you."

"He knows my business. Not my personal life."

She shook her head and crept toward the desk. Her hand slid along the back of the chair. "You are so wrong. There would have been a million conversations that he'd heard over the years. Conversations you thought were private. Assistants hear everything. They always know the best gossip. When I did the real estate bit, the agency's owner had this insanely organized assistant who knew everything. And I mean *everything*. Where the owner took his mistress for dinner. How many times the guy had cheated on his wife. Where every single body was buried." She reached for the top desk drawer. Pulled it open. Tried to, anyway. It was locked.

"You think Pierre knows where I bury bodies?" An amused rumble of laughter. Dark laughter. "Obviously, darling, you don't get that when I bury bodies, no one finds them again."

Her head whipped toward him. "Are you making a joke?" A bad one.

"Maybe I'm sharing all of my deep, dark secrets with you. You wanted to hear them, didn't you?"

She wanted the truth.

He closed in on her. "Pierre nearly fainted when one of the interns tripped as she was—literally—running with scissors, and she cut a gouge in her hand. The man can't stand the sight of blood. I hardly think he's the type to set me up for a torture party."

She tried another drawer. Locked, too. "Is he the type that would know you were looking at buying Abyss?"

He didn't have a ready comeback.

Her head turned toward him. "Is he?" She'd bet that Pierre was. "Because a good assistant always knows where his boss is. In a company like yours, I bet he's always aware of any potential acquisitions that you might make." Her hand had pulled away from the locked drawers. "I bet he was aware of, say, when you flew down to Savannah to meet your brother."

"He didn't know why I went to Savannah. Only James knew about Royal. But..." His eyes flickered.

She edged closer to him. "That seems like a really big *but...*"

"All this…" His hand gestured toward the empty desk. "Because my assistant happens to be late?"

She caught his hand. "All of this…" Her hold tightened on him. "Because you may have tried to sideline me, but I have actually still been working your case. I don't have full access to your life, but I can still come up with suspicions. When I think of people who would know your travel schedule, who would know about your acquisitions, who would know where you would be and when…a couple of folks pop to mind for me. People at the top of my suspect list." A slow exhale because he was not going to like what she had to say, but the words needed to be spoken. "People like James, of course."

His expression tightened. "Of course. Let's not overlook James."

She wouldn't dream of overlooking him. "He was with you in Augusta, after all. I doubt there are many moves you make that James isn't aware of."

"He didn't know I was considering buying Abyss. I don't normally discuss every acquisition with him. Besides, the place is a bit out of my normal wheelhouse."

And that was interesting. "So why even consider it?"

"Maybe I was looking for something new."

No emotion. So that meant he was probably seething inside. She got it. Hearing that the person closest to you was on her suspect list—the list of the people she thought might want Declan tortured and killed—would hurt. It would even hurt the man who liked to say he didn't feel. *I'm starting to think you feel too much, Declan. Not too little.* "Cade and Hunter."

He didn't even blink.

"They are both extremely dangerous men. They are at the top of your security team. They each have full clearance to all aspects of your world. Again, they were with you in Augusta. They were supposed to protect you and yet, they weren't there when you needed them." Another fact that bothered her... "I was the one to spot the shooter in the alley. I would have thought one of them would do the job." She liked the men. She did. But liking them didn't mean that she couldn't suspect them at the same time.

"So you don't think the enemy is from the outside, huh?" They could have been talking about the weather because he seemed so very casual. "You think it's an enemy within my inner circle. You think people close to me hate me enough to arrange my abduction and torture."

"I think the mastermind knew your favorite drink. So that means it's either someone close to you or the perp we're after has been *using* someone close to you in order to gather intel about you. Intel like...where you'd be. What you drink. When you might be unprotected because you ditch guards and take off on your own because you need the occasional escape. To discover these details, you'd have to get access to someone who knew your habits incredibly well. Someone who knows you better than you know yourself."

"No one knows me well."

Not true. "I think Pierre knows your habits far better than you realize." She wet her lips. Didn't let go of him. "Last night, when I tried to get in to see you here, he told me that you never allowed visitors that weren't on your schedule."

"I don't. I don't like surprises."

Yes, well, considering his last surprise had involved him waking up drugged in a basement, she could understand that. Truly. "I told him you shouldn't be working so late. He told me that you never left before nine p.m. on a workday. And then he rattled off your schedule to me. Telling me when you normally arrive at work. When you leave for lunch. Telling me that I couldn't interrupt you at all because you were a busy man with commitments that had to be met. Then, you know, he tried to actually block me with his body so I couldn't get to you. At the time, I thought he was freakishly dedicated to his boss and his job."

No response.

"And then I opened your door later and told him to leave. He was...he was on the phone with someone." She played the scene in her mind again. "Cell phone. Not business. I could have sworn that he stared at me with some hot anger before the emotion vanished. I was planning to have a one-on-one chat with him today—"

"You mean you were going to interrogate him."

"I mean *we* were going to interrogate him." One of the reasons she'd so readily agreed to visit Declan's office. "But your faithful assistant isn't here. His desk hasn't been disturbed, and I suspect every single drawer that he has is locked."

"Pierre doesn't have the stomach to torture me."

"No, but he may have the stomach to take a ton of cash and sell you out to someone who does want to torture you. Someone who needed an inside man in order to learn everything possible about you. Pierre has access to every part of your life. Don't you think we need to investigate that? Investigate him?"

His square jaw hardened the tiniest bit.

And...

Ding.

Her head swiveled toward the elevator. She sucked in a breath because if this was Pierre, now would be the perfect time for her to grill him. Declan probably thought she was crazy to go off on this tangent, but she'd woken early this morning, and the more she'd considered the people closest to Declan, the more afraid she'd become.

Declan won't give me a list of his enemies. Is that because...is it because he thinks the enemies are close? She felt like he was holding back on her. Keeping his secrets when he should have revealed everything, and that crap needed to stop. Correction, it *was* stopping.

If he was afraid she'd turn from him if she learned all the dark parts he kept hidden from the world, then the man was mistaken. She never intended to turn from Declan. Wasn't even sure that she could.

The doors parted.

And Hunter McQueen strode out. "He's not answering his door or his phone, boss."

She let go of Declan's hand. "What?"

"I took the liberty of breaking in his house, of course," Hunter added with a shrug. "His place looks undisturbed. I don't think he went home last night. My gut is telling me that the guy could be in the wind."

She looked at Hunter and his stern, I-never-laugh-but-I-often-kill expression, then Marley peered at Declan and his unreadable face. "What is happening right now?"

Declan raised his brows. "I may have reached the same conclusion you did."

"What?" Marley hated that she seemed to keep repeating the same, sharp exclamation.

"I haven't been just sitting on my ass this past week either, sweetheart. I've been digging. Pulling financials. Ripping into the lives of those I should be able to trust. People like Pierre."

Her heartbeat began to drum faster. "You suspect him, too? You suspect him and yet you still let me do that whole spiel about why he could be in involved in this mess?"

"Yes...and yes."

"Declan," she snapped.

"I wanted to see why you thought he might be guilty. Him, James, Cade..." He motioned toward a watchful Hunter. "Hunter."

"Me, too?" Hunter grunted, but didn't seem offended. "Yeah, I could torture the hell out of a person. I know all the tricks." He sauntered forward, as if admitting he could torture someone for hours and wreck a person's life was just a common confession. "Glad to know I made your suspect list, PI."

She shook her head. Anger and confusion hummed through her. "You both think Pierre is guilty?"

"I found an offshore account the guy had yesterday," Declan admitted. "Took some time, even for someone with my tech skills and connections."

"Connections in all the wrong places," Hunter murmured.

This was the chattiest she'd ever seen the former Ranger.

"He'd buried that account," Declan added. "But I got access. And I saw the payments. Some that have been coming for a while now. One that hit the day after my abduction."

Her breath shuddered out. "It's him. Pierre's involved." She glanced back at the desk. "He knows you're on to him. He's run?" He must have. That was why he wasn't at work. Why he hadn't been at home when Hunter had checked that location.

And why does Declan trust Hunter so much? I thought he didn't trust anyone. But he'd told Hunter about his suspicions regarding Pierre, and Hunter had gone out to track down the assistant.

The missing assistant. Who'd run and was hiding—

"Or he's just, you know, dead," Declan concluded.

She jolted. "He was alive last night! Right here!" Her gaze flew back to him.

Declan stared straight at her.

Did you kill him, Declan? Her lips pressed together. She would not voice the question because, no, absolutely not, he hadn't. Declan had been with her all evening.

"Doesn't mean he's still alive," Declan said. "We've got a killer eliminating loose ends. If Pierre was another part of his hired help, he'd need to be eliminated, too."

"Security doesn't have a record of him leaving last night," Hunter revealed. "Probably need to start a floor-by-floor search. Considering just how many floors there are in this beast of a building, that could take some time."

They thought Pierre was dead. Dead somewhere in the building. Her breath huffed out. "This is the kind of crap I'm talking about," she fumed. "I need to be in the damn loop, Declan. You can't fuck me like your life depends on it one moment, and then keep from me the fact that you think your assistant is trying to kill you—and, oh, that *he* may be dead. That isn't how relationships work."

Declan glanced toward Hunter.

She did, too.

He grimaced. "This sounds like a you-two problem. I think I'm gonna go search the building for a dead assistant."

Who said things like that? Searching for a dead assistant as if that was a run-of-the-mill activity?

Hunter swung away. "Oh, and by the way, you might want to check the news when you get a chance. Big story out of Georgia."

"*Hunter.*" A snarl from Declan.

Hunter tossed a wave over his shoulder before he

reached for the elevator button. "Thought she had a right to know." The doors opened. He glanced back. Stared at Marley. "No more monsters."

Then he slipped into the elevator. The doors closed a moment later.

Of course, he would have access to get in and out of the private elevator and to go wherever he wanted in the building. "You trust him more than anyone else." Something she had not picked up on before. In fact, if anything, she'd thought he was closer to Cade. But...

Hunter. Hunter is the one who shares Declan's secrets.

A million thoughts seemed to crash and churn in her head. *They think Pierre is dead. So...what? They believe the killer was here last night? That he got in the building with all of its security and took out the assistant? And what in the hell is happening in Georgia that I need to know about?*

Then, beyond all that...

And why does Declan trust Hunter so much?

"We should talk in my office." Declan turned away. "Hunter will let me know what he discovers. Be certain of that."

"You mean if he turns up Pierre's body, probably with a bullet in his head and his heart..." Like the two men who'd taken Declan. "He'll notify you."

"Yes, that's exactly what I meant."

She didn't move. "You let me tell you all about my suspicions. For James. For Cade. For Hunter. For *Pierre*. And you said nothing. You acted like it was typical for him not to be here—like you weren't alarmed at all when you already believed the man had betrayed you!"

"I was going to bring you in on the interrogation."

"You were going to bring me in on—" Incensed, huffing, she broke off. Then she blasted past him, might have even elbowed him out of the way, as she stormed into his office. "What in the hell, Declan? What in the actual hell? This isn't how a partnership works! This isn't how a relationship works!"

The door closed quietly behind her. She spun around. He leaned back, letting his shoulders hit the door as he studied her.

"That's the second time you've used the word 'relationship,'" Declan noted, as if that was the most important part of their conversation. Spoiler, it was not. They were talking about a potential murder. More important, surely, than their relationship.

His arms crossed over his chest. "Does that mean you've accepted my proposal?"

Her eyes widened. She felt them widen. Or bulge. Whatever. "Declan!" Marley glanced around the massive office, frantic. Her gaze landed on the desk. The desk they'd been on when he took her for the first time. When she'd taken him.

Memories flooded through her.

"Is that a yes?"

"There was no proposal! There was you telling me, not asking. We've covered this, and you are not going to distract me." Her hands were on her hips. She needed to get him focused. "Why isn't Hunter a suspect?"

His eyes narrowed. Narrowed eyes did *not* equal an answer.

"Hunter is on *my* suspect list." Marley was sure she'd covered this, too, with him. "Why isn't he on yours? Why are you trusting him so much when I thought you weren't a trusting person?"

Declan rolled one shoulder. "Because I hauled his ass out of an inferno once upon a time. The man has this ridiculous idea that he owes his life to me. And now, shit, I'm pretty sure he'd take a bullet for me in a heartbeat."

Surprise had her hands falling from her hips.

"The guy is pretty jealous that you beat him to the whole taking-a-bullet-for-me punch, by the way. The last seven years, he's been jonesing to even the score for me. I carried him out. Bastard was mad at first, when I pushed his ass to do therapy to get back on his feet, but after he stopped raging at me, Hunter realized he was still alive. And he could go after the SOBs who'd set the trap for him." A pause. "He did go after them, by the way. I helped."

A chill skated down her spine. "Declan." Marley wet her lips. "What happened in Georgia?"

His brows lowered. "Someone else is on *my* suspect list."

"Who?" Who had she missed? "If you would *share* your list of enemies then we could get on the same page and—"

"Your police detective."

"Okay, first, he is not *my* police detective." Obviously, he was talking about Parker. And Parker was not hers in any way, shape or form.

"He's in Chicago right now."

That news had her edging back a step. "Since when?"

"Yesterday morning. I might have put eyes on him before we flew to Chicago."

She thought there was no *might* about it. "You had someone tailing him for that long because..." Because the only thing that made sense was... "You already suspected him before we left Augusta? Declan, you have got to stop being a secretive bastard and *tell* me things! Don't you get that? You have to tell me things because we are—"

"In a relationship," he finished.

She sniffed. "I don't fuck men that I'm not in

relationships with. So, yes, we are in a relationship. And that means you tell me everything. Good, bad, and all the messy stuff in between."

"You don't want to know the parts in between. Or the bad things."

She did, even as her stomach twisted. "Why do you think I can't handle bad things?"

He closed the distance between them. His hand reached up, and his knuckles skimmed over her cheek. "I don't want any bad part of me to ever touch you."

Her head turned. Her lips brushed over his hand.

Declan pulled his hand back. Fisted his fingers. "But there is so much bad in me."

"Stop seeing yourself that way. You are *not* bad."

A faint smile twisted his lips.

The twisting in her gut got worse. "Is your brother a suspect? In your mind, could Royal be guilty? I mean, he arrives in town and then your assistant—who we both believe was sharing intel with the perp after you—suddenly vanishes. That's a coincidence." *But, apparently, Parker is in town, too.*

At this point, who isn't in Chicago?

"Why would Royal want me dead?"

She could think of several million—possibly billion—reasons. "A long-lost brother might want your fortune."

"He doesn't give a shit about that. Besides, I've already set up the legal paperwork so that he gets half of everything no matter what. Whether he wants it or not, it's going to him. Once the paperwork is signed and the deal is sealed, he can give all the cash to charity if he wants. But it's going to him." A vow.

That news sent a little hum through her. "Did your

assistant know that you were giving your brother half of everything?"

"Yes."

"And Royal...you met him over a dead body, so I'm taking that to mean the man clearly has no qualms about killing."

"Royal killed to protect himself and the woman he loved. I completely understand that action." A roll of one shoulder. "Someone hurts you, and you can damn well bet they'll be getting a swift trip to hell."

That was dark. And intense. And very Declan. Maybe he thought the words would give her pause. They did not. "Someone hurts you," she returned, not missing a beat at all, "and I'll make sure they take that same trip."

He blinked. Then... "Marley..."

She waited for him to say something profound. Maybe emotional. A woman could hope.

His phone rang. He yanked it from the pocket of his fancy suit coat. A dark blue one today. Declan stared at the phone's screen. "It's Hunter." His fingers swiped over the surface. Turned the call on speaker.

Great. She wanted to hear this.

"Do you have news?" Declan demanded by way of greeting.

"Oh, I have news—I've got a fucking body."

She sucked in a breath.

"Bullet to the brain and bullet to the heart. Looks like our perp is definitely in town and eliminating loose ends."

"Where are you?" Declan wanted to know.

Marley would like to know that important fact, too.

"Conference room. Floor right below you. Pierre is spread out on the table. Guess he had one final, big meeting, huh?"

Was that supposed to be funny? It wasn't.

"Security cameras are offline for this floor," Hunter added. His voice had roughened. "That's how I knew to look on this level first. Apparently, security glitched a lot last night. Back on in most places pretty quickly, but not where I found Pierre." A rough exhale. "The bastard was right here. For all we know, he could have left some surprises around the building. Be damn careful. More than that...how about you get your ass out? As in...*now*." A sharp order.

Declan grabbed Marley's hand. He hauled her toward the door. Yanked it open.

"Surprises?" Fear flashed through her. "Where would he put surprises?" *What kind of surprises?* But a terrible, numbing thought rushed through her. *A bomb. He could have left a bomb in the building. Then waited for Declan to appear so that he could set it off.* Her gaze jerked to Pierre's desk. To the locked drawers. Why had the drawers been locked? "Declan?"

He slammed his hand into the elevator button. Hauled her in front of him. Shielded her with his body. "Hurry, fucking hurry," he bit out.

"Declan..." Marley stared into his eyes. "You think it's a bomb?"

The elevator dinged.

She jerked.

Declan shoved her into the elevator. He rushed in after her. His hand slammed into the control panel. He used his access code and then he grabbed her and curled his body against hers. He held her tightly in his arms. Tight as can be.

"Declan, I love you," she whispered.

And then she heard the terrible boom that seemed to echo all around her.

Chapter Eighteen

*D*ECLAN, *I* LOVE YOU.

Chaos. That was what he had. The entire building had been evacuated. Firefighters and the bomb squad and more cops than Declan could count filled the scene. Most of the street had been roped off. Security had locked everything down. *After* assuring that all personnel had safely exited his building.

And everyone was safe. No injuries. Except, of course, for the dead assistant. Pierre LaRene. The guy who had fallen on the conference room table after taking a bullet to the brain and one to the heart. According to Hunter, there had been one hell of a blood spatter scene to tell the story of what had happened.

The crime scene team wasn't actually even in the building yet. The bomb squad hadn't given the all-clear for them. Instead, the bomb squad had their dogs in the building. Sensors. All kinds of equipment. There was a whole lot of space to search. Too many floors. Too many places to hide explosive devices.

The structural integrity of the building would need to

be checked. Declan didn't want any risks taken with the people who worked in the high-rise. Already, though, he knew that most of the damage was restricted just to the top floor. The blast had taken out Pierre's work area. And the majority of Declan's office. One of the bomb guys had told him that the device had been positioned so that the bulk of the explosion would shoot straight toward Declan's office.

"Why didn't he just plant the device *in* your office?" Marley suddenly asked.

They were in the limo. Down the street and in the designated safe zone. Watching the chaos unfold. He hadn't yet told Andy to get them the hell out of there because Declan had been waiting, hesitating because he'd hoped there would be more news.

Cade had rushed to the scene as soon as he'd learned what happened. After checking in with Declan, he'd gone to grill some of the cops. And the bomb squad members. Certain individuals in those groups owed Declan. They would tell Cade as much as they could.

Maybe they'll give me something to track the bastard.

Meanwhile, Hunter was gathering his intel from his own contacts.

"Declan?" Marley touched his hand.

"My office has extra security. I always activate it when I leave." He could activate the system from his phone. A bit of tech he'd created. "Full camera surveillance and additional locking mechanisms on the door. No one gets in the office when I'm not there." So the SOB had just done the next best thing...

He'd gotten into Declan's assistant's office space.

"I'm guessing you have checks running on every security camera in the building?" Marley wanted to know.

Yeah, he did. "I already know that Pierre deactivated

some of the systems last night." Particularly on the floor where the bastard had died. "Cade is working to pull up footage from the stairwells and the elevators now."

Speaking of Cade...he was jogging toward the limo. Andy stood guard on the side of the vehicle, but he opened the door immediately for Cade. Cade ducked in. Slid into the seat across from Declan. Grimacing, he announced, "You chose wisely."

Declan frowned at him.

"Could have been the elevator or the stairs, am I right?" A nod from Cade. Also, a long exhale. A heavy expulsion of air that seemed too loud in the quiet limo. "You realize there is a bomb. Maybe *bombs* planted to kill you. You have seconds to figure out how the hell to get out with your lady." A wave toward Marley. "What do you do? Elevator or stairs? Usually, when there is a fire, you're told to never use the elevator. To always take the stairs."

What was the point of this ramble? "There wasn't a fire."

Cade grimaced once more. "There's a fire now. It's still smoking. The sky is black, and every news crew imaginable is just past the barricade point."

Yes, Declan was aware.

"Some people would have gone for the stairs. I think that's what he expected you to do." Cade held his gaze. "And when you opened the stairwell door, you would have set off another explosion. The perp was prepared. He thought that was how you'd flee, but you didn't. The bomb squad just found the device he'd left in the stairwell for you."

Declan felt a knife stab into his chest.

"If you don't mind me asking, boss, why did you choose the elevator?"

"Because it was right there. Because I wanted Marley behind the doors—I wanted to get her down and out of that place, and if I could do nothing else, I was just going to throw her inside so..." He stopped. *I was going to throw her inside. Seal her in. Make sure she was safe even if the blast hit me.* Rapid, churning thoughts. "Fuck it, I wasn't thinking clearly." Gruff. Rough. "I just wanted her out. My damn mind shut off."

We're lucky to be alive. A wrong choice would have killed her.

His head swung toward her. All logic had fled. He'd just wanted to get out. To get her to safety. He'd fucking panicked, and they were lucky as all hell.

Declan, I love you.

Had she really said those words? Or had he imagined them before the blast? When he'd felt the boom, he'd been terrified that the cables holding the elevator would snap. He'd pictured them plunging down, and Marley screaming.

Marley dying.

No. That would not happen. It could not happen.

"Yeah, well, good, panicked choice." Cade exhaled. A much lighter exhale this time. His hand reached up and rubbed the back of his neck. "Why do I have the feeling that shit is going down that I don't know about? Can't help but get the impression I'm in the dark and more is at play."

Because you're on my suspect list. You're on Marley's, too. How much do you hate me, Cade? "I know what happened." Flat. Seemed like the best way to get it out in the open. "I know why you started working for me."

Cade's hand dropped to his lap. His expression—normally warm, open—hardened in an instant. "*I* don't know what you mean, boss."

Yes, you do. "Collateral damage." It was everywhere he

turned. "Your parents were informants, Cade. They turned on my dad. Before they could testify to the Feds, they were killed." More bloodshed that went back to Conor Flynn.

Cade swallowed. "Bullet to the head and a bullet to the heart."

"OhmyGod." From Marley. She grabbed Declan's hand. "Seriously, you *knew* this, and you kept Cade close? You had him watching your back?" Her hold tightened on him. "Declan, what—*why?*"

Cade's mouth twisted into a half-smile. His gaze never left Declan's face. "I wanted to destroy you."

"*Not* going to happen," Marley retorted. "Don't you even think about it."

Ah, but he knew Cade had done more than just *think it.* Time to bring all his enemies out into the open. That bomb explosion had rushed his timeline. No more playing.

The limo door opened again. This time, Hunter slipped inside. Declan had seen Hunter approaching through the tinted window. Once Hunter was in, Andy closed the door behind him.

Hunter glanced at a tense Cade, and then, with no hesitation at all, Hunter pulled out his gun.

"*What is happening?*" Marley demanded. She surged forward.

Gently, firmly, Declan pushed her back against the seat. "I'm facing the past, sweetheart. Time for a reckoning."

"I hate reckonings," she whispered. "I think they really, really suck."

Yeah, well, Cade was on your suspect list, too. This reckoning has to happen.

"Don't mind me. I'm just making sure things don't get out of hand," Hunter announced to the group. "Uh, Declan,

I thought the plan was to *wait* until I was with you for this chat?"

"Saw you coming. Knew you'd jump right in the car."

"Yeah, well, it wouldn't have killed you to *wait* just a few more minutes." Hunter had his weapon pointed right at Cade.

"Are you shitting me right now?" Cade blasted at Hunter. "You have your gun on me? We are *friends*. I let you use my season tickets for the Bears!"

"So does Declan. He lets me use his tickets all the time." Hunter raised one eyebrow. "And he has box seats."

"Fuck." Cade's lashes flickered. "So what's the consensus? I'm evil, and I'm about to be driven away—while dozens of cops watch—just so I wind up with two bullets in me, *exactly like my parents?*" Rage infused his voice.

"I'm sorry for what happened to your parents." Declan meant that. He was damn sorry. "My father was a twisted bastard, and he let no enemies escape his wrath."

Cade wet his lips. "I used to think you were exactly like him."

"Many people think I am." The charge hardly surprised him. But it did piss him off. *I am not my father.*

"You *aren't* him." Fierce. From Marley. "Declan, stop playing the devil. You're not an angel, but you don't belong in hell, either."

He was far, far from an angel. And he'd been living in hell for a very long time.

"You paid for my college," Cade suddenly said. "Bought my older sister a new home, too. Took me ages to figure that shit out. To figure out how we went from having absolutely nothing one day to her almost winning the lottery and having money to get my niece the treatment she needed for her cancer. Luann—she'd raised me when my parents died.

She was eighteen, and she took over the care of a ten-year-old brat with way too many anger issues. We struggled and fought to survive...and in a blink, everything became easy." His chest rose and fell. "Nothing in this world is supposed to be easy, but suddenly, life was. We had all the food we could eat. New cars. It was all too good to be true."

I was trying to fix what my father had broken.

"Then I started digging, tearing through all the BS red tape and bureaucracy crap out there, and I realized it was you. You'd made your company into a success. You were paying all of our debts. You were helping my sister and her kid and you...fuck, I *hated* you. You were barely older than me, and you were doing that shit like it was nothing. Shoving blood money at us to wipe away your sins."

"Declan *earned* that money," Marley fired at him. "His dad left him with nothing but heartache and ashes, so don't you tell him that—"

"I *know*." Cade lifted his hands. His palms faced Declan and Marley. "Ease up on me. I realized that shit fast, okay? My niece got better. I quit college and joined the SEALs because I needed to do *something*. I was twisting in rage, and I was lost. I'd dragged my sister down for too long. It was time to stand on my own, and I did. But I saw things in my service...did things..." A swallow. "Life isn't black and white. And fucking *Declan Flynn* provided tech that helped my team, again and again. I saw you in hotspots, Declan. *I saw you.* You were in places where some rich prick should never have been." A shake of his head. "Why the hell were you over there? Why not stay in some safe high-rise far away from danger?"

Declan felt his own lips curl in a humorless smile. "High-rises aren't nearly as safe as you might believe."

A sharp bark of laughter came from Cade. "You crazy

sonofabitch." A shake of his head. "I wanted to hate you. I *did* hate you for so long. Then I got out, and I got a job at your company. Didn't think you knew who I was, but you did, didn't you? All along?"

"Yes, all along."

"Declan." Marley's low murmur. "We seriously are going to have a talk about hiring people who want to kill you. It is not good form. Your HR team needs an overhaul."

"I don't." A quick denial from Cade. His gaze was straight on Declan. "I don't want to kill you. You're not your father. Thank Christ. But your PI is right about one thing, though. You're no angel. You will never be a saint, either. But you're not the devil. I've seen the things you do. When you think no one is watching. I know you try to fix the chaos that your father left behind. And you try to stop the evil out there. Probably because you know personally just how fucked some monsters truly are. We can't let them keep attacking the innocent, can we?"

This time, Declan was the one to shake his head.

"What does that mean?" Marley whispered.

It means you are going to learn that I have more than a few bodies shoved in the ground.

"I'm not your enemy. I don't want you dead. Fuck me, but I think of you as my friend, Declan." Cade slanted a glance at Hunter. "You, too, asshole. Even though you're pointing a gun at me, I still think you're my friend. And with friends like you two pricks, why the hell do I need enemies?"

Silence. Tension.

"If I wanted Declan dead," Cade continued as his shoulders thrust back, "I've had plenty of opportunities. That's not what I want." His stare returned to Declan. "I'm not behind the attacks. But I do have some news for you about who might be."

"Don't keep us in suspense," Marley muttered. "Share with the group."

"I like her," Cade said. Then he clarified, "Most days." He scraped a hand over his jaw. "I talked to the lead guard on the lobby level. Called him at his house. I wanted to know if he'd seen anyone who didn't belong around here last night. He said a police detective was here. Wanting entrance to the building a little after ten p.m. Guy flashed his badge. Tried to act like he was on official business, but Fitz isn't a fool. He also knows he'd get his ass fired if he ever let cops stroll through your building without a warrant."

"Who was the cop?" Declan asked. But, come on, he already knew. It had to be—

"Parker Ellis," Cade revealed. "Fitz told me he knew some cop from Georgia didn't have jurisdiction here. He told the cop no way was he getting in without a warrant. He thought the cop left." Cade's eyes glinted. "I'm figuring he just found another way inside."

Parker has a motive. He has the skills to do the hits. And he was from Augusta. Now, the prick is in my town, and he was at my building last night. The evidence seemed to be piling up against Parker.

I also just don't like the bastard because he's stuck on Marley.

"Want me to hunt him down?" Cade asked. "I do enjoy that kind of work."

Yeah, he knew that Cade did. Tracking was his specialty. "Find him," Declan ordered. "Bring him to my house. It's time for a long one-on-one chat with the detective."

"Is 'chat' another way of saying we're putting him in the ground?" The question came from Hunter. "Because I like to plan out my full day in advance. And so far, this day is *not* going according to any plan I had."

It wasn't going according to Declan's plan, either. Nearly getting blown into a thousand bits hadn't been on the agenda. "Bring him to my house," Declan repeated. "Go together," he told Hunter and Cade with a wave of his left hand. "Track him. Find him. Secure him. I don't want the guy in the wind. Eyes *were* supposed to be on him." Anger seethed in his words. "Somehow those eyes lost him when he hit Chicago." A point he hadn't been able to mention to Marley until now.

"Uh, you had eyes on him?" Cade frowned. A furrow appeared between his brows. "Why didn't you give that job to me? You know that when it comes to stalking, there is no one better."

Yes, normally, that would have been Cade's job but... "I thought you might be a murdering SOB who wanted me dead. So I had to give the job to someone else in security."

Cade straightened. "And am I still on the suspect list?"

Yeah, you are. But... "Don't know why you'd wait so long for your vengeance if you wanted me dead. You could have killed me on day one. I gave you the opportunity. Met you alone in my office. Was unarmed. It was after hours." He ticked off all the pertinent details for that initial meeting. "You could have blown a bullet into my brain and walked out."

Cade seemed to pale. "Always wondered a bit about that meeting. Thought it might have been a test. That you had someone hiding close by. I was afraid you knew who I was—I mean, afraid you knew about my past."

"I did know."

"And you hired me anyway."

Yes.

Cade's lashes flickered. "I did things during my SEAL days that haunt me. Like I told you, I know the world isn't black and white. I also know what it's like to be right next to evil. Real evil." His stare cut to Marley. "You know, too, don't you?"

She nodded.

His gaze swept back to Declan. "Killing you isn't on *my* agenda. I don't think it ever was. But sure as shit not once you became one of the closest friends I've ever had." Emotion boiled in his voice. "I would not hurt you. But I would fucking kill someone who tried to take you out. Believe *that*."

Declan wanted to believe him. He also *did* believe that Cade wouldn't casually take out innocents. And the blast in that building? It had been too uncontrolled. Others could have been hurt. Cade wasn't the type of man who would allow collateral damage. Would he take out his enemy? In a heartbeat. But he wouldn't let an innocent die. He would never risk innocents.

"So, I still have a job, right? Assuming I do, since you want me to go with Hunter to find our missing Augusta detective."

"You still have a job."

"Great." A tiger's smile. "And, Hunter, good buddy, how about you move that gun so it doesn't keep pointing at me? Not that I think you'll get twitchy with the trigger, but friends don't point guns at friends."

Declan inclined his head.

Hunter holstered his weapon. "Nothing personal."

"Oh, I am sure it wasn't," Cade agreed. "Not personal at all."

"Just couldn't have you killing the boss. I like my paycheck."

Cade grunted. "You think I don't know he saved your ass? Try that shit with someone else. I know Declan was on the ground with your unit. Taking care of classified tech and drones and who the hell knows what else. He should have been a million miles away." Cade's brows rose as he studied Declan. "But you like to get your hands dirty, don't you? I know all about how you picked up chatter about the attack on Hunter. How you took a damn Jeep, hauled ass, and got him to safety. I also know that he'd probably murder in cold blood for you without hesitation because you saved his life. You can't buy loyalty like that. That's just not how it works." He flicked his fingers toward Marley. "And don't even get me started on her..."

Declan stiffened. "Yes, don't even *think* of getting started on her."

But Cade was studying Marley. A Marley who had gone uncharacteristically quiet. "Declan would murder for *you* with no hesitation," Cade told her. "What would you do for him?"

Declan opened his mouth.

"Whatever needed doing," Marley replied coolly. "And if you betray him, I'll make sure you regret that unfortunate life choice."

"Seriously, I can like you so much sometimes." He flashed a smile toward her. Then grabbed for the limo's door. "Come on, Hunter. Let's go track down that sketchy detective."

Cade and Hunter exited the vehicle. When they were clear, Andy ducked his head inside. "Are you ready to leave? Or do you need to speak with the investigators more?"

"Get us the hell out of here," Declan said.

A curt nod. Andy shut the door with a soft click.

"Marley, I—" he began.

His phone rang.

She quirked a dark brow. "Better get that. The way your life is *exploding*, it could be life or death."

He'd already yanked out the phone to peer at the screen. Royal. Hell. He put the phone to his ear. "I suspect the coverage is far worse than it looks."

"You sure about that?" Came his brother's dry reply. "Because where I'm standing—about ten feet from your limo, by the way—it looks like a clusterfuck. The sky is black, and I'm pretty sure someone just tried to blow you straight to hell."

Royal would not be wrong about that situation.

"No injuries?" Royal queried. "You and your PI good?"

Declan turned his head and found Marley's dark eyes on him.

I love you, Declan.

He swallowed. "We got out in time."

"How near of a thing was it?" Royal pushed. Tension bit through the words.

"You sound like you care. Touching. Really."

"*How. Damn. Near. Was it?*"

His grip tightened on the phone. "Pretty much as close as you can get." *And if I'd tried to flee via the stairwell, we wouldn't be having this conversation.*

"Heard there was a dead body inside the building." Low. Careful. More controlled. "Glad to know it wasn't you."

"Again, there you go—sounding like you care."

"Because I do. Don't get that fool ass of yours blown to

hell. Told you already, I don't want your cash or the creepy house. So stay alive, would you? Stay the fuck alive."

The limo pulled away.

"I see that you're on the move," Royal noted. "Let's plan to meet at your place later. I've got some leads I'm running down. Bet you do, too, huh?"

"I want you out of town, Royal." Flat. He kept staring at Marley.

She nodded. Then mouthed, *good idea.*

"Excuse me?" Royal's voice hardened as it poured into Declan's ear.

"I want you to pack your bags and get the hell out of town. Now. Don't run down leads. I'll handle things. Get out. Go back to Violet. Protect yourself. When it's safe, I'll notify you."

"You mean when you've killed the bastard, you'll notify me." No judgment. "Don't you get that eliminating murderous SOBs is literally my main skill set? I'm happy to do the grunt work on this for you."

Yes, he knew all about Royal's...hobbies. "Thought you'd given up that life."

"I can make an exception for this perp. He came after me. He came after my brother. Normal rules of engagement won't apply."

"He's mine, Royal." A vow. "Get out of town. Get back to Violet."

"Beau has Violet under careful watch. She's safe. *Always.*"

"Then go back to Beau." Royal's brother not of blood, but of choice. Beau was not a good man—not even *close* to good. But Beau was a man who would do anything for Royal. "I'll end this."

Royal laughed. "It's cute the way you think I'll do what you say. Nice try, *bro*. See you soon." He hung up.

Sonofabitch. Declan shoved the phone back into his pocket.

"Like...do the secrets you keep choke you? Because there are so many of them." Marley gripped her phone in her hand. He realized that she'd been holding it...

How long had she been holding it? He tried to replay the scene in his mind. He couldn't remember when Marley had pulled out her phone. *What is she using the phone for? Not to call someone. But to...shit. Shit. To search for info?*

Marley had gone silent while he talked to Cade. She'd gone silent because...

He tried to see her phone's screen.

"There's some news out of Georgia," Marley noted. Her voice broke a little on *Georgia*. "Sebastian Glass is dead. He got caught in a riot—he should never have been with general pop, *never*. But there was some sort of glitch. A *computer glitch* of all things. And his guards got orders to take him out and he..." She sucked in a deep breath. "He was killed. Stabbed with a shiv."

That's called fucking justice.

"Declan...what did you do?" Horror filled her eyes. Shock.

And he realized that, finally, Marley was seeing him for exactly who and what he was.

Chapter Nineteen

SEBASTIAN GLASS IS DEAD. THE MONSTER FROM MY PAST *is gone. Killed in a prison riot. Stabbed with a shiv.*

Stabbed...the exact same number of times that he'd sliced her with his shiv so long ago.

They were back at Declan's home. Behind the security guards and the massive gates and all the tech that he had to protect them. Declan and his tech. She was beginning to realize the tech was like a spider web that he'd spread out into the world. It let him do almost anything. Reach anyone.

Destroy anyone.

They hadn't spoken again during the limo ride. Not since she'd asked her question. *Declan...what did you do?* He'd just stared back at her, and she'd known the truth. *Declan did it. He arranged to have Sebastian Glass killed.*

The house felt cavernous and cold as she made her way across the marble floor in the foyer. She knew at once that he'd arranged for all staff members to be away. The better for them to talk in private about the little matter of a murder.

The murder of a man who'd spent his life terrorizing

others. The man who'd given her nightmares for years. Who'd nearly killed her.

Sebastian Glass.

And he was...dead.

She heard Declan's steps behind her, but didn't turn around. There was no need to turn around. Everywhere she looked, she saw Declan. *We had sex right here. And he carried me up the stairs and he...*

With a burst of speed, she entered the den. The lights were on. To the right, heavy, dark curtains blocked the French doors that opened onto a stone terrace that led to a garden—a garden she'd strolled in during the week when Declan had sidelined her. She'd expected the garden to be perfectly maintained. Filled with the most perfect of things but...

It had been overgrown. Unkept.

Cold and sad as if...*was this your mother's garden, Declan? Did it die without her? Like I fear a part of you died?*

She hadn't gotten the chance to question him about the garden. There had been far too many other questions to ask.

The coldness lingered inside. And then she realized that maybe it wasn't the house that was cold. Maybe it was her. Chill bumps covered her arms. *The cold is inside of me.*

"You're afraid of me." The first words he'd spoken.

She whirled around in a fury. "You killed him." Not a question. A statement.

His hands were shoved into the pockets of his expensive suit coat. Declan looked like he was posing for some business or tech magazine. The perfect executive. Handsome. Controlled.

And you killed Sebastian Glass.

"I believe another inmate is responsible for stabbing

Sebastian Glass. From what I can gather, Glass was swarmed by people who weren't—well, who weren't fans, shall we say?"

"Declan."

His chin lifted. "Marley."

"You did this."

He stared at her. She waited for a denial. She waited for something that would tell her—

A shrug. "He was dead the minute I learned about what he'd done to you."

Marley shook her head.

But he nodded. "He terrorized you. Stole your joy and replaced it with fear. You were still afraid when you said his name. I could hear the fear in your voice. You were afraid of him. Even though he was behind bars, you feared he'd come for you again."

How many nights had she woken up, choking on a scream, because she feared that Sebastian had gotten to her? How many times had Eb or Jake run to her and promised her that she was safe?

Only she'd never really felt safe because Sebastian Glass was still out there. Still alive and...

And there were whispers that deals were going to be made with him. A new attorney general who wanted to find the missing victims. A man sentenced to death, but talk of changing his sentence—something that should have been impossible, and there were rumors of letting him—

"He raped and murdered his victims. He attacked you, Marley. As far as I'm concerned, his death was too easy."

Her breath shuddered in and out. "How did you do it?"

"This will never be traced back to me. It can't be. It was a prison riot. How could I possibly be responsible for such an event?"

"Declan." She stormed toward him. Stood toe to toe with him as she tipped back her head and stared at his dark, dangerous features. "How did you do it?"

Everyone else had been sent from the house for a reason. She knew it. So that Declan could tell her his secrets.

"Sometimes, you just have to arrange a situation. Predict the behavior of others. Glass was hated by the other inmates. Everyone doing max time wanted the bragging rights to say they'd offed *Broken Glass,* as you called him. It was about creating the right moment. A technical glitch indicated that Glass should be out in the yard at a certain time. The guards simply followed the orders on their screens."

The chill bumps got bigger. The cold deeper. Technical glitch, her ass. "I'm guessing your tech is used in the prison."

"Your guess would be correct."

"Declan." She couldn't think what to say beyond that. "*Declan.*"

"He left marks on you, Marley. He killed all those other women. Are you truly going to mourn for him?"

No. She wasn't. She just—

"Right and wrong. James told me that he thought the line between those two was particularly thin for me. He's right. Because when it comes to eliminating a bastard who hurt you, putting him in the ground was the *right* thing for me."

She stared up at him. Marley didn't know what to say. Or do.

"I did try to warn you," Declan rasped. "Understand me now?"

Her breath came in and out. Not deep. Too shallow and fast.

"It's not the first time I've destroyed a life with the click of a few keys on the computer." His wooden voice was back. The unemotional one. And his gaze had gone unblinking. "I discovered that talent long ago. My father had other methods for eliminating enemies in his world. My father would have been ever so disappointed with my tactics. Bankrupting someone with the tap, tap, tap of my keys as I slide into their accounts. Setting up meetings that prove the SOBs are smuggling guns and trafficking women and children—getting the fools to talk straight with cops when then they think are talking to other dealers. It's all so easy, really. I can destroy a life and never even break a sweat."

Her breathing was shallow, but each beat of her heart echoed in her head like thunder. "That's what you do? Work with cops to put away criminals? That hardly seems so bad."

His hand lifted. He brushed back a lock of her hair. "Oh, sweetheart, I am the criminal, and we both know it."

They knew—

"*You sonofabitch.*" A shadow surged from behind the heavy, billowing curtains to the right—the curtains that blocked the terrace doors. In that desperate instant, she finally realized that the terrible chill in the air? The chill wasn't just from her fear. *A door was open.* Someone else had been using the garden terrace—using it to gain entrance to the house.

The intruder lifted a gun and pointed it—

Declan jumped in front of Marley. He shoved her behind him.

"*I knew you were guilty as fuck!*" A bellow from the intruder. "And I just heard your confession. Heard every damn word! You're going to jail, you bastard."

She knew the voice—knew the shadow. Detective

Parker Ellis. He'd gotten into Declan's home, and he was aiming his gun at Declan. "No!" Marley screamed.

"*Yes!*" Parker shouted right back. "He's dirty, Marley. As fucking dirty as they come—you *heard* what he did! How many times do you think he's tapped with his tech and ended lives? Snuffed out people like they were *nothing?* Just like his father! He's just like his father!"

She tried to surge forward. Declan shoved her back once more and—

Boom.

She screamed at the explosion of sound. Screamed because she thought Declan had been hit and his blood would cover her, and she'd lose him, and she didn't *care* about Glass or—or—

"Stay the fuck behind me, Marley," Declan rasped.

He...he hadn't been shot. He was still on his feet.

And still using his body to shield her.

But she peeked around him, and she saw that Parker was weaving on his feet. He had his gun in his hand and a mixture of shock and horror and pain covered his face. "How..." Parker's knees hit the floor.

"He set off the alarm the minute he entered the terrace door." James's voice. And James was striding into the den with a gun in hand. A gun he'd *fired* at Parker because she could see the blood on Parker's chest now. The deep bloom of red that spread too fast. "As soon as I got the alert, I came at once from the guest house. The cop's gone rogue, just like I warned you, Declan. He wanted you dead because of what your father did to his family."

"Marley..." Parker still had his grip on the gun. He waved it toward her and Declan. "H-help me..."

"Get the fuck behind the couch," Declan growled at her. "No, get the fuck *out* of here," he corrected. Then he was lunging forward. Rushing straight to Parker. "I didn't get a security alert."

"Maybe it was a glitch. Those do happen, I hear." An odd note had entered James's voice. "Don't worry. I'll end him," James promised. "I must have missed his heart. That's not like me. Let's try again—"

"No!" Marley yelled.

"No." A snarl from Declan as he—as he put his body in front of Parker's. "You're not killing a cop in cold blood."

James frowned at him. "But...he was going to shoot you, son! There is no *cold blood* about this. I just saved your life!" His breath heaved in and out. "We have to finish him."

Marley inched toward the couch. *Declan wants me to get the fuck out of here, but I—*

"Call nine-one..." A gasp tore from Parker. "Call—"

"No one is calling nine-one-one." James was definite. His gun was pointed at Declan.

A Declan who seemed to be the only thing between Parker and death. "You can't do this!" Marley cried out. "He's a cop! This is all a misunderstanding. Parker can't die!"

James shook his head. "Didn't I warn you about her, too, Declan? I told you that she was talking too much with the cop. I bet she told him to come here. Bet she promised him that they could get a confession from you."

Declan's gaze darted toward her. She could not read his gaze to save her life.

"No." Marley shook her head. She hadn't tried to set up Declan. Wouldn't.

"You can't trust her! I told you, over and over. I warned you. She probably *wanted* you to kill Glass just so she could get the confession—she and Parker are working to take you down. But I'm here to protect you. I'm the only one you can count on."

Marley thought that she'd been cold in that den before. She'd been wrong. Absolute ice seemed to pour from her veins as Declan stood with James's gun pointed at him...and a weak Parker still holding a gun behind him.

Either man can shoot Declan at any moment.

She stopped inching toward the couch. Screw that. She took a step toward Declan.

"Don't." A snarl from him. "Get the fuck out, Marley."

Her eyes widened.

"I don't want you here. You betrayed me, and we're done. Get out, *now*."

No, he didn't mean that. "Declan?"

"Go," he gritted. "*Go now*." And emotion...emotion broke through those words. The faintest hint of...fear.

Her eyes widened. She started to run.

And James's gun swung to point toward her.

Marley froze.

Hate glittered in James's eyes. "Dammit, Declan, I knew you were getting emotionally involved with her. The man who pretends he doesn't feel. Utter bullshit. You fell for her just like your father fell for your mother. Guess you could each love one thing in this world, huh?" He sent Marley a small smile. "You aren't going anywhere. Because if you leave this room, you'll just call for help. That's not the way things are going to end. You don't call in the cavalry. You don't get to save the day again for him, PI."

She put her hands up. It seemed like the right thing to do. To show she wasn't a threat. To try and calm James down. "You don't need to point that gun at me. I'm not armed."

"Come here, Marley," James ordered.

She didn't move a step.

"Come here, or I will shoot you in the heart right here and now."

"*No!*" A roar from Declan.

Marley sucked in a sharp breath.

But James smiled. He *smiled*, and she knew that he was going to pull the trigger, whether she came to him or not and she—

"You obsessed him, just like she obsessed his father. I killed her, and I'll kill you, too." His smile widened even more as he began to pull the trigger.

She tried to leap to the side. To just get out of the way even as her heart raced in her chest, and the thunder was so loud and wild, and it wouldn't stop and she—

Declan slammed into her even as the gun erupted with a blast of thunder far louder than her heartbeat. She hit the hard floor, the impact jarring her body, but it was just bruising. Aches. She hadn't been shot. She was safe.

Declan's head lifted. He stared down at her with eyes that blazed with his emotions. "*Get the fuck...out of here.*"

"I love you, too," she threw back.

His eyes widened. But then he was rising. Rising and whirling and he had a gun in his hand. Where the hell had he gotten that?

Her frantic gaze jumped across the room. Parker was slumped on the floor, his gun missing from his outstretched hand.

So that's where Declan got the gun.

James laughed as Declan faced off with him. Marley inched away. The last thing she wanted to do was distract Declan or present a target for James. She needed a gun of her own. Some sort of weapon. And she also needed some help.

Her fingers pulled out her phone. She had Hunter and Cade programmed into her phone, so she sent out a desperate text to them. *James is the bad guy. Get your asses here. Hurry!*

"You don't have the killer instinct, son," James said. He laughed. "You type out commands on a keyboard, but that shit is nothing like pulling a trigger and seeing the life fade from a person's eyes. That calls for a special kind of darkness. You're too weak for that. Your father always told me you were weak. He tried to beat that weakness out of you and he—"

The bullet blasted from Declan's hand and slammed into James's right shoulder. James howled in pain even as the gun fell from his fingers.

"He did beat out the weakness." Declan took a slow step forward. "I stopped being weak the day I killed him. You think he was the only one? You have no idea what I've done or where I've been. Hunter could tell you stories about our times in hellholes that would chill your soul." Another step. "Government contracts are given to me for a reason. Because I get shit done."

James was frantically trying to staunch the flow of blood that poured like a river down his arm.

"You always thought you knew me, but you didn't know jack. You abandoned me when I was a kid. Came back when you thought you could position yourself to get money. And that's what this is all about, isn't it?" Declan stood about two feet in front of James. "You decided to kill me when you realized I was leaving half my fortune to Royal. Pierre told you, didn't he? You were paying him to keep tabs on all my business, personal and professional."

Marley kept the two men within sight as she crept toward Parker, using the furniture to shield her body as much as possible. Was he still alive? He was face down, with his right hand in front of his body, and he didn't seem to be moving at all.

"That little shit brother of yours should have died years ago!" James raged. "Your mom wouldn't tell me where she'd stashed him. Not when I put my gun to her heart. She just stared straight at me...and she said I was as bad as Conor was. Can you believe that? I was just doing my job! He'd sent me after her when she ran. I was following orders. I was *never* like Conor!" Spittle flew from his mouth.

Marley sucked in a breath. She knew each word had to be torture for Declan. *James killed his mother.*

She reached Parker. She bent to her knees beside him. Her fingers slid toward his neck.

I can't find his pulse.

"All she had to do was tell me where the fuck your brother was," James snarled. "I got mad. Her dying was her own damn fault."

A faint beat shivered beneath her fingers. *Alive.*

"You hear me, Declan? It was her own damn fault!"

"The hell it was." Declan's voice. Burning with fury. So much emotion.

Enough hate to kill a man.

Chapter Twenty

"YOUR MOM WOULDN'T TELL ME WHERE SHE'D STASHED *him. Not when I put my gun to her heart. She just stared straight at me...and she said I was as bad as Conor was. Can you believe that?"*

Those words blasted through Declan's head as he stared at James. The man who'd stepped in to be his surrogate father. The man who'd sworn he'd never abandon Declan again. The man who'd been at his side, day in and day out.

"All she had to do was tell me where the fuck your brother was. I got mad. Her dying was her own damn fault."

Flames burned inside of Declan's body. So much hate. So much rage.

"I was never like your twisted prick of a father." James glared at Declan. Blood poured from his shoulder wound. Declan hadn't been shooting to kill. If he had, the bullet would have gone straight into James's heart.

My father taught me how to shoot perfectly long ago. A necessary requirement for Conor Flynn's son.

And, apparently, being a good shot had been a necessary requirement for Conor Flynn's stepbrother, too.

"When he hired me, I seriously thought I was going to be handling PR." James shook his head. His blood kept flowing. "Schmoozing with clients. And then, two weeks in, he has me meet him at some rundown warehouse. I'm thinking, okay, maybe we're doing some acquisitions. No, *no*. That prick had a guy in there that he *tortured*. Right in front of me." The words came out feverishly. "Your dad had goons. They tied the man up. They broke this prick's fingers. Hell, they used pliers to completely rip off a finger. The guy was screaming and begging and...he told your dad every damn thing he wanted to know in record time."

Declan's gun was dead steady on James. "You got a taste for torture that night, didn't you?"

"What? No." A fast, negative shake of his head. "I did not—"

"Yes, you did." From Marley.

Sonofabitch. Hadn't he told the woman to leave? If he was going to shoot his best-friend-slash-father-figure in the face, he'd rather she not see him commit the deed.

And I am going to kill him. James is not walking out of this house alive.

"You liked the power you got, didn't you, James?" She knelt beside Parker, with her hand on his throat. Parker didn't seem to be moving.

Apparently, James hadn't missed with his shot.

One to the heart and one to the head. Conor Flynn's preferred execution style. The way most of his enemies had been taken out over the years. But his father certainly wasn't the only one who enjoyed that style of death. It was a typical mob hit.

Marley wasn't wrong about my family's ties to the mob. I tried to sever them, but there are some sins that will haunt you forever.

"Did you help that night?" Marley asked. "Did you join in and torture that man so long ago?"

James was staring—no, glaring at her.

"Did Conor Flynn *make* you help?" Marley amended.

"Yes," James hissed. "And I fucking vomited when they started cutting that SOB open but...he was begging and screaming and..."

"And did you like the sounds?" Marley's careful question.

James smiled. It was a smile that Declan had never seen before on his old friend. James's eyes seemed to shine with a bright light, and his face held absolute joy. "I liked it better when he stopped breathing entirely."

"There it is," Marley said. Her hand pulled away from Parker's throat. She inched back. "I've seen that look before. Another man, another place. Some people are just really, really good at wearing masks, but even the best masks will eventually fall away to show what's inside."

James's smile dimmed. "What in the hell are you talking about?"

"Evil," she responded simply. "I see it in you. On you."

So did Declan. Why hadn't he seen it before? Because James had been good at wearing his mask? Or because...

Because I didn't want to see it?

"Did you become one of Conor Flynn's hitmen?" Marley asked as she rose to her feet. "Torture and death. Is that the kind of work you did for him?"

James licked his lips. "It was more fun than PR."

Declan knew he was staring at a dead man. And he *would* be pulling the trigger to end James's life. But he wanted answers first. He needed them. His brother needed them. "My father told you to kill my mother."

Laughter burst from James. He took a step to the side. A step that put him closer to Marley.

"Stop," Declan warned.

"You aren't going to kill me." James wagged his left index finger at Declan. His right arm was totally limp against his body and soaked with blood. "You can't. I know the truth about your mother and father, and if I die, that big mystery will never be solved. The mystery that has haunted you for your whole fucking life." Another wag of that thick finger. "If you wanted to kill me, the first shot would have done it. You didn't. You just don't have the taste for—"

Declan fired.

This time, the bullet thudded into James's right thigh. The leg gave out on him, and he slammed to his knees.

"That's an awful lot of blood," Declan noted, aware that his voice was ice cold. "Wonder if I hit an artery?"

James howled as he clamped his left hand around his thigh. Blood streamed from between his fingers.

"I believe you were telling me what happened to my mother," Declan continued politely. "Because you see, you and my father aren't the only ones who can use torture in order to get answers." He took a step toward James. Rage wanted to blind him, but he fought to hold it in check. "You kidnapped me. You tied me up in a fucking basement. You were going to torture me for hours." Another step.

James threw back his head to glare at Declan.

"I will not hesitate to do the same to you," Declan promised. "Hours." A promise. "I will spend hours giving you pain until you tell me what happened to my mother. What happened and *why*."

"Declan?" Marley's hesitant voice. "We have to get help for Parker. He's still alive..."

James smiled. A twisted smile of pain and glee. "She's

seeing you now, too. Seeing the evil that *you* hide." He huffed out a breath and kept his hand clamped to his thigh. "Tell her that you don't intend for the cop to get help. You're content to..." Another huff of breath. "To let him bleed out right in front of you. N-not like you can let him s-survive. You'll go to jail."

Declan didn't take his gaze off his prey. But from the corner of his eye, he was aware that Marley had bent next to the cop again. She struggled to roll him over. Parker's body was completely limp.

But when she did get him to turn...

"That's so much blood," Marley cried out.

Declan took another step toward James. At this point, he could almost lift his gun and press it to James's forehead. "You found out that I was leaving half the estate to Royal. You wanted everything. You wanted all my fortune, didn't you?"

"Before he came along..." Sweat trickled down James's temple. "*I* was the heir."

"Guessing I was gonna die before you did, huh? So you could inherit everything."

"You do have a lot of enemies."

The front door flew open. It thudded into the wall. Then slammed shut. A loud, echoing slam.

"*Declan!*" A wild shout.

Declan's body jerked in surprise.

"We're in here, Cade!" Marley called back. "*Hurry!* Parker has been shot, and we need help!"

Cade rushed into the den with his weapon drawn.

"A lot of enemies," James repeated. "More than you know." And the smirk was back on his lips.

Cade took in the scene in one frantic glance.

"He's dying!" Marley yelled. She'd put her hands on Parker's chest to try and stop the blood flow.

Cade rushed toward her.

"No!" Declan bellowed.

But it was too late.

Cade grabbed Marley. Wrenched her to her feet. And he shoved the nozzle of his gun into her side.

Everything shifted focus for Declan in that instant. He didn't look at Marley's face. Couldn't. If he saw the fear in her eyes, he'd lose his control. The control he'd always worked so hard to maintain. The control that had kept him sane when the world went to absolute madness around him.

Cade wasn't looking at Declan. His frantic gaze was on James as he stared in growing horror at the blood covering the older man.

"Fuck," Declan breathed as he understood just how deep the betrayal had really been. "It's always about family, isn't it?" He could see it now. In the angle of Cade's jaw. The eyes were a different color. So was the hair. But the jaw was the same. The shape of the eyes were the same...

He just hadn't *seen* it before.

"Like father, like son, am I right?" Declan mused.

"Declan?" Marley's trembling voice.

Do not look at her face. Not yet. You have to kill these two bastards and get her out alive.

He also had...dammit, he had to keep standing. A hard task because James *had* always been a good shot. And when Declan had tackled Marley earlier, the bullet meant for her —it had gone into him. Blasting into his abdomen. His suit coat covered the injury or, hell, maybe it was getting soaked with blood. The pain had been red-hot at first. Surging through his body. But now it was a steady throb. Pulsing as the blood left him and weakness wanted to slither through his veins.

Keep standing. Kill the two men you thought were friends. Save the woman who is your fucking life. An easy enough to-do list, huh?

Because suddenly the past didn't matter. No, no, it *did* still matter. Getting the truth about his mother mattered, but it didn't matter more than Marley. Nothing mattered more than her.

"Thought this was supposed to be an easy scene," Cade muttered. "Set it up to look like Declan found Marley with the cop. He killed her in a jealous rage, and then Declan and the cop shot each other. Put a nice little bow on the scene, and we were *done*."

James's hand was inching down toward his ankle.

Did the bastard really think Declan had forgotten that James kept a knife strapped there? *You're the one who told me how important it was to always have a weapon on you, James.* He'd learned so many lessons from James over the years.

"Cade, you were on my suspect list," Marley said. She didn't sound scared. More angry. "I really wanted to be wrong about you."

"He's my father," Cade retorted. "Sorry, but family comes first. Told you before, I realized that this world is not black and white. We have to make our own shades of gray. And like Declan just said, it's about family."

"Not exactly." Declan got the big picture. "It's also about the money. Just so you know, that's all it has ever been about for James. Let me guess...he's the one who found you, isn't he? He's the one who convinced you to come and work for me? While he was doing all of that convincing, did James tell you that *he* was a hitman for my father? Hell, he could have even been the one who killed your mother!" A total bullshit guess designed to throw off Cade—

"He killed her because she *left* him!"

Sonofabitch. His guess had been right?

"She went to the Feds. She stole me from him!" Cade's voice rose. "And she lied to me for my entire life. She told me that lame bastard who raised me was my dad, but she was lying. She'd cheated on him—cheated and then hid me from my real father. I knew...fucking knew when my niece got cancer. We did all of these tests. My sister and I—we were only *half*-siblings. I hated not knowing who my real dad was—or where he was. Or who the hell *I* really was."

"So you went off to battle. You learned about your shades of gray and you got really good with weapons and your dear old dad finally came to you." Marley's voice held disgust. "Got a news flash for you. James didn't pull you into his world because he missed his son. He did it to *use* you! I'm betting he always knew about your existence. He didn't care. He still killed your mom when the time came. And he left you alone for years."

"You don't know *anything*," Cade jerked her. Hard.

"He's getting you to do his dirty work!" Marley claimed. "You just told us he *killed your mother—*"

"Shut the bitch up!" James yelled. "Now, shut her—"

That's it. Done. "No one calls her names. Enjoy hell," Declan told him.

James let out an inhuman shriek. He jumped to his feet. Tried to, anyway, but mostly stumbled as he drove his knife toward Declan's stomach.

Declan fired.

One shot to the heart.

Because you fucking broke my heart, you lying piece of shit.

James stumbled back. His eyes were wide open. Stunned. "S-son—"

"I'm not your damn son."

"*I am!*" Cade roared.

James fell to the floor.

Declan whirled toward Cade. He knew he had to fire. Fast. But he couldn't risk hitting Marley. She had to get the hell out of the way—

Marley had already broken free of Cade as he stared in shock and fury at Declan. She surged toward the wall.

Declan smiled at him. "Guess we're taking each other out, huh?"

"You aren't leaving this room, you sonofabitch. *Everything you have should be mine! Everything should be—*"

Marley slammed a painting into his back. The wood of the frame hit his head and shoulders. Cade jerked and shuddered, and he whirled toward her even as Declan tried to lunge forward.

"*Hey, asshole.*" Royal burst from the curtains near the terrace. "You don't screw with my brother, got it?"

And when Cade started to fire at Royal...

Royal took the shot first. And so damn fast.

Two hits. One to the heart. One to the head. Zero hesitation.

Cade hit the floor with his mouth hanging open in a scream that he never got to voice.

Declan's breath shuddered out. His grip was too tight on the gun, but he couldn't force his fingers to relax. He was too tense. Too certain that another attack would come.

A door slammed into a wall. *The front door? Again?*

Footsteps pounded toward them. "Declan!"

Hunter's voice this time.

Don't be another betrayal. Don't be.

"Need me to kill him?" Royal asked.

Hunter burst into the den. Took in the scene with wide eyes. Then... "Declan?" Wooden. "Declan, all that blood on you...is it theirs or is it yours?"

A sharp cry escaped Marley as she bounded toward him. She reached for his coat.

Fuck that. He reached for her. He hauled her against him even as he heard Hunter calling nine-one-one.

"Yeah, yeah, I told you heroes to get here fast—I need faster. My best friend is bleeding his ass out all over the place. Hurry," Hunter ordered, voice blasting.

"You were shot." Marley shuddered against Declan. "Why didn't you say something?"

Little too busy killing my father figure, sweetheart. Little too busy. "Guess I'm like you," he managed instead. "It's just a scratch." No, it wasn't. "No need to mention it."

She pulled back. Stared up at him. "I love you, Declan Flynn."

"Am I dying?" He felt his body weaving. "That why you're lying to me now?"

"It's not a lie, and you're not dying." Her jaw hardened. "You're *not*, understand? Because if you try, then I will follow you to heaven and drag you back to me."

His legs gave way. Shit. He hit the floor.

Or almost did. Hunter grabbed him from behind. Carefully lowered him down. Went to work on the wound that Declan couldn't even feel any longer.

"How the hell was he on his feet?" Hunter demanded.

Marley touched Declan's face. *"I love you."*

"Not going to heaven." He knew this. She did, too. "Always bound for hell."

Marley bent toward him. Her lips brushed over his ear.

"Then I guess I'll just go to hell and fight the devil until he gives you back to me. I'm not scared of evil, and I know it when I see it." She pressed a kiss to his scar. Lifted her head. "I know it when I see it," she repeated. "And I know love when I feel it."

He did, too. His love for her was something that had been there...hell, since the basement. Growing and growing until she filled the heart that had always felt cold and withered but now beat so incredibly fast. Fast not because he was afraid of dying, but because he didn't want to leave her. He wanted to be with Marley. To have a life with her. To have something more than ashes and pain and a past that gutted and twisted.

He wanted his Marley. Maybe he didn't feel love the way others did. Who cared? She was it for him. The one he would always love. "I would die for you...a thousand times."

"You'd better not," she snapped back. "Not even once, understand me? *Not even once*."

Royal's head was suddenly next to hers. "Yeah, bro, so... we have two dead bodies here. Need me to hide them before the cops arrive?"

One cop was already there. Was Parker still alive? "Save...the detective..."

"We're not burying any bodies." Marley was adamant. "We're saving Parker, and Declan is going to recover fully. You hear me, Declan? You are recovering *fully*."

His eyes wanted to drift closed. He didn't let them. He couldn't. If he was going to leave this world, she would be the last thing he ever saw. No darkness. Only light.

Only his Marley.

"I love you," he told her.

"About time you said it." Marley's fingers skimmed over his cheek. "About time."

Chapter Twenty-One

"I'm his fiancée." Marley's voice drifted through his head. "Where he goes, I go."

He was moving. No, *he* wasn't the one moving. He was *being* moved? Pushed. Lifted? A siren wailed and lights flashed and—

Marley's soft fingers squeezed his hand. "Where he goes, I go."

* * *

"I'm his fiancée!" Marley's voice. Loud. Angry. Definitely angry. "What in the hell do you mean I can't go in the operating room with him? Did you *miss* the fiancée part? Where he goes, I go and—*Declan! Declan! Don't you dare die on me!*"

* * *

"I'm his fiancée." Flat. "I'll be staying here all night long and all day long. I will be here when he opens his eyes. Try to move me. I dare you."

* * *

Declan opened his eyes.

Marley released a long, slow breath as she perched on the edge of his hospital bed. Her eyes felt grainy. Probably from all the tears she'd shed and the sleepless night. But she hadn't been able to risk sleeping. Declan needed her.

And she'd been afraid he might slip away from her.

She waited a moment as he took in his surroundings. The bright, white walls. The low hum of voices coming from outside. The antiseptic smell.

His head turned. His gaze focused on her.

"Hi." Way too hoarse. Marley cleared her throat. "Fancy meeting you in yet another hospital."

His eyes narrowed.

Her heart drummed hard in her chest. He'd lost so much blood. His skin had turned deathly pale, and she'd been utterly terrified.

"Pro tip." Still too hoarse. "If you're shot, tell someone. I had this stupidly sexy billionaire guy tell me that once. Life changing info, right there. Lifesaving, too. Because if people know you've been shot, they can, oh, I don't know—*help you*." She wanted to pounce on him. To hold him tight and never, ever let go.

But he hadn't smiled at her feeble joke. He just kept staring at her with that hard, fierce expression on his face.

Marley released another breath. "Do you remember me?" She'd asked him the same question the first time he'd awoken in a hospital and found her at his bedside. Surely, he remembered her, though. There had been no blows to the head. No brain injuries. *Just massive blood loss.*

Declan stared back at her with his dangerous gaze, and the hazel swirled. In the next instant, his hand flew out and clamped around her wrist. Sure enough, just that touch from him had her pulse racing like crazy.

Different hospital, same story.

"I absolutely remember you." Gruff. Deep. Rumbling. "Not like a man can forget his fiancée."

If possible, her pulse thundered even faster.

"Pretty sure I also remember..." Declan winced. Hissed out a breath. "I remember you telling me that you loved me."

"Yes." Not like she would deny it.

"Did you say it...because you thought I was dying?"

She leaned closer to him. Her hair trailed over her right shoulder. "I said it because it's true." She searched his gaze. "I love you, Declan Flynn."

He lifted her hand. Brought it to his lips. "And I would kill and die for you, Marley Jones."

Yeah, he already *had* killed for her. As for the dying... "Don't you plan on dying anytime soon, understand? Maybe eighty years from now when you've long since skated past your one hundredth birthday and we have a swarm of grandkids and great-grandkids around us. *Then* you can die, with me at your side and with a smile on your face." She leaned forward and brushed her lips over his. "But not before that, understand? Don't leave me, Declan, not when I just found you."

"Marley, I don't *deserve* you." His voice was slightly hoarse. Probably because he'd had a tube down his throat during the surgery. The long surgery that had terrified her.

"You should have left me when you had the chance," he added.

No. "Leaving you was never in the cards for me."

He blinked. "It was...when you found out about Glass..."

"I wasn't going to leave you. I was pissed that you'd taken risks like that for me. You didn't need to handle my monster." *What if the attack had come back on Declan?*

"I will always face your monsters."

Damn him. Being sweet and scary at the same time for her. "You and my brothers are gonna have to talk."

A furrow appeared between his eyes. "They won't... like me."

"No, they'll probably love you." He had no idea what would come his way with Eb and Jake. But he would find out, soon enough. "I love you, so they will one hundred percent love you, too."

He shook his head. "I don't...fit in."

"You fit with me," Marley told him, meaning those words with all of her being. "You fit me perfectly. I love you, Declan." She needed to give him those words again. And again. And again.

The faint lines near his mouth deepened. "I don't know that I feel love—the way you do."

"You don't have to feel it my way. Feel it yours. Feel it your way, Declan."

"I feel...like I breathe better when you're near me. Like I want to fight anyone who'd ever hurt you. Like...like I've been in the dark, and someone finally turned on a light for me."

Tears stung her eyes. "I like the way you feel love."

"I want to be good, for you, but I'm scared I can't be."

"You are *plenty* good, Declan. You stood in front of

Parker so that James wouldn't shoot him. You saved Parker even though you knew he wanted to destroy you. And you—"

The door opened behind her.

She glanced back.

Speak of the devil.

Parker had just been pushed into the room. Parker still wore his hospital gown. He looked far too pale—just like Declan—and an IV pole wheeled beside him. And, behind Parker, Hunter was the one pushing the wheelchair.

"Well, well, well..." Hunter chimed. "Look who is back in the land of the living. I call that perfect timing." His words were mocking, but his expression showed his relief at seeing Declan awake. "Someone wanted to come and tell you how damn grateful he is to be alive. You see the detective here? Turns out he doesn't remember exactly what happened in the house before he was shot. He remembers going toward the house. He remembers slipping inside—can't believe a cop would commit a B&E, but he confessed to doing the deed—and then...*bam.* End of memory."

Parker flinched.

"Poor guy doesn't remember anything else. Docs say it is probably because of the trauma from the gunshot."

Marley started to move closer to Parker.

Declan tightened his hold on her wrist. "Stay. Please."

Ah, it was that rough *please* that got to her.

Parker glanced at her, then at Declan. "Heard I have you to thank for the fact that I'm still alive."

"You do." Marley was adamant. "He shielded you with his body."

Parker's jaw clenched. "*Thank you,*" he bit out.

Behind him, Hunter flashed a broad smile. "Was that

hard? It wasn't, was it? Didn't kill *anyone*." He began to reverse the chair. "Let's give them some privacy—"

"I remember everything," Declan said.

"Good for you," Parker muttered.

"I suspect you do, too. You owe me no favors. If you want me locked away, do it."

Parker opened his mouth to speak—and the hospital door opened again. Royal strolled in, easing around Parker and his wheelchair with a quick, side glance. Then he paused at the foot of the hospital bed to study Declan. After a long moment of study, Royal nodded. "You'll survive. Good to know." He paused. "I was afraid that you'd die and leave your whole fortune to me. Do you have any idea what a pain in the ass that would have been for me?"

"Glad I stayed alive and didn't inconvenience you," Declan returned. And he...smiled. A real smile. Not a dangerous one. Not a menacing one. Not a smile that never reached his eyes. This smile—it tilted his lips, it flashed his strong, white teeth, and it lit his gaze. He looked happy. Really, truly happy.

I want him to smile like that so much more.

Royal blinked, as if caught off guard, and then he pointed at Marley. "You."

"Me—what?"

"You scared the hell out of me." He shuddered. "For a minute there, I thought you'd attacked the bad guy with the *Van Gogh*. New rule, we don't use the *Gogh* on our enemies. Not ever. We use much, much cheaper art."

Fine. She'd just make a mental note of that request. *No, I won't. I'll use whatever is handy.*

Royal glanced back at the detective. "Feeling grateful because my brother saved your life?"

Parker frowned.

"Marley told me the story." Royal rubbed a hand over his chin. "How Declan bravely stood between you and a bullet. And to think that you were trying to send him to jail. I hope someone learned a valuable lesson."

Parker growled.

"Parker mistakenly thought Declan might have something to do with the death of a prison inmate called Sebastian Glass back in Georgia," Hunter explained to Royal. "Don't worry. I helped him to see the error of his ways. The guards at the prison have admitted they made a mistake letting Glass in with general pop, and Glass—being the asshole he was—he antagonized the wrong prisoners. No way Declan could be involved in something like that."

Parker's gaze was on Declan. "No way."

"Now, I'll just get him back to his room..." Hunter wheeled Parker back a bit.

"Wait." Declan pushed up in the bed. Then winced in pain.

"You have to take it easy," Marley murmured. She *hated* his pain.

"He was shot, too," Declan groused as he eyed Parker. "And he's rolling around. I can't let the cop get ahead of me." He pushed up a little bit more. "I don't want you always gunning for me, Parker. If you've got an issue, say that shit now. I'm tired of my enemies hiding."

"Your latest two enemies are dead," Royal pointed out. "They aren't hiding. They're in a morgue."

Declan kept his gaze on Parker.

Parker inclined his head. "You...aren't what I thought."

Marley tugged on her wrist. Reluctantly, Declan let her go. She stood by the side of the bed. By Declan's side. "People are seldom just one thing in this world." Something she'd learned long ago.

"That's right," Royal affirmed with a solemn nod. "One person's hero is another's villain...and another person's villain..."

Might just be the love of my life, Marley thought. "Is someone's hero."

Parker gripped the arms of the wheelchair. "I doubt that anyone thinks James was a hero."

"Bet his son did." A retort from Hunter. For a moment, sadness slid across his face and whispered in his voice. "I... liked Cade." His shoulders straightened. "He got past my guard, boss. It won't happen again."

Declan shook his head. "He got past mine, too. And so did James." It wasn't sadness whispering in his words. Anger rumbled in his voice. "That sonofabitch killed my mother. And then he walked back into my life and pretended to care about me—like a freaking father—for years."

Royal and Hunter exchanged a long glance.

"I think this might be a private conversation." Hunter whirled Parker toward the door. "Let's get you back in your hospital bed. Don't tell the nurse you went for a ride, will you? I don't think you were supposed to move at all. Some shit about you being critical."

The door closed behind them a moment later.

Marley reached for Declan's hand. She needed to touch him, especially when he faced his past.

"The Ice Breakers have been digging non-stop since you got rolled into the hospital. Apparently, James was our father's hitman of choice back in the day." Royal shoved his hands into the pockets of his jeans. "They're connecting kills to him, left and right."

Declan nodded.

"Our mom—I don't know what happened yet. I have

some guesses. But that's all they are. We may never know the truth." Royal exhaled. "I think our mom ran with me. I think Conor Flynn sent his best guy after her. I think—"

"James put a gun to her heart and demanded that she tell him where you were. She refused. And James became enraged and shot her." Declan squeezed Marley's fingers. "He staged the car explosion to cover his tracks. But then he became terrified that Conor would realize what he'd done. See, our dad loved our mom. He was evil and twisted, but she was his obsession. I don't think he wanted her dead. James crossed the line, and he realized that Conor would kill him if he ever found out the truth. So he ran. And he hid. And he stayed hidden until I took care of *his* monster for him."

Silence.

All Marley wanted to do was comfort Declan. To pull him close. To tell him that she would always be with him so—

So she did. She crawled right back into the bed with him. She threw her arms around him and held tight. "I will always be with you," she promised. "You're not going to have to fight alone. You won't face monsters alone. You are going to be happy with me, Declan. We're going to have a crazy, wild, fantastic life." Then she kissed him. A little too hard. A little off-center. A little too desperate.

His fingers pressed to her cheek. "My Marley." A rasp. "My world."

"Ahem." From Royal. "That's one version of events. One that pretty much works in my mind, but I'll still have the Ice Breakers keep investigating. They are top-notch. Especially since we have your hotshot PI on the team. Who knows what else she'll uncover? She's already making waves, I can tell you that. The woman who saved

Declan Flynn—she's building quite the reputation for herself."

Marley pulled back so she could stare into Declan's eyes. "I didn't save Declan. He was the one who took a bullet for me."

But Declan shook his head. "Yes, sweetheart, you did save me. In ways that you will probably never fully know, you saved me."

She had to blink away the tears that wanted to fill her eyes.

"I love you, Marley." His gaze searched hers. "Will you marry me?"

Her breath caught.

"I'll get the ring soon, I promise, and I *asked* this time. Dammit, it's not romantic. Wrong place. I can do better, I swear I can. I—"

"Yes." Marley kissed him. "*Yes!*"

"Good," Royal groused from the foot of the bed. "Because I'm pretty sure that for the last sixteen hours, the woman has told everyone she met that she's already your fiancée."

Yes, she had. A woman had to do what a woman had to do...in order to protect her man. "I love you," she told Declan.

"I love you," he said. No hesitation. Instant. Real. "*I love you.*"

Epilogue

THE TWO MEN FOLLOWING HIM WERE MAKING A FATAL mistake.

Declan strolled past the shuttered bars on the Augusta, Georgia, street. Lamplights shone down on him, and he caught the faint pad of their footsteps as the men closed in on him.

He really was not in the mood for this shit. Marley was waiting for him, and he did not like to keep her waiting.

An alley branched to the right. He could duck into it. Let the fools follow him. Take care of them in less than a minute and be on his way to meet up with his fiancée—

"Declan!" A hard shout. "*Declan Flynn!*"

Or he could just go toe to toe with the stalkers right then and there. Sighing, he spun around. As he spun, he palmed the knife he'd been carrying.

The two men were tall, with broad shoulders. Both seemed to have dark hair. They stayed just out of the lamplight so he couldn't see their faces clearly.

"You really fucked things up for me," the one on the right groused.

Declan shrugged.

"Do you have any idea how long I waited for that kill?" he continued. "What shit I had to do in order to get close? And then you just eliminate the bastard with a few clicks on the keyboard?"

Declan's eyes narrowed. "Sounds like we have a problem."

"Yeah, yeah, we have a—" His words ended in a gasp. Probably because a knife was now at his throat. Courtesy of Hunter—Hunter had slipped up behind the man speaking and now had his blade killing close.

"Problem?" Hunter finished.

Declan waited for the second figure to attack. The guy didn't. Instead, he burst into laughter.

"Aw, shit, Eb, someone got the drop on you!" More laughter. "Wait until I tell Marley. She will never let you hear the end of it!"

Eb. And...Marley. He's going to tell Marley.

Declan's mouth dropped open. And he realized that... "Hunter, I think you have your knife to the throat of Marley's brother."

"Fuck," Hunter cursed.

Yes, exactly.

Hunter withdrew the blade. And *Eb—as in Ebenezer—* swiped away a drop of blood.

"Told you that Declan would have a shadow close by," the other guy said.

And Declan realized that if he was staring at Ebenezer Jones, then the man with him had to be—"Jacob?"

"That's me." He ambled from the shadows, offering his hand. "Hope we can be friends. Not like I want to be enemies with my sister's soon-to-be husband."

Declan stared at the hand. Then at Jacob's face. Hard,

intense. Strong. The guy looked *nothing* like Marley, but Declan knew he was, in fact, staring at Jacob Jones. After all, he'd seen a picture of Marley and her brothers. *Back at her place. When a knife was plunged into the photo.*

Jacob and Ebenezer. Twins.

Ebenezer—Eb—moved more into the light. "You beat me to the punch," he said simply.

Declan shook Jacob's offered hand. Released it. And raised a brow at Eb. "What punch would that be?"

Jacob slapped a hand on his brother's shoulder. "Eb has been undercover in max security. You really think we were just gonna let Glass get away with what he'd done to Marley? Hell, no."

"Hell, no," Eb echoed.

"So we pulled some strings with people we can't talk about, and we were just about to take care of the problem...when you went tap, tap, tapping on your keyboard."

The brothers had planned to kill Sebastian Glass?

Shit. We might have more in common than I thought.

Eb flashed a smile at him. "I know you're supposed to meet our sister soon, but...how about we buy you a beer? She's usually late for meetups with us. We should have time for a round before she shows up."

A knife had just been at Eb's throat, and he seemed completely unfazed.

Okay, I might just get along with her brothers after all. "I love your sister."

"Well, sure, you killed for her." Eb nodded.

So did Jacob.

"Figured you had to love her to do that. And she saved your ass—figured she has to love you in order to do that." Then Eb waved toward Hunter's still form. "You're the first

SOB who has gotten the drop on me in five years. That means your drinks are on me."

Hunter ambled forward. "I don't drink."

"Fine, then your cheap pretzels are on me." Eb brushed past Declan. "Better hurry. We'll have our first round, then meet up with Marley. If you get me drunk enough, I might just tell you where all the bodies are buried."

Where all the bodies are buried.

Hunter caught Declan's arm. "He's joking, isn't he? Not like Marley and her brothers have *buried* bodies."

Declan frowned after the brothers. Jacob had joined his twin. They were walking in perfect sync and blending easily with the shadows.

Damn. He knew trouble when he saw it. "Marley might not have buried any, but I think they have."

Hunter whistled. "Are we going to like them?"

"Let's go find out."

And they headed off after the brothers. But when they reached the bar, Marley was already there. Declan didn't have time to talk about buried bodies. He was too busy staring at the woman who was his world. Celebrating his engagement. Laughing with her brothers and Hunter and...

Too busy being happy.

So this is what it fucking feels like.

And he smiled as he toasted his soon-to-be bride.

In the mood for another romantic suspense from Cynthia Eden, then check out WHEN HE HUNTS.

She's a dead woman walking.

Luna Black knows that she's being hunted. The price on her head is astronomical. She was in the wrong place at the wrong time, and she saw some very dangerous people doing some very, very bad things. Now she needs to reach the Feds, stat, *and* get a new identity and a new life. Because her old life? Definitely *over*.

It's not personal. She's just a job.

Ronan Walker lives in the shadows. His job? Simple—to deliver death. And the latest hit has him tracking down the very elusive and unpredictable Luna. But he's not the only hitman on her trail. Luna has valuable intel. The kind of intel that can never see the light of a courtroom. When the other hunters swarm in on her, Ronan has no choice but to intervene.

Death wasn't supposed to be so...dead sexy.

After he defeated the group trying to abduct her, Luna expected to die by the gorgeous stranger's hands. Even as he kissed her, Luna was sure that the tall, dark, and fierce predator would kill her. Only...she woke up, very much *still* alive, and handcuffed to his bed. Before she can even scream, he offers her a deal...protection, but for a price.

Is he a hitman with a heart?

No, he's not. Not even close. His heart never gets involved in a job. Ronan faked Luna's death, and now he has to keep her with him in the shadows until the Feds are ready to use her in order to bring down a massive criminal ring. The problem? He's not exactly used to sharing close quarters with anyone. Especially not someone like Luna...a woman who pushes him to the edge and makes him want to let go of the fierce control that he's kept in place for years.

On the run. Hiding in the shadows. Pretending to be a couple in love...

Sometimes, it's easy to pretend. To act like lovers. But what happens when the pretending starts to feel all too real? The longer they are together, the more Luna realizes there is so much more to Ronan than meets the eye. He protects her, he defends her from every threat, and she...just might be falling hard for the hitman who swears he can never love...

The story of her life. To fall for the man who delivers death.

Author's Note: Ronan deals with death. He's worked undercover as a hitman for years, only seeing the darkest side of life. Then he meets Luna. A woman named for the moon but who feels like sunlight in his arms. No way should he want her as badly as he does. No way should he start to think of Luna as his. But...he does. And anyone coming after Luna will find that Ronam will take "protecting and defending" her to a whole, new level. No one else will touch Luna, no one will hurt her, and he will deliver death to anyone who tries to take her from him.

Author's Note

Thank you for reading CRUEL ICE! I hope you enjoyed reading Declan and Marley's story—and solving the case with them. I love writing the "Ice Breakers" books. I get to mix romance and suspense and slip into the darkness a bit with the characters. I've always been addicted to both romances and cold case solving...so these books let me enjoy the best of both worlds!

If you have time, please consider leaving a review. Reviews help readers to discover new books—and authors certainly appreciate them!

If you'd like to stay updated on my releases and sales, please join my newsletter list. (I give all new subscribers a free Cynthia Eden book!)

I'm also active on social media. You can find me on Instagram and Facebook.

Again, thank you for reading CRUEL ICE.

Best,

Cynthia Eden

cynthiaeden.com

More Books By Cynthia Eden

Protector & Defender Romance
- When He Protects

Ice Breaker Cold Case Romance
- Frozen In Ice (Book 1)
- Falling For The Ice Queen (Book 2)
- Ice Cold Saint (Book 3)
- Touched By Ice (Book 4)
- Trapped In Ice (Book 5)
- Forged From Ice (Book 6)
- Buried Under Ice (Book 7)
- Ice Cold Kiss (Book 8)
- Locked In Ice (Book 9)
- Savage Ice (Book 10)
- Brutal Ice (Book 11)

Wilde Ways
- Protecting Piper (Book 1)
- Guarding Gwen (Book 2)
- Before Ben (Book 3)

- The Heart You Break (Book 4)
- Fighting For Her (Book 5)
- Ghost Of A Chance (Book 6)
- Crossing The Line (Book 7)
- Counting On Cole (Book 8)
- Chase After Me (Book 9)
- Say I Do (Book 10)
- Roman Will Fall (Book 11)
- The One Who Got Away (Book 12)
- Pretend You Want Me (Book 13)
- Cross My Heart (Book 14)
- The Bodyguard Next Door (Book 15)
- Ex Marks The Perfect Spot (Book 16)
- The Thief Who Loved Me (Book 17)

The Fallen Series
- Angel Of Darkness (Book 1)
- Angel Betrayed (Book 2)
- Angel In Chains (Book 3)
- Avenging Angel (Book 4)

Wilde Ways: Gone Rogue
- How To Protect A Princess (Book 1)
- How To Heal A Heartbreak (Book 2)
- How To Con A Crime Boss (Book 3)

Night Watch Paranormal Romance
- Hunt Me Down (Book 1)
- Slay My Name (Book 2)
- Face Your Demon (Book 3)

Trouble For Hire
- No Escape From War (Book 1)

- Don't Play With Odin (Book 2)
- Jinx, You're It (Book 3)
- Remember Ramsey (Book 4)

Death and Moonlight Mystery
- Step Into My Web (Book 1)
- Save Me From The Dark (Book 2)

Phoenix Fury
- Hot Enough To Burn (Book 1)
- Slow Burn (Book 2)
- Burn It Down (Book 3)

Dark Sins
- Don't Trust A Killer (Book 1)
- Don't Love A Liar (Book 2)

Lazarus Rising
- Never Let Go (Book One)
- Keep Me Close (Book Two)
- Stay With Me (Book Three)
- Run To Me (Book Four)
- Lie Close To Me (Book Five)
- Hold On Tight (Book Six)

Bad Things
- The Devil In Disguise (Book 1)
- On The Prowl (Book 2)
- Undead Or Alive (Book 3)
- Broken Angel (Book 4)
- Heart Of Stone (Book 5)
- Tempted By Fate (Book 6)
- Wicked And Wild (Book 7)

- Saint Or Sinner (Book 8)

Bite Series
- Forbidden Bite (Bite Book 1)
- Mating Bite (Bite Book 2)

Blood and Moonlight Series
- Bite The Dust (Book 1)
- Better Off Undead (Book 2)
- Bitter Blood (Book 3)

Mine Series
- Mine To Take (Book 1)
- Mine To Keep (Book 2)
- Mine To Hold (Book 3)
- Mine To Crave (Book 4)
- Mine To Have (Book 5)
- Mine To Protect (Book 6)

Dark Obsession Series
- Watch Me (Book 1)
- Want Me (Book 2)
- Need Me (Book 3)
- Beware Of Me (Book 4)

Purgatory Series
- The Wolf Within (Book 1)
- Marked By The Vampire (Book 2)
- Charming The Beast (Book 3)
- Deal with the Devil (Book 4)

Bound Series
- Bound By Blood (Book 1)

- Bound In Darkness (Book 2)
- Bound In Sin (Book 3)
- Bound By The Night (Book 4)
- Bound in Death (Book 5)

Stand-Alone Romantic Suspense

- Waiting For Christmas
- Monster Without Mercy
- Kiss Me This Christmas
- It's A Wonderful Werewolf
- Never Cry Werewolf
- Immortal Danger
- Deck The Halls
- Come Back To Me
- Put A Spell On Me
- Never Gonna Happen
- One Hot Holiday
- Slay All Day
- Midnight Bite
- Secret Admirer
- Christmas With A Spy
- Femme Fatale
- Until Death
- Sinful Secrets
- First Taste of Darkness
- A Vampire's Christmas Carol

About the Author

Cynthia Eden loves romance books, chocolate, and going on semi-lazy adventures. She is a *New York Times*, *USA Today*, *Digital Book World*, and *IndieReader* best-seller. She writes romantic suspense, paranormal romance, and fun contemporary novels. You can find out more about her work at www.cynthiaeden.com.

If you want to stay updated on her new releases and books deals, be sure to join her newsletter group: cynthiaeden. com/newsletter.